The Long Way to Mexico

Thank You
Alexis

A Novel

By

Roger Rodríguez

The Long Way to Mexico

By
Roger Rodríguez

Café con Leche

The Long Way to Mexico

Published by

Café con Leche

3 Griffin Hill Court
The Woodlands, TX. 77382
281-465-0119
www.cafeconlechebooks.com

Dedication

For my father — my biggest fan.

Chapter 1

Boy Jenkins

"I lose it sometimes, Curtis. I just lose it."

Tomball, Texas, September, 1978

Since childhood, Boy Jenkins had always been a violent person. His real name is Peter, but in elementary school, the other kids would tease him a great deal about looking like a girl. His folks always kept his hair fairly long. It was rumored that his family might move up to Minnesota, and maybe they were trying to keep him warm. In Minnesota, that would have been alright. In Texas, it opened the cattle-gate for insults from his peers. He remedied the situation by kicking each and every one of their asses and forcing them to call him "Boy" for the rest of their lives—and that they did! In fact, everyone in Tomball, Texas, came to know Peter Jenkins as "Boy."

Something about me was agreeable to Boy, and nothing I ever did made me deserve any of his classic beatings. Ironically, nothing he ever did bothered me much either. He acknowledged my tolerance of him one night when his honest bones let their guard down under the influence of the best tequila brought over to Texas from Mexico. "Eddie, ain't no other friend in this whole world gonna take such liking to me as you." To this day I have no idea who Eddie is or even if he knew

1

he was talking to me, but I took the compliment as my own and Eddie can wait to hear something nice from Peter "Boy" Jenkins another day. My name is Curtis Cash, and I am known by many in Tomball, Texas as Boy Jenkins's only friend. Few knew me as anything else, and even fewer knew there was indeed one thing about Boy I could not tolerate very well even if I never spoke up about it. I didn't like it when he would unleash his fury on Mary Beth Crawly. She was a beautiful woman, who many believed married Boy more out of fear of saying "no" than out of love, but one wouldn't know this for the first two years of their marriage. I thought for sure Mary Beth had converted Boy into a modern-day Ward Cleaver. I hooked up with Mary Beth's cousin Angela Gilley, and we took fishing trips together to Texas City. Boy was just as kind as any man could be to his wife, and if Mary Beth didn't love him before, she certainly seemed to have grown to love him over time.

We were on a camping trip one summer at a state park while in Oklahoma visiting Mary Beth's parents. Angela and I were having sex, trying to make as little noise as possible when we heard Boy and Mary Beth yelling in their tent.

"You bitch! Sometimes you make me want to kill you."

This strong sentiment was followed by the sound of a slap, and the night suddenly became engulfed in silence. It wasn't until the morning that we knew who had slapped who. Mary Beth was preparing bacon on an open fire with a fresh bruise under her right eye. She engaged us as if nothing had happened. I figured if she didn't think she was loud enough to have been heard fighting, then I should feel comfortable knowing they didn't hear me and Angela having sex. Since then, I would see Mary Beth show up at the house with a fresh bruise. It was a small light bruise, but it was a bruise, nonetheless. Angela and I would fight so much over my not confronting Boy with his problem that we eventually broke up without either one of us ever hitting the other. I started to believe for a moment that maybe violence does save relationships, but the fast deteriorating demeanor in Mary Beth's eyes quickly changed my mind about that. The night I decided to talk to Boy about his violent temper happened to be a decision I made much too late.

I hadn't seen Mary Beth in two months before the night she stopped by while Boy and I were watching Monday night football at my house.

"You think the Oilers will make the playoffs this year?" he asked me knowing the answer already.

"Maybe. If they stay healthy enough, I reckon they will," I told him. It brought a smile to his face. He hadn't really made eye contact with Mary Beth until she asked if he'd like something to eat.

"Yeah, baby. Why don't ya run out and get me and Curtis here some brisket sandwiches from Cooters?"

"Oh, I ain't really all that hungry, Mary Beth," I told her.

"Suit yourself, skinny boy. Then, bring two anyway, and I'll eat Curtis's," he said while reaching for his wallet.

I didn't see any fresh bruises on Mary Beth, and Boy slapped her hind end with an affection that made her toy with him by exposing her tits in my presence. "Don't you be showing those at Cooters," he joked.

"Why not? Maybe I'll get a discount," she added humorously.

Boy waited for her to be out of range before answering, "They'll probably charge you more. Ain't that right, Curtis?" he asked laughing. It was a response I chose to keep to myself. Everything seemed well between them, and I postponed my concern for their relationship at that time.

It was halftime when Mary Beth came back and laid the food on the table. "I got you those potato wedges you like so much, baby."

"Oh, I love those things soaked in ketchup," was his reply.

I was getting ready to use halftime to take a shower, so I could get my sleep right after the game. My entire life I had made my living as a welder, and one thing that can always be said about welders is that we put in some long hours. I was walking toward the shower hoping they wouldn't start having sex on my couch when without one single exchange of words I heard a loud slap and a thump on the floor. I returned to the kitchen quickly and saw Mary Beth on the floor with her arm over her face in defense.

"Where's my fuckin' ketchup?"

"In the bag."

"Ain't no fuckin' ketchup in the bag. You know I don't eat wedges without ketchup!" He continued, and with a fury I had never seen in him, picked Mary Beth Crawly up and threw her to the ground.

"Boy, wait a minute–just wait. I have ketchup here, man. Relax!" I walked over to my cabinet and handed the ketchup to Boy. "Relax. Hey, come on now, Boy. These slaps have to stop. This is your girl."

"I lose it sometimes, Curtis. I just lose it." He looked down at Mary Beth, who appeared to be using the floor to cover her face from any further damage. "Come on, baby, get up. You know how I get. I'm sorry. You know how much I love you."

"Just let her be, Boy. She'll get up in a minute. I'm going to take a shower. Come on now. Take your food to the living room."

"Okay."

I went toward the shower, but Boy walked close behind me and turned me around by my shoulders. "Curtis, you know I ain't never hit her hard. I always slap her with my bare hand the way mama used to slap me. I never hurt her."

"She ain't your daughter, Boy. Stop slapping her, and no make-up sex in my living room either."

"Nah, we'll go to your bed, ain't that right, baby?" Boy tried to get her to talk to him. I gestured to him to give her some time to gather herself and signaled him over to my living room with my finger. My shower was longer than I had previously planned. The warm water paralyzed my muscles, and I was prepared to lean against the shower wall and fall asleep there. I reckon if Mary Beth could flash her breasts in my face, I could come out wearing only a bath towel. The Oilers were beating Kansas City by a touchdown. I must have been in that shower much longer than I thought. Boy had fallen asleep on my sofa, and I figured Mary Beth had taken that opportunity to leave. I turned toward my bedroom to get some clothes and realized Mary Beth hadn't left at all. She was still on the floor as motionless as a gofer in a coon's nest. I walked over to her and placed the palm of my right hand on her back. The warmth of her body had escaped her, and my pulse started to race.

"Mary Beth," I called out softly. "Mary Beth, get up, honey. I'll take you home, so you don't have to drive."

She was silent as anyone could ever be, and as I placed my forefingers on her neck to feel for a pulse, I could see small droplets of blood escaping from underneath her nostrils in a small trail toward her upper lip. I rose immediately in fear and called out to Boy as calmly as I could without taking my eyes off Mary Beth's hardening body.

"Hey, Boy. Get up."

He didn't move at all, and I had to walk over and move him physically to shake some of the alcohol out of his brain. "Boy, get up!"

"What the fuck, man?"

"It's Mary Beth. She ain't moved yet and is bleeding from her nose."

"She's just being a bitch, man. She'll get up after a while."

"I don't think so, Boy. Not this time."

Boy rose slowly and reluctantly walked over to the kitchen. He immediately saw the blood that was trickling to the shallow end of the uneven kitchen floor. "Curtis, what's going on, man?"

"What do ya mean?"

"I mean she's going to be okay, right?"

Neither one of us had walked any closer. Instead, we looked over at Mary Beth from the living room.

"I don't know. She seems done for to me."

"Done for? What the fuck do you mean done for? What does that mean, Curtis?" he asked in a frantic voice. He had taken hold of my collar and shook me as he asked these questions.

For a moment, I considered that I was in the room with a killer and feared what he would do to me in efforts to eliminate any witnesses. "I mean she's dead, Boy, and she ain't coming back!" My good senses took over when Boy acknowledged that it was an accident.

"Jesus Christ, Curtis! What do I do? I can't go to prison. It was an accident. I didn't mean her any harm."

"Well, why the hell do you go and get so pissed off over ketchup for?"

"I don't know, Curtis. I just lost it, okay? I didn't mean her no harm, I told ya. All my life I've been labeled as some crazy mad man with a short fuse. I sorta liked that rep and just kept it going. Half the time I wasn't even angry. In fact, the fuckin' ketchup got me more pissed off than anything else I ever went through with Mary Beth. You gotta believe me, Curtis. You got to."

"I believe you, but that ain't gonna solve nothing."

"So, what do I do? I can't survive no prison. I just can't. I ain't as mean as people think. So I lose my temper now and again . . . that don't make me no killer. I ain't no goddamn killer, Curtis!"

6

He yelled with an intensity that left me no choice but to believe him. A loud silence hovered over our heads. Boy never got close to the body but leaned his arms and head against the wall. I had given my back to him and sat on my sofa. There was only a minute left in the game. It was tied now. I opened a bottle of warm beer that had been sitting on my coffee table. It wasn't until the game had finished that I decided to break the silence. "I reckon you ought to go fetch us some shovels while I clean the kitchen up."

For a moment, Boy didn't respond at all to this suggestion. He never made eye contact with me, but I watched him walk out slower than an old mule with molasses stuck to her heels. His shirt was outside his jeans and the buttons open from the front. I could see his chest was sweating like if he had just finished bull riding in July. He reluctantly put on his cowboy hat and gulped what was left in his bottle. He opened the screen to my front door and wobbled out the house. "I'll be back by midnight," he said softly.

I began to clean. Without having any conversation about what had just happened, it had been decided: I was going to help Boy Jenkins get away with murder.

Chapter 2
Old Man Winters

"Poor guy looked as nervous as a cat with a long tail in a room full of rocking chairs."

With only trees as my neighbors, it was easy to load Mary Beth onto Boy's pickup truck. We decided on a patch of land just outside Harris County where Boy and I used to fish when we were kids. There's a lake on that land that houses some of the largest bass in Texas. Boy and I used to sneak in there when Old Man Winters wasn't looking, but there wasn't any need for hiding anymore since the old chap died about five years ago after being kicked in the head by his own horse. His son inherited the land but had no interest in it whatsoever. He took in a male lover in an apartment somewhere near Manhattan. Boy and I used to joke about city boys having no business in a ranch since we both knew the ranch remained vacant. One of the most successful ranchers in Texas lived near Tomball and was known to prefer male companionship, but we had no reason to believe that was Old Man Winters's son. The abandoned house had since decayed and become useless, but the lake was as beautiful as ever.

We arrived in this area at about two in the a.m., and the night was so quiet that it was bothersome to hear it. "Hell, say something, Boy. It's too damn quiet."

"Well what do ya want me to say, Curtis? Shit."

"Anything, man. Tell me where to park."

"Kill your headlights."

"I can't see shit."

"Don't care. I think I heard something."

"You're nervous. There ain't nobody out–"

"Shhhh! Listen."

I had to adjust my eyes in what seemed to be complete blackness. Once I did, I was able to make out a horse hazing on a patch of grass near the lake. "It's just a horse, Boy." We looked at each other. Now that we were completely out of public view, Boy seemed to be a little more relaxed. "Maybe it's the horse that kicked Old Man Winters in the head."

"Yeah, now he's got the property all to himself, don't he?"

"Hell, he's doing a much better job with this place than Old Man Winters could."

We tried to laugh, but it was difficult to make light of what was happening. We gave each other a serious look and got two shovels out the bed of the pickup. We dug what we felt was at least three feet. We both paused for a moment knowing what came next. I looked at him curiously. "You still want to do this?"

Out of nowhere, he began to panic like a one-eyed raccoon in a cactus patch. I'd never seen Boy scared before. Besides anger, I'd never seen him express any kind of emotion. "Of course I don't want to do this, Curtis. I ain't no killer! But what do I do? What can I do?" He'd asked me that before, but I truly didn't know how to answer him.

After a moment's hesitation, I answered him softly. "Come on, partner. Let's get Mary Beth."

"Can't we just let her be out here? Do we have to put her under the ground like that?"

"And what do you suppose people will think?"

"Who the hell is gonna find her? Ain't nobody coming out here."

The poor girl was as light as a feather. Boy didn't have the heart to lift her, and when he went to the passenger side of the truck to wait, I knew he wanted me to put her in the ground myself. I could not do it either. It was a difficult thing to toss dirt on her like I planned to do, so I did it slowly until I eventually just stopped. I did it so slowly, in fact, that Boy got down in a rush and started shoveling dirt over the grave like a madman with the other shovel. He walked rapidly back to the truck, he threw the shovel into the bed, and was back in the passenger seat before I could even start walking back.

He rolled down the window. "Let's go, Curtis. What the hell ya waiting for?" He began to panic again. We both got out of the truck knowing exactly what the other was thinking. We dug Mary Beth back out and left her on a small patch of green grass near the abandoned house. We were sure burying her would not be necessary.

We drove for thirty miles before any one of us said anything. I didn't feel much like breaking the silence this time around, so I let Boy do it.

"You know there was a saddle on that horse," he mentioned while lighting a cigarette. "What?"

"The horse. The horse back at Old Man Winters . . . it had a saddle."

"So?"

"Why would it have a saddle unless someone's been riding on it?"

"Boy, that place ain't been tended to for a long ass time now. I doubt no Manhattan gay boy would be coming back to unsaddle a horse. Shit, he didn't care about that property much less a horse."

"What about them noises in the brush?"

I decided at that time to pull over to the side of the road. "Listen here, it's done, alright? What's done is done. If you're going to live in paranoia the rest of your life, we best go back for Mary Beth and drive straight to the police. I don't want to live like this the rest of my life and shouldn't either. It's too late, Boy . . . it's done, alright?"

"Yeah . . . okay."

I'm not sure if I believed what I was saying or if I was reacting to the fact that what Boy was saying made sense—and it scared me. The rest of the ride was spent in complete silence until we got into the greater part of Tomball. It was approaching four o'clock in the morning.

"You hungry?" I asked.

"I don't think I can eat much right now."

"Well I'm stopping at Lucy's for eggs and bacon. I'm hungry."

"I'll have some coffee."

No one really knows how Lucy's got its name. The owner's name is Betty Thompson, and she moved over to Tomball some thirty years ago from Louisiana after her daughter overdosed on cocaine and Jack Daniels. The place served a simple lunch but was notorious for its breakfast.

"Hey, gentlemen, I haven't seen you fellas around for some time. Where y'all been?"

"Just working, Betty," I answered for both of us.

She poured us a cup of coffee each and initiated a conversation Boy may not have been prepared to engage in. "So, how's Mary Beth? You guys having any babies soon?"

"Um, let me have some eggs over easy with a side of bacon, fried potatoes and a side of stacks, will ya, Betty?" I interrupted.

"How about you, cowboy? Eating anything?" she asked Boy. Apparently, he had changed his mind about how hungry he was. "Yeah, let me have the biscuits and gravy and a small cup of oatmeal."

"Coming right up, cowboys," Betty said as she directed her attention toward the entrance to the diner. "Well, good morning, Dawson. Come on in for some coffee."

"Thank you, Betty, that'll be great."

Tim Dawson was by all accounts a jerk, but he also happened to be a deputy sheriff. His father was the actual sheriff and wasn't half as arrogant as his son. The rules against nepotism were obviously not enforced. He went to high school with me and Boy and always made it a point to remind him that he never got Boy to call him "Boy." Instead, he referred to him by his real name just to try to piss him off.

"You didn't think you'd get away with it, did ya, Peter?" he asked him.

We both kept our eyes on our coffee mugs, and Boy answered softly. "Get away with what?"

"Your tag."

"Tag?"

"Yeah, on your truck. It's expired."

"I'll get it fixed."

"Of course, that's not half as bad as hitting a woman."

"Fuck off, Dawson!" Boy exclaimed jumping out of his chair.

"Relax, Boy," I suggested. I figured the last thing in the world he needed at the time was to get arrested. Most would count on Mary Beth to bail him out and wonder where she was if she didn't.

Dawson kept picking at Boy, provoking an arrest. "My, my Peter, that sure is quite a temper."

I decided to interfere before Boy showed what he was capable of. "That's enough, Dawson. Ain't nobody here looking for any problems."

"Is that so, Curtis?"

"Yeah, that's so."

"Hey, aren't you running with that Angela girl no more? I thought I pulled over a convertible Mustang the other night with her and some other fella in it."

"No, ain't running with her no more. She can do whatever the hell she pleases." I helped Boy back to his seat as our breakfast had already been placed at the bar in front of us. Customers began to fill the place, and I didn't care much for an audience to our conversation. "We ain't got nothing more to say to you, Dawson. Just go about your business, alright?"

Dawson took one last sip from his coffee and apparently received a call on the radio that he had to tend to. He gulped yet another drink and made his way out. "Take care of that tag, Peter." Neither Boy nor I looked back or even acknowledged that we heard him.

We had our breakfast in silence and the morning was advancing quickly. The roosters began to sing throughout Tomball, and the smell of coffee began to caress the morning dew falling off the large trees in and around Harris County. I was worried about Boy—poor guy looked as nervous as a cat with a long tail in a room full of rocking chairs. "Come on Boy, we gotta get to work." I wasn't sure if Boy was going to be able to get through this. I believed him. He just wasn't the killing type.

Chapter 3
Angela Gilley

"If I was a genius, I would have quit this friendship
a long ass time ago."

I couldn't even get through my shift that day. I had been awake for longer than I cared to remember and played sick to go home at noon time. I fell asleep the moment my head hit the pillow and put in about five hours before I was interrupted. The sound of knocking on my front door was the most annoying sound in the world. Visitors had the tendency to knock on the screen door rather than the house door itself, and the screen would slam into the main door with every knock. It was especially annoying when visitors knocked with extreme urgency.

"I'm coming . . . good God, did you strike gold or something?"

I opened the door, and before me stood Angela Gilley. Her hair had been straightened and dyed a darker color. She was still just as beautiful as ever, and the blue in her eyes penetrated my soul like an Apache's arrow.

"Are you drunk, Curtis?" she asked me point-blank.

"No, I ain't drunk. I'm tired." I responded, making no signs or gestures suggesting she ought to come inside.

"Have you seen Mary Beth? I've been looking all over for her."

"You're asking the wrong guy. Shouldn't you be asking Boy?"

"I don't know where he is. I've been looking for him, too."

"Well just wait for him to get home from work."

"He didn't go to work. I looked for him there."

This got me nervous because I wondered what Boy was doing with his time. "Well, I don't know, Angela, maybe they went off together somewhere."

"Huh! Yeah right–that bastard wouldn't take Mary Beth anywhere if his life depended on it."

"Look, Angela, he ain't all as rotten as you think. He loved Mary Beth with all his heart."

"You'll go to your grave defending that son of a bitch!"

"We already had this conversation, Angela . . . it was supposed to have been our last one. I'll tell Mary Beth you're looking for her when I see her."

"Yeah, you do that, Curtis." She finally left my house, but before I could twist the cap off a beer, she returned with a knock at the door.

"What?"

"You said loved."

"What?"

"You said loved. You said Boy loved Mary Beth."

"So?" I finished twisting the cap off my beer.

"So why would you say it in the past tense. Did they break up or something?"

"I don't know what you're talking about Angela. I gotta go."

"You call me when you hear from Mary Beth, Curtis . . . you call me!"

I arrived at Boy's house at about seven that night. He was outside loading things onto his pickup like a madman. "What's going on, Boy? Where ya been all day?"

"I'll tell ya what's going on . . . we gotta get outta here and fast."

"What are you talking about ? We can't just up and leave."

"We got to. Someone saw what we've done!"

"What? No way, man, you're being paranoid again," is what I suggested to him.

"You can call it what you want, Curtis, but this ain't no paranoia!" he said while pulling a sheet of folded paper from his back blue jean pocket and slapping it against my chest. It was a handwritten letter simply stating that if we didn't want to do prison time to meet the writer of the note at Blue Bear Creek about six miles east of Old Man Winters's land.

"Look, this is some kind of prank. They ain't talking about what we did. There was no one there."

"You're just a modern-day smart ass aren't you, Curtis? You're a real fuckin' genius. Someone was there! I heard it! I saw the saddle on the horse! You tried to convince me I was going nuts, but that horse wasn't dying of hunger either. It was nice and healthy like someone has been tending to it. You were wrong, damn it, and now we gotta split."

"Hell, there's nothing but grass out there for the horse to feed on."

"You're just gonna keep dancing to the same song until we're in prison, aren't ya?"

"Well, Boy, if this is real don't ya think we ought to meet this person?"

"Are you sick? Are you plain sick? I ain't going to no Blue Bear Creek where cops will jump out of the bushes and take my ass off to prison."

"Where'd ya find this note?"

"On my windshield, why?"

"Don't you think that if this person knew how to find you, they would have already called the cops? There would be no need for them to set you up like that when they could just tell the cops where you're at."

He paused for a moment, but I knew that some of what I had said made sense to him. Some of what he said sunk into my head as well. I must admit it sunk well. It couldn't have been a prank. There was indeed a saddle on the horse.

"So, what are you saying we ought to do, genius?"

"Stop calling me that. If I was a genius, I would have quit this friendship a long ass time ago. According to this note, we still got until tonight to meet the fella. Let's go get some barbeque and then go meet this shit hole and see what he wants. If he saw anything, he probably wants a million dollars or something. We'll take care of it. Come on."

Barbeque and Texas are one and the same. We decided to avoid our usual choice of Cooters and went to Bimbos, expecting it to be much quieter. We managed to eat in peace, but it wasn't long after we started a game of pool that our friend Dawson walked in.

"Hello, gentlemen. How are things tonight?"

"Don't you ever go home, Dawson?" I asked. Boy never took his eyes off the pool table and just went on with his game.

"Nope, pulling a double shift today, but don't worry guys, I ain't giving you no problems no more."

"Oh yeah, and why is that?"

"Well I figured on taking a kind heart to . . . well your kind."

"Whatcha mean our kind?"

"How long you boys figured on keeping it from the public."

"Dawson, you're more confusing than a bird with half a wing. What the fuck are you talking about?"

"I mean you and Peter here . . . queers."

"Fuck off, Dawson. You ain't got the know-how to crawl under our skins."

"I'll bet Peter here gets your skin all the time."

"You need more than that, Dawson. Let us be."

"Oh, I got more, you little pussy. Had some obvious gay guy walk over to me at the truck stop. He asked me where I can find the cowboy who drove the pickup with Peter's license plates on it. Oh, how sweet it was for me to know the truth about our man Peter here. He's got a boyfriend and everything. That's really sweet."

Boy continued to his game and walked around the pool table closer to Dawson. He cranked back on his pool stick and slammed it to the back of Dawson's head. Dawson fell to the floor, and Boy started kicking him in the stomach and the face. Whether it was out of sincere hatred that I had for Dawson or out of desperation to get him to shut the hell up I don't know, but I started kicking him too. I made sure the tip of my boot sunk in deep toward the inside of his rib cage. I wanted it to hurt for months. By the time we finished with him, he was unconscious.

We were very fortunate the place was usually empty. We looked around and couldn't see the waitress or the bartender. Something about the entire assault we had just committed triggered an evil inside Boy I had never seen in his face even in his worst of tempers. He removed Dawson's .357 revolver from the holster and leaped over the bar. He forced the register open and removed the cash that was in it. Just at the time, the bartender came out from around the back with supplies.

"Hey! What do ya think you're doing?" he yelled out.

Boy looked at him straight in the eye and pointed the revolver. The bartender dropped his supplies and just lifted his arms to demonstrate his helplessness. "You boys best be gettin' on. The deputy sheriff usually comes in at around this time."

"He's already here. When he gets up, tell him to fill out the report," Boy responded. He shoved the gun in between his jeans and his stomach. He walked around the bar and toward the front door right past me. "Let's go, Curtis," he said. At that point, I was afraid of him.

Chapter 4

Young Johnny Winters

"That lie cost him his life."

Dawson was always trying to pluck our chords like a secondhand guitar, but I'd have to admit he played the right note with what he said to us, and both Boy and I found it suspicious.

"Did ya hear what Dawson said?" Boy asked while lighting a cigarette.

"Which part?"

"The part about some gay guy going over to ask where he could find me."

"Don't pay no mind. It's just Dawson being an ass."

"Didn't you say Old Man Winters's boy was into men?"

"Yeah, what of it?" I said raising the volume on the radio hoping to filter Boy out just a little.

"Could be he was at his old man's place and saw what we done. Now, he's trying to profit," Boy reasoned. I had no response for that because it made sense to me.

It was late when we got to Blue Bear Creek, and the clouds started to cave in on us. From a far distance, I could hear thunder rolling in. The area was very dark, and visibility was minimal. A short distance later, we could see someone signaling with a flashlight off the side of the road. We pulled over to a gentleman leaning against the trunk of a luxury car. Boy opened the revolver he took from Dawson to make sure it was loaded and snapped it back shut.

"Why are you taking that thing for, Boy?"

"Well, do ya have a million dollars to pay a bribe?" he replied with authority. He shoved the gun back inside his pants and got off the truck. By now, I could catch the scent of wet dirt being pushed into my face by the far-off winds warning us about the rain and thunder. I followed Boy to meet the young man who took out a Cuban cigar and lit it.

"Who the hell are you, and what do you want?" Boy started.

"Just call me John, and that's all you need to know."

"No, you little shit, I need to know more than that."

"Let's just say I got some nice footage of you boys doing some bad things on Old Man Winters's farm, and I think I ought to get paid for it."

"Why do you call your own father Old Man Winters?" I interjected fishing for the truth about his identity. I obviously played on a loose nerve because he was quick to snap at me.

"That asshole is not my father!"

Boy thought he would play a few nerves of his own. "Oh, so you hate your old man, huh? Was he playing with your pecker when you was a kid or what?" Boy lit a cigarette of his own. "Is he the one who made you a queer?"

"Shut the fuck up! The both of ya." Boy looked at me and started laughing. He looked back at John and started playing some more nerves like Dawson's own guitar. "What the fuck you bring us out here in the wilderness for, Johnny? We're cowboys and all but this ain't a queer convention in New York. If you're looking for some kind of bargaining for information, I'll just shoot my dick off right now."

"You're very funny, cowboy, but what I want has nothing to do with your pathetic pecker."

"What do you want?" I asked.

"I want you fellas to kill my father."

"Thought he was already dead," Boy asked, flicking his cigarette toward John's feet.

"No, the son of a bitch ain't dead. He faked his own death to avoid a shit load of taxes he owes the government. Now he brought my ass over here from New York, making me think I was getting some kind of inheritance. The bastard didn't give me shit, and I'm working my ass off in his freaking ranch."

"Ha! You?" Boy laughed. "You city slickers don't know shit about no ranching."

"And I don't care to learn either. But I can't go back to New York unless I can find where he keeps his safe. But the fucker hardly sleeps, and he won't drop that damn shotgun."

"You say he's got money in there?" Boy turned to look at me and casually redirected his attention to John while taking out another cigarette. "So, what you going to give us if we do this?"

"Give you? I'm not giving you cowgirls shit. I just won't go to the fuckin' cops. That's what I'll give ya."

Boy started laughing and looked at me. "Huh, this queer is calling us girls, Curtis. What do you make of that?"

"I don't know, Boy. He seems like an angry one."

"Well, let me tell you something, city slicker. I don't know what you think you know or why you would think that we're killers, but we don't take human lives."

"Oh, you just bury them, right?"

"Go to hell!" Boy shouted and pulled out his revolver. "We ain't no killers, and we don't make no deals." He fired a shot, and John fell to his knees almost instantly. He tried crawling toward Boy but didn't get very far. Who knows what he planned on doing if he had reached him?

"Damn it, Boy! Are you crazy, man?"

"What'd you want me to do? He's got us on tape. You know they have projectors with reels and shit for that now."

"What do ya think he was crawling toward you for?"

"How the hell should I know? He probably wanted to suck my dick before he died . . . who gives a shit? Come on, help me get him in the trunk."

The body was just as light as Mary Beth's, and though it took us a while to figure out how to pop the trunk on a luxury car, we finally did. We completed the drive to Blue Bear Creek, and Boy drove the car as I followed. We popped the car in neutral and pushed it into the lake. By that time, it was thundering hard, and the creek would certainly overflow.

"Damn it, Boy. You shouldn't have gone on and shot him like that."

"I ain't leaving anyone around who can send me to prison."

"What, then, you gonna kill me, too?"

"Damn it, Curtis. Why do ya have to go on and complicate things? Just shut up and let's get over to Old Man Winters's farm."

"What? What are we going there for?"

"There's money to be found, and we got to get it so we can get the hell out of Tomball."

"What about the footage?"

"He probably ain't got shit. Why the hell would he be prepared to tape something way out here at night?"

"I don't know. Maybe he just saw it and lied about having it taped."

"That lie cost him his life."

Chapter 5

The Fire

"Poor Johnny didn't live long enough to learn that shotgun wasn't fit to shoot a blind rabbit in a squirrel's nest."

The rain began to fall hard, and I started to wonder whether John was being truthful or not about his father still being alive. If not, searching for him in a storm would have been a waste of time. The house was so decayed I couldn't imagine anyone living in there. I couldn't understand anyone wanting to have us kill someone who really wasn't alive, so it must be true. Boy was getting pissed that he couldn't light a cigarette in the rain, and I was contemplating exactly what it was we were going to do if Old Man Winters was there.

It didn't take much to get into the house. The top hinge to the doorway wasn't even tightened, and the screen door was all torn. It took even less to find Old Man Winters sitting at a rocking chair, smoking a pipe and watching reruns of *The Andy Griffith Show*. I didn't mind standing there a bit, being that I had been an Andy Griffith fan since I was just a boy, but after thinking about it, we decided it was time to pursue our unplanned endeavor.

"How ya doing, old man? I didn't think the dead watched television," Boy said, finally being able to light his cigarette. The old man rose quickly to his feet and rotated the shotgun in his hand.

"U-u-u no, no, I wouldn't do that, old-timer," Boy said, already having had Dawson's revolver pointed right at him.

"Who the hell are y'all, and what do ya want?" Old Man Winters asked.

"Who are we? Why, we're from the Internal Revenue Service, old-timer, and we're here to collect. Now, put that worthless piece of shit gun down, or you'll make the front page." Boy threatened convincingly. The old man put down his shotgun. Poor Johnny didn't live long enough to learn that shotgun wasn't fit to shoot a blind rabbit in a squirrel's nest. But he was a city slicker and didn't know any better.

"What do y'all want?" he repeated.

"Well seeing as you're already dead, old-timer, I imagine killing you wouldn't raise much fuss, would it?" Boy said with a cigarette still in his mouth.

"It's Johnny, isn't it? Johnny is trying to have me done, idn't he?"

"Yeah, he sure is, Winters. He said something about you playing with his pecker when he was just a boy and turned him the other way," I said just to crawl under his skin a little.

His reaction was passive, and his face revealed some truth to that statement. "So, what are you assholes gonna do to me? Y'all gonna kill an old man, are ya?"

"Nah, Winters," Boy said, trading in his cigarette for chewing tobacco he had in the inside pocket of his blue jean jacket. "You ain't no threat to us. What are ya gonna do? Go to the cops? Shit, the IRS and the police would have your ass bent over in a prison cell before you could even tell them about us. We just gonna tie you up and look for what we came for."

"What do y'all want?" Old Man Winters asked again. The question went unanswered. Both Boy and I knew that negotiating for him to tell us where the money was would waste more time than a dog chasing his own tail. Old Man Winters had proven how stingy he was by faking his own death to avoid having to pay taxes. If he wasn't willing to pay the government what he owed them, there was no way in God's green earth he would tell us where he kept his money.

"Tie 'em up, Curtis."

It was the wrong time for Old Man Winters to keep such strong rope simply laying around. It was the solid rope that can burn the skin straight to the bone if you fight it too much. I remember having used this type of rope while roping bulls in my younger days. Old Man Winters didn't do much resisting. His tender age wouldn't allow for much retaliation, and he seemed quite content with having his life spared. I'd just completed the last knot on Old Man Winters when Boy came out the back end of the house with a large duffel bag.

"Bingo!"

"You found it already?"

"Yes sir, I'm afraid Old Man Winters ain't very creative, and his son is just stupid!"

"Hell, Boy, give the man some credit. The IRS ain't found him yet."

"Yeah, I suppose so."

Boy tossed the bag to me. I could tell by the weight that it contained a good amount of money. Boy went back into the rear of the house and returned with a gallon of gasoline. He started to spread it throughout the house and on the sleeves of Old Man Winters's pants.

"What the hell are ya doing?" the old man said with a great deal of panic in his voice.

"I don't like leaving no witnesses, old man," answered Boy.

"You said yourself I can't go to no cops, you moron."

"Now Winters, you ain't in no position to be hurting my feelings with name-calling."

"Okay, alright. Look, just leave me a couple of hundred dollars to get outta here, alright?"

"No deal, old man. I'll spare your life, but that's it." Boy turned to look at me and motioned with his head for us to get going. We got to the outside of the house and looked inside the bag. For the first time since we started this entire web of lies, I was beginning to feel comfortable with our chances of getting out of Tomball and starting new somewhere else.

"Whooo Weee, Curtis! We done went and got ourselves rich!"

"Come on, let's go, Boy." I had just made the suggestion for us to leave when we heard a shot come from the house. We turned to see Old Man Winters reloading his shotgun. "You bastards are gonna pay. Give me back my money, you fuckin' morons!"

"I thought you tied his ass up!"

"So did I." Apparently, Old Man Winters had successfully undone the noose I thought I'd secured carefully. Boy pulled out the revolver and fired a shot. He missed Old Man Winters, but the bullet landed somewhere that ignited the gasoline Boy had showered the house with. It didn't take long for the flame to reach Old Man Winters's pants, and he was totally engulfed in flames. Poor old man was yelling his ass off without a soul around for miles to hear him.

"Come on, Curtis. We gotta get outta here now and fast."

We ran to the truck and raced off the roads where no fire trucks were likely to pass through. After about twelve miles, Boy pulled off to the side of the road abruptly. "What are you doing, Boy?"

"My leg is burning like a cowgirl skinny dipping in acid."

"What's wrong?"

"Shit, Curtis! The fucker shot me."

"What!"

"I said the ass Old Man Winters shot my leg."

"Let me see." I looked at the injury and it was bleeding quite a bit. "It's just on the skin."

"What's that mean?"

"I mean it's just a flesh wound. You'll be alright. We don't need no hospital. We just need a first aid kit."

"I got one behind the seat. Patch me up and let's go."

We had plenty of practice patching people up. We'd often have to patch up friends who suffered snake bites while hunting. It was quiet while I wrapped his calf muscle until he broke the silence.

"I thought you tied him up."

"I did."

"I thought you said you were some kind of roper in your younger days."

"I was. But I never said I won anything for it."

We got in the truck and proceeded east on the farm road. "Where are we going, Boy?"

"Mexico."

"We're going the wrong way."

"I know. We're taking the long way to Mexico."

Chapter 6

Millie Kirchner

"It's not enough to keep the fox out of the yard. You gotta lock the hens in the hen house too."

We got to a small place somewhere in between Tomball and no-where by five o'clock the next morning. I had a mixture of feelings about everything that had transpired over the course of the last few days. I had a stale fear inside me that made me feel sick. To be honest, I wasn't even sure what it was I feared. Too many people had died, and nothing pointed to me or Boy. But beating on the deputy certainly was something they could be looking to find us for. On the other hand, there was something refreshing about coming into so much money and being able to simply not go to work. It hadn't been import-ant to mention that my boss was a real dick, and nothing I ever did was to his liking. I worked my ass off for him for the past five years and he had never heard me complain like most do about better hours or a pay increase. Carter Kirchner was his name. He wasn't that much older than I was, but his uncle left him the business after being sent to prison for some money scheme he tried to pull off. Maybe I never complained because I felt indebted to him. I slept with his wife at an employee Christmas party the very first year I started working for the ass. Ironi-cally, he was at that exact same party—not in the same room, of course, but he left his guard down long enough for me and young Millie Kirchner to find a quiet spot. I imagine my drunken father was right. "It's not enough to keep the fox out of the yard. You gotta lock the hens in the hen house too."

We had not been driving too long, but we had used some unpaved farm roads that didn't offer a pleasant ride. We found an old motel that seemed suspiciously out of place. There was no traffic running through this area, and the establishment was poorly kept. I always thought that a motel that went by the name of "Motel" was not likely to be a place that would offer much comfort. I learned some time ago that when one is tired, they can lay on a thorny mattress with a cactus pillow and sleep like an angel. And that is exactly what Boy and I did until 5:45 p.m. that evening. We rose at the setting of the sun with extreme hunger.

"Is there a diner somewhere in this place?" Boy asked me while lighting a cigarette.

"Hell, I don't know these parts any better than you."

"Well go ask, will ya?"

"Sure, boss. You want me to shine your boots when I get back?"

"I'll shine it myself up your ass, you sarcastic shit."

I was just toying with Boy. Every once in a while, I'd cut a little more off the top of his already short fuse. He was a good man inside, though, and I was quite hungry myself. I went to the front office, and there stood a tiny woman on top of a stool giving me her back.

"What can I do you for today?"

"Just looking for a place to eat."

"Nearest diner is about twelve miles down the road. I wouldn't try everything there unless you're on a death wish, but their pot roast will do," she advised me while she continued to mingle with her back to me. I was just getting ready to head for the door without even thanking her when I saw what it was she was mingling with. It was at that time I realized the seriousness of our situation. I ran to Boy like if I had sat on a pile of fire ants. "Hey, Boy! Boy!"

"Can't a guy take a shit in peace? What's wrong with you, man?"

"Get your ass out here, man. We're in for it now, Boy!"

"What's going on?" He seemed more concerned with my reaction now. "There's a flyer going up on the lobby wall with our pictures on it."

"Don't be fuckin' with me, Curtis. I don't take a liking to people messing with my head."

"I ain't messing with ya. We're up on that wall, alright."

"What the hell did it say?"

"They want both of us for roughing up Dawson."

"Oh, come on. He's a fuckin' deputy with pride. You knew that shit was gonna happen."

"And that ain't it. They wanna ask you about Mary Beth."

"Hell, why do they wanna ask me about Mary Beth?"

"Don't know. Maybe Angela stirred up some trouble."

"Angela? What does she got to do with this?"

"She'd been looking all over for her and didn't straight out and ask me if you hurt her, but –"

"Dammit, Curtis. Why don't you tell me shit like this?"

"You get all nervous, and when you get nervous you lose yourself, man. I didn't think nothing would come of it."

"Well we gotta get going before someone remembers we slept here."

"This place doesn't bring a whole lot of folks. I reckon they will remember us just fine."

"How'd they get a notice of us out here so quick, anyways?"

"Maybe they called local departments to make a flyer for them. You know these small-town cops stand by each other like that."

"Was our picture on it?"

"Yeah, them drawings didn't look nothing like us, but I'm sure the one that looked like a girl was you."

"You're gonna start that shit right now of all times, Curtis Cash?"

Once again, Boy and I were on the road heading in any direction. We seemed to be headed west through country roads. I had mentioned to Boy that we couldn't be going to San Antonio because it was full of people and law men. He didn't pay much mind to what I was saying and continued down the road. Sleeping throughout the day gave us the night to travel. We got to a point on our trip where Boy made some awkward turns. I am not sure he would admit it, but I do believe we were lost. Being lost was not an entirely bad predicament. If we couldn't find ourselves, maybe others couldn't find us either. My concern was more for Boy than for myself. If we were caught, I would probably spend a couple of nights in jail for what I had done to poor Dawson. Boy could go to prison if he was found accountable for Mary Beth being gone. I told Boy that denying any involvement would mean more if her body was never found. We were both confident that it wouldn't be. The only problem was that the entire town of Tomball associated Mary Beth Crawly with Peter "Boy" Jenkins. One would hardly hear one name without the other.

It seemed as if every time we were in the truck neither Boy nor I ever had anything to say. The rides were so quiet between us that I felt married to him. I imagine poor Boy had a lot of things going through his mind. Things had escalated to a level I had never expected it would reach. Overnight, I went from a drunken cowboy working double shifts to a criminal on the run. My life had never been so exciting, but my freedom never so compromised.

"We can't trust no hotel, Curtis," he finally said.

"Let's find a campground then."

We drove another three hours before coming across a camp site that had no closing time. As we drove into the area, I saw a sign that read El Campo, Texas. It had been the first time in a while that I didn't feel completely lost. Some years had passed since the last time I had set boot in El Campo, but I remember spending Easter Sunday there once with family. My father and mother got into quite a match in front of family. Aside from that episode, the water was great, and the fish coming out of the river were large.

The night was quiet, and Boy and I found a great area near a river. The current was strong, and I could feel small droplets of water dancing on my hot neck. We settled in before midnight and built a small fire. Both Boy and I had delayed a great deal on our hunger but not because we were tough cowboys. More than anything we were scared that at any given place someone would recognize us. At one stop, we had to take a chance—we left the store with a good amount of provisions and drinks. We mostly got beer, but we invested in some water as well. Boy got just about anything God made for no other purpose than clogging arteries. It was pretty much how we ate when we weren't running from anything. We figured it wasn't the best time to change our diets.

The smell of sausage and steaks served as a calling to a family of owls perched just above our heads on the trees. We paid them no mind and went on with our dinner. A pound of beef and six beers later, we could hardly move. "You think we oughta change the way we look, Curtis?"

"Hell, I don't know that it'll make no difference."

"It might."

"Maybe we oughta get rid of the truck."

"What? My grandpa gave me that truck."

"Then what you oughta do is cut the long girly hair."

"Why you always feel you have to rag on me like a woman?"

"Well, why do you keep your hair so long, anyway? People can spot us from a mile away like a goddamn snake in a weasel's nest. You still waiting to move to Minnesota?"

"You listen here, Curtis Cash. I ain't got nothing to lose by getting rid of your ass."

"Why do you get all defensive? It was just a suggestion, alright?" He didn't respond to that. I had my suspicions that Boy hated to be called defensive, but there were times when that's exactly what he was, and someone had to tell him. He dropped the rim of his hat over his eyes, leaned against a tree, and ignored me. I couldn't help but notice that there was blood moistening Boy's jeans on his injured leg. He had been limping earlier, and I couldn't help but wonder how long before he'd need some genuine medical treatment.

"That leg hurt much?" I asked.

"A bit," was his only reply. He waited a few minutes and continued. "Old Man Winters probably couldn't get his piss inside the toilet without missing, and the bastard gets a shot off on me."

"You best be glad that's where he hit you."

"I reckon that's the smart way to look at it."

"Well I'm gonna jump in the river. I ain't showered in a while."

The river was divinely cold. For that moment I felt the joys that only a free man can feel. It was the pleasure that could only be understood by a man whose recent past excluded any pleasantries life had to offer. Up until that moment, all had been downhill. The reasons to live had been revealed to me on that beautiful night. But that moment was stolen from me by some commotion taking place down by the river. I had already removed one boot and limped over some stones and pebbles that were still hot from being under the Texas sun all day. I got to the edge of the river with one boot in my hand where I heard all the noise. There was a couple arguing over some meaningless crap that probably had nothing to do with anything else aside from the fact they didn't really love each other. The girl's man embraced her with both hands from her upper shoulders and started to shake her up a bit. "Tell me, bitch! Tell me again what you just said, and I'll send your ass down the river."

"Go to hell, you jerk!"

At this sentiment, he threw her to the ground and kicked her to the lower body. I felt no other recourse but to get involved before he killed her.

"Now, that ain't a very nice way to treat a lady is it?" I startled him as I lit a cigarette and waited for a response.

"Fuck off, cowboy. This ain't any of your concern."

"You know, I have friend who once told me that very same thing."

"Well, you should learn to listen to him."

"Oh, I do. But you see, you ain't my friend."

"That'll make it easier to kick your ass!"

"I was hoping you'd say something like that," I told him. I began to take off my other boot, and this brought a great deal of curiosity to him. "You some kind of Indian who fights barefoot or something?"

"No, sir. This is where I keep my gun." He waited to see the shiny silver brass before deciding I wasn't fooling with him. The beautiful moonlight repelled off the steel frame and gave the gun a more powerful effect. I guess Dawson was good for something after all.

"Okay, look, mister, we'll just be getting back in our cabin." He reached over to pick up his girl.

"No, sir, the girl stays here," I told him, cocking the hammer back on the gun. He waited a moment not sure what to do. I feared for a moment that the girl would take his side and tell me to mind my own business. If that were the case, I was prepared to shoot them both. But that is not how things played out. In fact, there seemed to be a sense of relief in her eyes that someone came to bail her out.

"What are you going to do with her?" he asked.

"Well sir, with any luck, we'll skinny dip in that lake for an hour, and then go back to my truck and fuck all night. If not, I'll settle with standing by her side all night just to make sure you don't get no ideas."

"You son of a bitch!" he said while retrieving to his cabin.

With any good fortune, he would drop like a fly from all the alcohol he had consumed and make no more trouble. I walked over to the girl and helped her up from the ground.

"Thank you," she said with droplets of blood dribbling down her cheek from her forehead. "Glad to help, young lady."

"I thought you were going to kill him when he called you a son of a bitch."

"Nah, I didn't even know he knew my mother, and I'd never shoot an honest man."

Chapter 7

Sophia

"Most people who ain't white get offended when they get mistaken for some other race."

The young lady looked shy and nervous. Her skin was caramel, and her eyes were a golden honey kind. She didn't look like she could make up her mind to trust or distrust me. I couldn't blame the poor thing. I was a barefoot stranger in a campground with a gun and a flask of whiskey.

"So, what's your name, lady?" It was the only thing I could think to ask. Poor girl still seemed upset over all that had occurred, and I wasn't about to play the role of a counselor. In the past, most people have wanted to kill themselves after letting me speak to them. I wasn't about to cause any more problems for the girl. "Maria."

"You know I thought you looked like a Mexican girl. You are Mexican, aren't ya?"

"Yes."

"Oh, thank God. Most people who ain't white get offended when they get mistaken for some other race. I was afraid you were Chinese or something. So, where you from?" I continued to ask questions because she wasn't saying much, and I didn't take to kindly to inviting a mute to my open fire. I had been preparing some coffee all this time, but she seemed to be looking at my flask of whiskey, so I took it and stretched out my arm to her with it. Boy had already fallen in the back of the pickup truck, drunk as hell. I know he had been examining his injury and comparing one leg with the other because his boots were on the wrong feet. Sophia took two drinks from my flask before deciding to answer me.

"Monclova."

"Where the hell is that?"

"Mexico."

"It sounds like a poison or something."

"It is."

"So, how'd you end up with that trailer trash over there? He don't speak no Spanish."

"He promised to make me a U.S. citizen and find me a job. As it turned out, he just wanted to have sex."

"Hell, you can't blame a man for that. You're a good-looking lady."

I initially thought it was a stupid thing to say, but she smiled at me when I said it, so I guess it wasn't too bad. We spoke for what seemed like hours before she began to feel comfortable with me.

"So, were you serious about that skinny dippin'?"

"Well, hell yeah, little lady. You just show me the way."

She wasn't so shy after all, and I guess good deeds do go rewarded if you take the time to do them. We walked over hand in hand to the river. She proved to be a little less shy than I previously thought. She wanted me to get into the water first so that she could know that I was really going to do this. I left my clothes near a tree, so I could remember where to go back for them. The water was very cold by that time at night, and I couldn't help but yell a little and disturb some of the people. I swam a little deep down and emerged soaked and wet. I didn't think skinny dipping was a good idea anymore on account of possibly getting pneumonia or something. I looked around for the Mexican gal, but I couldn't see her anywhere. I cleared my sight and adjusted to the darkness as the moonlight exposed my swim partner running off with my pants and wallet.

"Hey, bitch where the hell do ya think you're going?"

If things weren't bad enough, I could see that her old man was in on the con job they made me part of. He drove past her, and she jumped into the passenger side so swiftly that I knew she had done this before.

"Mother of God! Why does this shit happen to me?" I had to walk through a crowd of people who had been woken up by the noise. I was naked as a jay bird, and the short walk to the truck seemed like miles away. I was fortunate enough to find my clothes and boots scattered throughout the campground. I was afraid they had taken the gun, but it was still inside the boot. Many people were coming out of their tents, and I was standing there, naked as a newborn. Even Boy, in a drunk state, woke up.

"What the hell happened to you, Curtis?"

"Some bitch just stole my wallet."

"Damn it. Why do ya let this shit happen to ya? Was any of our money in it?"

"A couple of hundred."

"You idiot!"

"Screw the damn money, Boy. We got more of that. I'm more worried about my driver's license being out there. I don't know how many posters with our face on it are out there by now."

"Well, what the hell you doing running around with strangers? We can't be making friends out here. Someone could get to know us from the news or something."

"Just trying to help out a lady, that's all."

"Just trying to get laid is more like it."

"And so, what if I was, Boy? I'm a man, ain't I? I'm tired of this. I wanna go home. Why the hell am I running for, anyway? I didn't kill Mary Beth!"

"Shut the hell up!" Boy erupted suddenly. "I don't ever want to hear Mary Beth's name again–do you understand me, Curtis?" He pulled the gun out of my boot and pointed it right at me. I had thrown my clothes and boots on the bed of the pickup. I was terrified, but I think I did a good job of hiding it. Boy had nothing to lose by killing me.

"Yeah, Boy, I hear you man. Put that damn thing away."

He put it away slowly, and he lit a cigarette. The flame from the match illuminated his leg, and I could see how he was bleeding a little more. I didn't want to make any suggestion at the time because he was still fairly upset at me for mentioning Mary Beth's name. The entire situation had gotten seriously out of hand, but there was nothing to say or do until the morning.

Chapter 8

The Witch Doctor

*"It seemed to me that everywhere I went, there was a small
diner that advertised something that was 'world-famous'
but that I had never heard of. Perhaps it was their own world
they were referring to."*

The following morning felt awkward to me. I felt as if half of my head was drunk and the other half still asleep. We had driven a good hour before Boy said anything. "You want breakfast?"

"Yeah, that'd be alright."

"I saw an advertisement some miles back showing a diner."

"What time is it?" I asked, not having realized at exactly what time we left El Campo. Boy looked down at his watch and shook his head as if he had discovered that his watch stopped, so he didn't answer me. We pulled into a diner that advertised "world-famous apple pie." It seemed to me that everywhere I went, there was a small diner that advertised something that was "world-famous," but that I had never heard of. Perhaps it was their own world they were referring to. Our waitress was a little older, but she had breasts I couldn't squeeze a dollar between and a gorgeous smile. I flirted a little with a smile, and Boy was annoyed by my lack of decorum. "Why are you such a hound lately? You wouldn't get any back home, so why the hell are you in such heat?"

"What the hell you talking about? I had my ladies."

"You didn't have shit, Curtis, and all this hounding just about draws more attention to us than Ray Charles at a Klan rally."

I didn't want to be so passive, but he had a point. We couldn't afford to be acting in a way that would allow people to easily recognize us. The waitress came back, and this time, I avoided eye contact with her.

"Okay, boys, what'll it be?"

Boy went first without looking at the lady. "Yeah, bring me three eggs, maple bacon, fried potatoes, and coffee."

"What about you, sir?"

"A stack of wheat hot cakes and pork links." I did what I could to avoid eye contact, but my previous personality put the waitress in a comfort zone.

"So, where you cowboys from?"

"Just passing through," I said shyly.

"Well, that's not what I asked you, cowboy."

Boy interfered immediately. "Lady, can you just get our orders going? We gotta hit the road."

"Well, I don't know where you boys are from, but you ain't the friendly kind, so you ain't from Texas."

She left quickly, and I gave Boy a stare that he didn't care much for.

"What the hell are you looking at?" he asked me.

"Well, genius, did it ever occur to you that being angry with the lady is just as likely to make us as memorable as me flirting?"

"She just said she doesn't think we're from Texas, so don't worry about it."

"Yeah, she'll think that until she sees the notice with the descriptions of our face on it hanging inside this very diner."

To this, there was no response, and little was said between us until we finished our breakfast. I was beginning to worry about Boy's change. He appeared to be getting more hostile every day, and he was limping a little more from his injury. He had on a new pair of jeans, but I was beginning to see tiny droplets of blood seeping through them. I decided I would try to discuss more encouraging matters with him when we got to the road again. "You know, we ought to go deep into Mexico, where the *señoritas* swoon over American men and the margaritas taste like the sunshine.

"What did you have in mind?"

"Hell, I don't know. I've never been to no Mexico, but I do know all these wannabe Jesse James criminals are all too happy just to cross the river—then they get their ass caught within days."

Boy chuckled as if he agreed with me, and it seemed as if I was restoring a little of his more pleasant nature. "So, what do we do when we get there?" he asked me in curious fashion.

I didn't know how to answer that in a satisfying manner, so I ignored that question and took advantage of his calmer state to ask him something more important. "Boy, I need to know how you're feeling with that leg, and I don't want to hear no fussing about my asking."

"It hurts, Curtis, but there are times when it's so numb I forget it's there."

"Well, we gotta find a way to get you to a doctor."

He didn't reply to this, but he didn't refuse either. Taking back roads was taking a toll on our bodies, and we were clearly driving miles further than we had to if we took a more common route. We both knew it was necessary to take those roads, and we both knew we were getting closer because the atmosphere began to change. Once we got by Victoria, Texas, things began to look more Mexican. Stores, people, and restaurants were slowly transforming into a Mexican atmosphere. By nightfall, we came to El Nopal Motel which was also owned by a Mexican. It was a great place to stay with only a few customers and carefully concealed off a farm road.

Only a few of the rooms were taken. The man at the counter plucked some strings to a guitar as he waited for the rare customer to come in looking for a room. He spoke in a heavy Mexican accent. "What can I do for you, fine gentlemen?"

"Well what the hell do people come here for?" Boy asked agitated. I gave him a slight elbow to remind him that our behavior could make us an easier pair to remember. Luckily, the hotel clerk may not have known English well enough to understand the complete sarcasm of his comment.

"I have a great room for you two *muchachos* with free television channels and a view of the back woods."

Neither one of us said anything. Boy just put the money on the counter. The clerk handed us the key as he wished us a good night. Our room smelled old, and the light bulbs inside were dim. Neither of us cared much since we intended on going to sleep right away.

"Hey Curtis, go get some ice for my leg, will ya?"

"Sure thing. You just take it easy." I took the ice bucket and walked around the building, looking for an ice machine. I finally found it, and as one could expect, there was no ice in it. The room next to the ice machine had its door open, but it didn't seem like much of a room. It looked more like someone was using the room for business, so I took the liberty of peeking inside. The area was decorated with all kinds of figurines and amulets that I had never seen before. There was a slight smoke coming from within the room, and I could barely see the figure of a man chanting things to himself, sitting Indian style on the floor.

He was instantly aware of my presence, without having turned back to look at me. He looked Mexican but spoke good English.

"Come in, *señor,* and tell me what I can do for you."

"I was just looking for some ice. I didn't mean to–"

"Ice? I do not have ice, but if you go get your friend, I can heal his wound without it." To this remark, I froze. There was no way for this man to possibly know that Boy was in need of medical attention. We hadn't been at the hotel for twenty minutes and hadn't conversed with anyone. The idea of getting such discreet attention for Boy's injury was an attractive offer. I went to the room, and Boy had already thrown himself on the bed without removing his boots.

"Come on, Boy. I gotta show you something."

"Where are we going?"

"Just come with me. I have something that will help."

"Where the hell is my ice? I ain't going nowhere. This television has color."

"Just come on."

He came with me reluctantly, and I walked him over to where the odd man sat and chanted to himself. He got up from his position and asked Boy to lie on his back.

Boy was taken by the sudden change of environment. "He ain't no queer, is he?"

"Just let him help you. Relax."

The man put an amulet around Boy's neck after dipping it into some ointment he prepared. There was no mention as to what the lotion consisted of, but it had an agreeable smell to it and seemed to have relaxed Boy. The man chanted and recited what sounded like prayers. After about twenty minutes, the chanting stopped, and the man woke Boy up. He gestured toward the door with his hand suggesting that we were free to go.

"How much do we owe you?" I asked him. He shook his head to say there was no fee and returned to the position he was in when I first saw him.

Boy got up with ease from the bed and made a face to say that maybe there was something to the man's practice. "You sure we can't pay you nothing?"

"No, *señor,* your money is no good." I was not sure what he meant by that. I turned my attention back to my friend.

"Do you feel anything?"

"No actually I don't. It's probably some temporary pain reliever or something. Come on, Curtis, we gotta get some sleep."

For a reason I could not explain, I couldn't get any sleep that night. I tossed and turned as if I were taming a wild horse in the water. I looked out the window and saw nothing but dead wilderness as far as the eye could see. The man at the counter made it seem like a view of the woods was a luxury. All I saw was something to give us a refund for, but there was an essence about the view that made me miss home. Finally, after about an hour or two of thinking about what I left back in Tomball, I fell asleep.

The morning came quickly, and when the sun arose, it brought with it a new adventure that I could never be prepared for. Before Boy woke up, I thought I would go fetch us a pack of smokes. On my way to the lobby, I saw several State Trooper patrol cars parked randomly throughout the parking lot. My natural instinct was to assume they were there for me and Boy, but I saw them taking out a man and a woman in handcuffs from one of the rooms. I adjusted my position and was shocked to see the couple was the Mexican girl and the white man who had conned me out of my wallet. The witch doctor who did a ritual on Boy the night before was walking back to his room from the lobby with a cup of coffee.

"Hey, excuse me, but what's going on over there with that couple?"

"Um, a very bad thing, *señor*. They paid for their room with counterfeit money."

"Counterfeit?"

"Yeah, they said the money came from a wallet that wasn't theirs, but you can't convince the police of things like that."

"Is that what you meant about my money not being good? You know who we are, don't ya?" He didn't answer this question, much to my annoyance.

"How's your friend's leg?"

"Um, it's good. Thanks for your help." I quickly returned to the room and looked out the window. The first thought in my head was that if they retrieved the wallet that was taken from me, the troopers would be sure to recognize me if those two kept my driver's license and if Dawson sent a sketch of me that far down the state. If they didn't recognize me, I still had to worry about the possibility that the money we had been using is also counterfeit. The troopers were having a conversation with the clerk at the front desk. I closed the gap between my face and the curtain, but I was able to see the clerk pointing toward our room. I realized that it was time to wake Boy up.

Chapter 9

Cactus Water

He brought over a large cactus plant and milked it like a cow.

I woke Boy quickly and he didn't take a liking to such an abrupt disturbance. This was one time that I wouldn't allow him to intimidate me since we needed to get out quickly. "Hey Boy, there's some cops outside pointing this way. Let's go!"

"What?"

"Let's go, Boy!" I said gathering what I could and putting it into my duffel bag. I opened the rear window that led out into the brown, dry Texas woods.

"Where the hell you going?"

"We ain't got no choice, cowboy. Now, let's go!"

The window had probably never been opened so it took more than simply lifting it. I did what came to mind and put my right boot through it. Boy saw I was serious and didn't ask any more questions. He gathered what he could and followed me out the window. We ran as fast as we could through the miles of brown bush without any sense of direction. I knew we hadn't gotten as far as it felt we did because I could hear the troopers identifying themselves and kicking our room door in. It would be a matter of minutes before we would hear dogs barking after us with our natural scent leading the way.

We ran for about thirty minutes before the soles of our boots became a warm skillet. The bottoms of our feet were hot, and the inside of our boots were burning enough to heat beans. We found what appeared to be the only shade for miles and threw ourselves on the ground near the bark of the only tree in the entire area that was taller than us.

Boy waited to catch his breath before coming out with something. "What the hell was that all about, Curtis?"

"It's fake–the money is fake."

"What money?"

"Damn it, Boy! Our money–Old Man Winters's money–it's fake!"

"What the hell do you mean fake?"

"Yeah, the old shit must have been dealing in counterfeit."

Boy pulled his cowboy hat over his face and leaned back against the tree in disbelief. It took me a while to come to terms with what happened before I finally realized that, technically, Boy and I had no money in addition to having lost the truck. I mentioned this to him, but he did not respond.

"I don't hear anything," was all he said.

"No, I don't suppose they ran after us all the way."

"Hell, they got the truck. They know who we are."

"Don't you think I've thought of that?"

"Of course, you have. You're the smart one, ain't ya?"

"Now, I ain't saying you're dumb, Boy." There was silence for a moment. Nothing could be heard but the far-off singing of South Texas locust.

"It sure is quiet-like out here, ain't it?"

"Yeah, kinda reminds me of my father's ranch when I was small. He used to make us load all the watermelons, onions, and corn from the field onto the truck. We'd lean on this giant mesquite tree that set off quite a bit of shade. We'd drink RC cola under it until our bladders couldn't take it anymore. I could feel the cold soda run down the inside of my chest like Niagara Falls. It was great."

"Shit, I could use something to drink now." Boy had always been a full-blown cowboy and knew how to extract water like a soda fountain from the right cactus. He brought over a large cactus plant and milked it like a cow. The water inside tasted clean—nothing at all like tap water. The after taste was a little grainy, like dirt, but it was clean, cool water as if it had been in a refrigerator.

"My father bought me a canteen once when I was just a boy. Cactus water kinda tastes like water that's been setting in a canteen for a few days."

"You know, Boy, I've known you for quite a spell already, and this is the first time I can remember you ever mentioning your pa."

"He isn't much to talk about."

"You still talk to him much?"

"He's dead."

"Now, why didn't I know that knowing you so long?"

"Didn't tell ya."

"Well I'm sorry, Boy."

"I ain't. Dumb ass got kicked by a bull at a rodeo. It shouldn't have happened, but he didn't show up nowhere without being drunk. A drunk ain't got no place in a rodeo."

I stopped Boy for a moment when I heard something far off. We both stood to our feet anticipating Texas Rangers coming around the brush to greet us. We couldn't tell exactly which direction the sound was coming from so that we could go away from it. The Texas woods often have a way of making sound disappear too quickly. Before we both knew it, it was too late. There was a truck directly behind us.

"You boys alright?" There was an older white man driving a white pickup with Mexican workers on the bed. Boy and I looked at each other both probably wondering the same thing. The white man spoke again. "Well, are you fellas alright, or ain't ya? You know, this sun will cook your nuts by two o'clock. Both of you better jump on back with the gentlemen here so I can give you guys a ride back to the main road. Besides, this is private property, and Crazy Jake Simmons ain't gonna take a liking to you being here. He's bound to shoot you boys upon sight."

Boy and I reluctantly climbed onto the back of the pickup truck. In less than half a day, the entire environment of our journey changed considerably. We had gone from driving in a pickup truck toward Mexico as wealthy men to being packed on the bed of a pickup with no money among illegal immigrants. Most of them did not seem to be interested in sharing their space. They looked at us with great suspicion, and whether or not Boy and I were safe was something I had not decided on yet. For the moment, this predicament was not negotiable. I wasn't so much afraid of being shot by landowners as I was of being crushed by the Texas heat. At the very least, our current position would afford us a cup of water.

The ride was long and hot. The immigrants seemed very comfortable with the heat and the horrendously bumpy ride. They sat just as comfortably as a cowboy on a wild bull. They didn't even budge in the tough terrain. The most annoying thing was the dead silence for over an hour. It was a gratifying feeling when we finally arrived at a farm with large gates at its entrance and a large yard decorated with Mexican pottery and nice furniture. Beautiful Mexican women worked throughout the yard like in the old days. Some were making home-made tortillas while others cooked on an open fire. Others decorated the inside of the barn as if preparing for a feast, and the aroma in the air suggested that whatever was being cooked would be as delightful of an experience to the palate as it was to the nostril. Finally, I had reason to converse with someone when the driver got off his truck.

"Welcome home, boys."

"Where are we at?" I asked.

"I'd rather not say, cowboy. I don't want no one calling on no authorities saying where my boys are. Immigration would be here in less than an hour."

I wanted to laugh at the prospect of either me or Boy calling the authorities, but I didn't think it would be a good idea to hint at our troubles and risk losing our only source of life in the Texas desert.

"So, what do they call you, boys?" he asked.

Boy intervened quickly and said his first words after more than an hour. "I think we're entitled to our secrets if you're entitled to yours," he said in a serious tone while lighting a cigarette.

"Fair enough, fellas. You guys stay out a minute, and there'll be another truck coming by for ya."

Chapter 10

The Hidden Farm

"You ask any one of these Mexicans to milk a cow, and they'll take it by the ears."

The road to the immigration farm was narrow and disappeared behind a family of trees that made no geographical sense. I imagine they were placed there intentionally to camouflage the beautiful farm that was behind it. Long lines of different crops covered the land in perfect synchronized rows. The truck kept driving for another five miles or so. It finally came to a stop near a farmhouse that seemed to be freshly painted. It was white with yellow trim and had the appearance of the typical 1800s Texas house. It was much newer, though, and the entire property seemed like it was paid much mind to. I felt as if I was in a completely different country. "You ever seen anything like this, Boy?"

"Not here in Texas. Are we still in Texas?"

"I don't reckon we've driven that long to be out of it."

"I suppose not."

We all got off the truck. Our co-riders went on as if they knew exactly where they were going. Boy and I stood our ground until we were approached by an older gentleman who appeared to be Mexican but spoke perfect English. "You boys here to work?"

"We'd be in debt to you for it, Sir." I wanted him to know we were ready to make an earning. If there was something Boy and I could never have enough of, it was money.

"Well, we always need the help. You guys ain't feds, are ya?"

"No sir, we're about the furthest thing you can get to being a fed."

"I'm glad to hear it. Well, we can drop the formalities if we're gonna be working with each other. They call me Cotton around here because I can pick it faster than any man without pricking my fingers with any thorns. Who am I talking to?"

"I'm Curtis Cash, and this here is my good friend Boy Jenkins."

Boy looked at me with a great deal of frustration. I imagine neither one of us will ever kick the habit of introducing ourselves by our natural names. I am not sure it mattered much in these parts. They seemed to be rather primitive in their lifestyle and very hardworking as well. It did not take a genius to understand we were surrounded by a great number of illegal immigrants who were there to make an American living. The last thing they wanted was to have law enforcement on their farm.

"How handy are you boys with cattle?"

"We know our way around them quite well, Cotton."

"That's where we hurt the most. Folks around here tend to be useful in growing things. They can take a cactus and make a watermelon of it. But cattle–that's the problem. You ask any one of these Mexicans to milk a cow, and they'll take it by the ears."

"We'd be glad to help."

"That's great, Curtis. We are running short on milk, cheese, and cream."

"You can count on us, Cotton."

He then looked over to Boy. "How about you? Ya think you can tame a horse?"

"I've been known to settle down quite a few."

"Follow me, then. I'll take y'all to where you need to be. I'll drive around to pick you guys up in the evening, so you can wash up for our festivities tonight."

"Festivities?"

"Oh yeah, it's Friday. We have a feast every Friday. We have a good old-fashioned cookout with some of the best meat you've ever sunk your teeth into and all the Mexican beer you can imagine." Boy and I made eye contact at the thought of having some good food. We never felt comfortable being separated, but there was something comforting about the environment at the farm. No one questioned us, looked at us with suspicion, or even cared to judge us. People were friendly, hardworking, and went about with day with a smile no matter how difficult their task was. It was a sight I had never seen before. Back in Tomball, I worked with a bunch of overpaid sons of bitches, with wealthy daddies, who always complained about their workday. Most didn't work half as hard as I was seeing these people work.

I squeezed quite a bit of milk, washed the cattle, and laid out some feed. Their bulls seemed like they needed some attention, and I took care of that as well. For a brief moment, I felt like I was tending cattle in my own ranch. It was an amazing feeling. I felt like a free man. As the sun began to show signs of fading, the truck came around with Boy already in it. It was Cotton.

"Hop on, Curtis. Let's go get washed up."

I hopped in the bed of the truck with Boy. "How'd it go, Boy?"

"I'm a bit sore, but their wild horses weren't nearly as violent as the ones I used to tame out in Tomball. How'd it go for you?"

"It went by quick. I have never seen folk take so much joy out of working as the people around me."

"Yeah, I noticed that."

"Ya know, Boy, I ain't never been one to judge others. But my granddaddy was in the Klan and my own father took to some of his ideas, but I don't see any of those things they used to try to get me to believe."

"They look like good folk to me."

"You bet."

"They're just trying to make a living like everyone else."

The Friday night affair was much larger than I had expected. It was held on a large barn on the opposite side of the land. It was neatly decorated, and the entire place smelled like food. People danced to Mexican music and talked about their day. Boy and I tried some foods that we had never had before, and we ate until we were close to busting.

"Boy, you tell me of a time you found food like this in a Mexican restaurant."

"I can't. Some of this stuff I've never even heard of. The beer is good too."

"We need to get down to Mexico."

"We're going. We're just kinda taking the long way."

Our introductory experience to this hidden farm was an amazing one. It was so incredible that it would be another two years before we even thought about leaving. It would have been much longer if what happened next hadn't changed the course of our lives in ways we never thought possible.

Chapter 11

Modesto

"Sometimes all the fight in us just ain't enough."

Somewhere in South Texas, 1980

The two years lived at the farm were not entirely spent in isolation. Boy and I both advanced in our Spanish speaking skills and made a good number of friends. We played horseshoes, drank together, played cards and shared stories from our past. No one cared whether the nature of the stories were fact or fiction; we just needed some good tall Texas tales to go with our Mexican beer. No new acquaintance had a more important impact on me than that of Lorena Azevedo. I met her the same night we had the first Friday night cookout two years before. We often took walks together and taught each other our first languages. She'd cook me something special every now and then and snuck food to me and Boy late at night to the barn where we slept.

It's a funny thing about how Boy and I slept. Our first evening we got comfortable in the barn, and it just became a customary place for us to hang our hat for the night. I don't think we ever thought about requesting a bed in the bunkers where all the workers slept because Boy and I always preferred to be alone. The less people knew or asked about us, the more comfortable we felt. This is one thing about Lorena

I really took to very quickly. She was very respectful-like when it came to asking personal questions. She never asked any. Everything at the farm appeared to be going very well. If things were any better, Boy and I could remain there forever instead of ever going to Mexico. If we didn't know any better, we would think we were already in Mexico anyway. Three things, however, were a thorn on our side. The first was that Boy didn't care much for my association with Lorena. She was the niece to one of the foremen that we didn't see very often, and Boy was afraid that he wouldn't approve of her relationship to someone who wasn't a Mexican and expel us from the farm. I cared deeply for Lorena, but I must admit that if Boy's worries ever came to fruition, that would not be a good scenario for us.

The second thing that was very difficult to constantly have to explain away was that Boy's leg never took to healing properly. One would think that after so much time, it would have not been an issue anymore. The witch doctor did a good number on it, yet the healing didn't last but a month. The lack of proper medical attention to it kept Boy limping. People often asked what was wrong with Boy's leg. I simply didn't know how to explain it. If anyone ever saw the actual skin, they would know exactly what it is. At times, it would dry up a bit, and Boy would be just fine. Other times, a hard day's work would open a little gap in the skin and droplets of blood would spew out slowly. Our first winter at the farm, Boy got a fever that was something awful. I thought his leg was infected, but Cotton gave him some antibiotics thinking he had the common flu. He felt better after a while, but we needed to do something soon about that leg. It was a conversation Boy and I needed to have soon. I'd heard along the way as a child that getting a raccoon to piss on a bullet wound would heal it, but I hadn't had the occasion to come across one at the farm.

The biggest issue on my mind had to do with why we were still on the farm after two years to begin with. Sure, the farm was nice and beautiful and even better once I met Lorena. I just was not sure if this was enough to keep two wanted men in the same place for that long. The problem was that the wages earned for a day's work wasn't enough to feed a dead billy goat. Cotton would often go into town to get us things we needed for hygiene and personal things. The small earnings would take more than half of what we earned just to survive, and this was truer for Boy who had to continuously treat his leg. Very simply, we just weren't earning enough money to continue on our route to Mexico. But nearly six months into our two-year anniversary, our fate would experience a drastic change.

It was the customary Friday night cookout. It was cold that night, and we had to close the barn doors halfway so that the cold night breeze didn't race through the barn where people danced and ate.

"Sure is cold tonight, Curtis."

"Yeah, the time is changing."

"Speaking of change, how much longer you reckon we're gonna be here?" I looked around and saw a few people too close for my comfort. I took Boy by the arm and led him outside the barn. I pulled out two cigarettes as if we went out to smoke. Everyone knew smoking inside the barn was not allowed for fear the hay may catch fire. "Listen Boy, I've been thinking over that very question. I love being here and the good Lord knows I love Lorena with all my heart, but we just ain't earning here."

"You bet we ain't. I don't know what the hell all these politicians are complaining about. Ain't no American I can think of is gonna want these jobs. What jobs are they taking? Who the hell would want to work for this?"

"Hell, I don't know. Any American who wants these jobs is in bad shape already without immigrants being here."

"So, what do we do?"

"We're gonna have to think it over. The very reason we haven't been able to put two coins away is the reason we're still here. How would we live in Mexico?"

"I reckon we'd need to get us some work."

"That's without saying, but if they pay like this or even less, we need something to start with."

"You got some smarts about you, Curtis." We heard some commotion at this point coming from the road that led to the entrance of the farm. The immediate thought in my head was that the border patrol had discovered this little hidden paradise, but that wasn't the case.

Cotton had a new crew in the back of his truck, but one young man in particular appeared to have sustained some serious injuries. Cotton acted quickly to get him off the bed of the truck and took him to a small shed in the back where they often kept some horses. Fortunately, the horses had been moved because of how cold the night was, and there was room for the young man there. Boy and I rushed over. "What happened, Cotton?"

"Well, Curtis, this young man went on and got himself into a fight and got roughed up pretty good."

"Roughed up?" Boy interjected, "He plain done got his ass kicked. He looks horrible! You'd think he'd want to throw at least one punch back!"

"Sometimes all the fight in us just ain't enough. Now fellas, I'm supposed to drive up to Abilene to see my daughter. The only person in this farm who can tend to something like this is Francisco. He was a doctor in Mexico. He's been around a couple of times, but you boys haven't met him yet. I called him up, but he won't be here until the morning. Can you boys make sure this young man is comfortable until then? I'll be sure to pay you guys for your service. Modesto is his name, and he knows a lot about irrigation. We need him to be ready to work for us."

I couldn't deny Cotton. He was a good man. "You bet, Cotton. We'll make sure he's okay."

Poor Modesto was in serious bad shape. Boy and I used two old buckets as seats and sat next to the young man while we smoked and drank Mexican beer. We continued our conversation about what we should do next Suddenly, we heard young Modesto murmur something under his breath.

"What did he say, Boy?"

"I don't know. I can barely hear him. Let me try and get closer." We both moved our buckets closer to the small army bed Cotton placed Modesto on.

"What did you say?"

"The ring. Get the ring."

Boy and I looked at each other in confusion. "What the hell does that mean, Curtis?"

"I don't know. I reckon only he can tell us."

He didn't say a thing after that and went back to sleep.

The morning arrived and brought with it a little warmth. We didn't sleep very comfortably in the shed, but we kept our promise to Cotton and kept young Modesto company. His eyes were open in the morning, so I decided to greet him.

"Top of the morning to ya. How are you today, Modesto?"

"My ribs hurt."

"Well, you took a hell of a beating. What did you go on and get into a fight for?"

"I had to. The boss made me do it."

"Your boss? You mean Cotton?"

"No, my previous boss. He makes a lot of us Mexicans fight each other for entertainment." Boy and I looked at each other in disbelief.

"Have you ever heard of anything like that before, Curtis?"

"No, I can't say that I have."

"Yes, he would make us fight," Modesto continued. "It was his sick way of entertaining his rich friends."

I was curious. "Why on earth would you agree to that?"

"We have no choice. The boss would not keep us on to work if we did not comply with his demands. Most of us coming from Mexico really need those jobs."

Boy was curious about something too. "So, tell me, Modesto, how come you don't have an accent or anything like that? I mean you speak all proper-like."

"I came to America at a very early age to go to private school. My parents were both schoolteachers, but I went back to Mexico to live with my grandmother, hoping to get my hands on the lost ring of Napoleon Bonaparte."

"The what of who?" Boy asked.

"The ring of Napoleon Bonaparte. He was a military leader for France long ago. A ring maker by the name of Pierre Arnoult crafted the ring in secret. Rumor has it that they were lovers. The ring got lost with time, and hundreds of years later, I have reason to believe that the ring is in my professor's home in Nuevo Laredo, Mexico."

Boy looked at me with a curious eye and asked Modesto something we both wanted to know. "So, how much is this thing worth?"

"It is priceless. It would be an incredible find."

I wasn't sure if Modesto was delusional from his injuries or if he was telling us something factual. I pulled Boy over to the side. "What the hell is this kid talking about the military leader of France?"

"Hell, Curtis, I don't know anything about no leader of France, but I take a good interest in jewelry worth something."

"How do ya know he ain't full of shit?"

"Well, let's ask him."

Boy walked over to the weak young man. "Hey Modesto, what makes you think this priceless ring is in your professor's house?"

"That is a long story, my friend."

"Oh, hell, we ain't going nowhere.

Chapter 12

Modesto's Account of the Ring

Mexico is a very superstitious country with strong beliefs that to speak of evil is to welcome it into one's home.

Nuevo Laredo, Tamaulipas, 1969

On a secluded side of Nuevo Laredo, Tamaulipas, near the Rio Grande and away from the dishevelment of the bridge to America, there is a road that makes no geographical sense. There is no main artery that would lead one to this part of Mexico unless they have prior knowledge it is there. The angle is mathematically confusing, and the road itself is a soft red dirt that will rise into a plume of floating dust with any slight wind. It is quiet. Nothing in the area appeals to anyone of sound mind. Only the slightly disturbed care anything at all about what rests at the end of this road. Few know the road is there. Thick brush and spiny thorn bushes conceal it. This is not intentional; rather, it is a warning from nature that perhaps one's curiosity is best reserved for another time and another place in the world.

Most people preferred not to speak of the place. Mexico is a very superstitious country with strong beliefs that to speak of evil is to welcome it into one's home. *Mal ojo* is what some will call it. I did not call it anything yet; I was only ten when I first came across the road and had never heard anyone mention it. My name is Modesto Valencia, but most people call me "Desto" because for some reason, acknowledging someone by their true name went out of style in the 50s. I was a quiet boy with a mystery inside me no one could ever solve. My parents did well for themselves, and we commuted to the American side daily so that I would attend St. Mary's, a private school few could afford. The Mexican children in my neighborhood considered me eccentric for speaking English well. Others simply envied the large red brick mansion I lived in. Large, white pillars that looked like huge tree trunks held up the balcony that led to my room. Flamingos roamed freely in the yard with less care in the world than those people living in the impoverished streets of Nuevo Laredo.

Their feathers were a dark pink with circles of engine red penetrating through the transparent quills on their tails. Some plucked the ants off the yard while others laid lazily looking toward the Rio Grande into American soil. I was the only one who cared for these exotic birds but, for some reason, had never grown emotionally attached to them. I had never grown emotionally attached to anything, for that matter. It was not in my nature. I did care for my parents, but I could never bring myself to say I loved them. Even at ten, I had already learned that "love" was a dangerous word. Someone who does not love you can still say it. My parents did everything for me, and they would not let me forget it. They used their means to send me to a private school to justify my enslavement. I had to do what they said, read what was given to me, eat at the same hour, and go to bed at the same time every night. I blame them for not being able to keep friends even today. The superstitious world is more important to me than loyalty to any one person.

My father owned a small school that taught English to the wealthier children in Northern Mexico. Some would attend the school simply to perfect their American accent when they were prompted to say "American Citizen" at the bridge. Others hoped to go to college in America and learn English early in their life instead of later. Whatever their reasons were, the school did well and had brought a considerable fortune to my family. The Valencia family was admired by the people in the area and thought of as prominent members of the community. But I did not feel privileged. Instead, I felt imprisoned with money as my warden. My only escape were the beautiful sounds of Bach and Mozart pouring into my ears from what was probably the only record player in this part of Mexico. I was not the only Mexican enrolled at St. Mary's, but most other parents had to struggle more to send their children there.

I did not care much for making new friends, but something about Jimena Abundis made me feel special. Her parents did better than most in Mexico but not nearly as well as my parents. Her family owned a bakery that had achieved a favorable repute. They were most known for their *empanadas de camote*. It was a light crusted pastry filled with yams. They are extremely popular during the holidays. Jimena seemed to like me as much as I liked her. She would often take the three-block walk from her bakery to my house just to say hello. I always looked forward to the day she would arrive with free pastries. School had just ended for the year, and I knew exactly what demands lied ahead for me throughout the summer. Despite the money my parents had, I was not expecting a summer trip to go camping or to the beach. I had no hopes of throwing a football around or working on a two-seam curve ball with my father. There would be no large-mouth white bass at the end of my fishing line either. I would be cleaning out the basement, running errands on my bike, and doing extensive homework to prepare me for the following school year.

I had been contemplating all these chores on my doorstep for an hour when Jimena arrived with a small bag of cookies. I was reading a comic book but saw her right away.

"Hey, Desto," she said to me.

"Hi."

"You want some cookies?"

"Sure." I said. I looked behind me to see if my parents were anywhere near. I knew they would tell me to not eat sweets before dinner. I did not want to be embarrassed that way in Jimena's company. "Can we go eat them somewhere else?" I suggested with a smile so slight, one would have to be acquainted with me well enough to know it was not the natural map of my face. Jimena agreed. She agreed with most of what I suggested we should do with our free time. The blue ribbon that kept her ponytail in place flickered from the slight breeze coming from Texas. A profound dimple caved in on her left cheek every time she smiled, and her green eyes accentuated her caramel complexion, which was lighter than most Mexican girls I knew. It had more of a light brown color. She never had problems crossing to the American side because of it.

She followed me as we made our way down a narrow-pebbled path that swung around my father's mansion and curved back the other way along the Rio Grande. Jimena pulled out a lollipop.

"You're going to lose your teeth eating lollipops and cookies altogether." I scared myself realizing I was sounding like my parents, but it was too late. I had already delivered the lecture.

"It's okay. I prefer candy. The cookies are for you." She handed me the small brown bag filled with *biscochitos* and *polvorones de canela*. I loved cinnamon especially around Christmas time. I shyly took a small bite out of the first cookie and continued on through the narrow path leading to the river.

Jimena followed loyally wanting to spend more time with me. "Are you going somewhere this summer?" she asked.

"No, I think my father is too busy."

"We are going to Monterrey to visit my grandmother."

"Who's going to run the bakery?"

"We have people," she answered confidently. We continued along the path to a family of *carizzo* that tended to grow rapidly along the Rio Grande. *Carizzo* was also known as Spanish Cane. My grandfather once told me it grows faster than any other form of vegetation in the world. I was used to making my way through it and had even taken some home with me to make bedding for my birds.

"My father said you could come work at the bakery over the summer if you wanted."

"I'll be too busy doing whatever my father says."

"What are you going to do?" Jimena asked.

Her tongue was completely red by this point, and her cherry lips revealed her love for candy. She impulsively licked her lips to get all the flavor she could from them.

"I don't know yet, but my father always has something."

We both stopped at the sound of a commotion taking place near the river. I walked slowly toward the sound of voices and gently moved the long stems from the *carizzo* to the side.

Jimena was too frightened to look for herself but wanted to know what was happening. "What is it?"

"I don't know. There are some men down there."

"What are they doing?"

"I can't tell yet." I continued to navigate the area with my eyes. I was finally able to see the dark yellow capital letters running across the men's jackets: POLICIA FEDERAL. "It's the police."

"What are they doing?"

I did not hear this last question, so there was no answer from me. A large officer was in the way of a better view. When he finally moved, I could see they were pulling a body from the river. "They are getting a dead man out of the river."

"A dead man?" This alarmed her.

"Shhh, don't be so loud," I cautioned Jimena.

The men debated about something; I could not hear. The police searched the victim's pockets and removed his watch, boots, and belt.

"What are they doing now?" Jimena whispered.

"I don't know, but I no longer think they are taking the body out of the river."

"Then what are they doing?"

"I think they are putting it into the river."

"Why do you think that?"

"Because the body is still dry."

"Why would they be putting the body into the river?" She continued to whisper.

I did not answer and focused on my observations. The men turned the body over face down into the water half submerged. They carried out this act with lack of compassion and with a discourteous decorum that no creature without life is deserving of. What possible folly can any one man partake in while alive that would merit such ill-treatment of his figure after life has escaped him? Yet, there was the abused remains of perhaps a father, one's husband, brother, or friend. The fumes of his prior existence escaped through his nostrils into the dark, muggy waters of the Rio Grande, and there they would remain as part of a collection of Mexican souls that were never awarded the occasion to relate their story.

"*Vamonos!*" One of the men called out to the others as they prepared to leave.

The discretion Jimena and I so hoped to maintain to avoid breaching a conversation between figures of questionable character proved to be in vain. At the most inopportune moment in our concealment, Jimena lost control of her senses and was unable to govern a sneeze provoked by the many stubborn allergens one encounters in such a moist environment. Had it been a single sneeze, she may have been able to deliver its hasty manner of exiting the body to a manageable degree. For Jimena, however, it was not one but a family of sneezes that could not be so easily contained.

The men were quick to discontinue any dialogue between them. A group of five men remained close behind the apparent leader, moving forward to examine the premises. The fully automatic weapon suggested to me that the leader had a predetermined design for eliminating anyone who may compromise their current operation. I was very frightened for both me and Jimena—we were only ten, after all. I paced backwards while reaching out for Jimena's hand. My eyes never once abandoned their post. I looked directly ahead of me, fixed on the tall dark figure moving at a fearsome pace. The pernicious man used the barrel of his weapon to push aside the thick *carizzo.* We were both quickly exposed to the large Mexican looking down at us with one glass eye and a scar running evenly down his face from the top of his shaggy brow to where his jaw ends.

"Run, Jimena!" I had no other alternative than to break the silence I had tried so passionately to preserve.

A command was issued with one stroke of the arm by the tall, scarred figure for his companions to give chase. I pulled Jimena through thick brush. "Let's run through here," I said practically dragging Jimena between two thick bushes that any normal sized adult would endure great difficulties to penetrate.

"But Modesto," cried the frightened little girl. "We do not live this way!"

"We cannot go home, Jimena. They will follow us and know where we live."

"No Modesto, I don't want them to kill my family."

"They won't. Just stay with me." Suddenly, gunfire pierced the thick bushes randomly. Jimena began to cry. I stopped to face her. "Jimena, you must stop crying. They will hear us. Let's run across the opposite end to those tall trees. The men are too big to follow quickly."

We ran as fast as we could through the thick brush until we arrived at two large trees. The space between the two large trees was completely covered with heavy brush. "We will hide in here."

Jimena buried her face on her knees and waited patiently. I looked calmly through the bushes and could not see anyone approaching. Still, I feared going in the same direction as the men in pursuit. "Come on Jimena, let's follow this road. We will find a place to use the phone."

Jimena was quite scared and became very quiet. Suddenly, she bolted through the woods in the direction from where they came.

"Jimena, do not go that way. Come back!" I pleaded. My heartfelt request had fallen on deaf ears, and the young girl continued to run. I felt helpless. I knew my scared friend wanted nothing more than to get home. It was my every intention to follow her, but I reasoned that doing so would compromise both of our safety and decided to abandon the idea and follow through with my previous plan. It was the most difficult decision I ever had to make in my young life. Watching Jimena vanish from my view was like watching that beautiful butterfly one can never catch because its flight is so directionless. You just don't know how to go about it. "I'll see you later at the bakery," I said to myself.

I followed the road until it ended at an intersection of yet a smaller path. I stopped and looked toward both ends only to realize that fate had taken me to the mysterious road made of red dirt. No one I knew had ever been that deep into this area. So many had avoided the topic of this secluded road. There were rumors that a witch occupied this patch of forest and that she would fly out at night to dance with the souls of those who had perished in the Rio Grande. But whether these tales were owed more to fact or fiction could not, in any way, overshadow what had already been confirmed with greater certainty: that returning toward the direction from where I came could lead me directly to the man with the scar down his face.

I walked reluctantly down the red dirt road and came upon an old home. The pillars were white, but the paint was cracked consistently from top to bottom. The rest of the home was a faded olive green. The shade was dying as if at one point it was a green of a much darker shade. Nothing about its appearance frightened me. Everything I had heard about the home was inconsistent with the essence of the environment. I walked up the waterlogged steps that led to the main porch and could hear the faint sound of classical music. *Beethoven!* I told myself excitedly. It was then I realized that somewhere between my front porch and being chased through the *carizzo*, I had lost my comic books.

I walked the length of the porch which ran alongside the house. I got to the last window at the end and noticed it was partially open. Inside was a man playing the piano. I had never actually seen anyone playing classical music. I would usually only hear it through my set of earphones. I was instantly drawn to the man at the seat of the grand piano. It was as if the sound of *Moonlight Sonata* had transported his soul into a heaven designated for classical artists. For me, it was a revelation that something greater existed outside my record player, and my having the only one in my area somehow became insignificant. The man moved his body to the change of every note with the elegance of a wave spitting the moonlight's shadow against the depths of a raging sea. His fingers caressed the ivory with the genuine grace of an angel plucking the stem of a rose from Eden's garden. Every note, every movement, and every gesture that came from the man was as if he was releasing every ounce of sentiment, joy, and passion that his body preserved to release only at the perfect time in his life. That time was then—at that moment sitting in front of that beautiful piano: an instrument I was certain had been created by God himself.

The man hit the last notes, and long after the piece had come to its conclusion, he remained in a poised position with his fingers resting flaccidly on the keys as if he did not want to damage them. He wanted to take in every glorious note extracted from every key so that he could take it with him when he left the piano. It was as if the keys of the piano injected this man with life and pierced every vein leading to his heart with the thunderous sounds of classical joy that few humans ever come to appreciate. For me, being as young as I was at the time, it was the most beautiful thing I had ever heard in my life.

The man stood and looked at the piano with the admiration a father feels when he looks at his own child. He placed the palm of his hand flat and gently on top of the piano as a sign of respect for the pleasure he derived from the relationship he had with this object. He then left the room quietly. I could simply not resist the temptation of wanting to feel the piano for myself. I pushed the window open a little more to give me the space I needed to make my way into the home. I walked slowly toward the piano, but every step advertised my presence with the sounds of the decaying wooden floor. The foundation was strong, but the boards were old and loud to walk on. I made it to the piano without being heard. I had never seen one that close before and was amazed at its appearance.

I looked around and was instantly overwhelmed with the number of classical paintings on the walls and antique books on the shelves. Beautiful statues were raised high on alabaster pillars at every corner of the room with a much larger glass box displaying a ring. I reached over to place my palm on top of the piano, but before I could do so, a voice emerged from within the dark hall that led to the piano area.

"That ring is from France. It once belonged to a great French leader, the one-time Emperor of France. Do you play the piano, young man?"

I was stunned and slowly began to pace backwards toward the open window.

"Don't be frightened, child. I asked if you play the piano."

"N-no, sir. I don't."

A tall, thin man emerged from the hallway holding a glass of white wine. He was light-skinned for a Mexican and spoke the perfect English. He was slightly bald from the top of his head and supported a thin salt and pepper mustache, which fit his facial dimensions quite nicely.

"I didn't mean to—"

"That's quite alright, young man. I just want to know if you play the piano."

"No, but I heard you play *Moonlight Sonata* and wanted to hear."

"So. you don't play the piano, you say?"

"No, sir."

"Yet you know of *Moonlight Sonata*?"

"Yes, sir, I heard you play the first movement, 'Opus 27, Number 2.'"

"So, you have yet to acquaint yourself with the art of playing this instrument, yet you are familiar with the classical arrangement I just played?"

"Yes, sir. I love classical music."

"Who introduced it to you?"

"Myself, sir. I once saw a performance at my school in America. I fell in love with it and wanted to learn all there was to know about classical music. The performer was far, and I never got to see the piano up close."

"Yet you don't play?"

"No, sir."

"Why not?"

"My father," I said softly. I hoped the polite man would not inquire into the nature of my relationship with my father. It was far too lugubrious to relate to a stranger.

Much to my satisfaction, he did not pursue the subject of my family any further and, instead, probed into my sudden presence in his home. "What is your name?"

"Modesto, sir."

"Tell me, Modesto, is there anything besides this piano that so compelled you to enter my home unannounced?"

"Well, I was hiding, sir."

"Hiding from what?"

"*Federales,* sir."

"And you thought it good judgment to lead them here?"

"I'm sorry, sir. Can I go now?"

"Yes, but on one condition."

"Yes, sir."

"The next time you are to ever enter this house, it will be because the door is open and not the window."

Boy and I listened attentively to what Modesto had to say. "What do ya think, Boy?"

"It all sounds good, but how does he know that darn ring is worth a rusted horseshoe?"

It was a legitimate question, so I thought I'd ask. Both Boy and I had doubts about Modesto's account. "Hey, kid, how do you know it's worth anything?"

"Why do you guys keep calling me a kid? I'm not any younger than you guys. I happen to know its worth because I did a lot of research on this. I know you guys look at me and think I'm just another ignorant Mexican, but I'm well-read and got a good education in a private school. The only reason I am here is because I was forced, and it all has to do with that ring. I know it's priceless. I looked into it myself."

"How did it get to Mexico if it's clear across from England?" I asked.

"It's France, and how it got to Mexico is only a theory, but this is what I believe."

Chapter 13

Modesto's Theory

"Long live the Empress!"

In Veracruz, on the Gulf of Mexico, the captain announced the *Novara* was ready to embark on its journey. Among the passengers were Ferdinand Maximilian von Habsburg of Austria and his wife Marie Charlotte Amélie Augustine Victoire Clémentine Léopoldine, who went by the much shorter title of Carlota, Princess of Belgium. Respect was paid by way of cannons being fired when they arrived less than a hundred miles from Mount Orizaba. The Mexican people had been hoping for restoration and leadership that could bring their country to a new economic height and military power.

Two years before their arrival, French and Austrian troops had arrived in Mexico to put an end to Benito Juarez's campaign. Maximilian and his wife Carlota looked over Veracruz and could see the failed attempts to restore Mexico. Many cemeteries had been established randomly to accommodate victims of yellow fever, or *vomito prieto*. The neighborhoods appeared destitute but hopeful. Upon exiting the Austrian vessel, Maximilian addressed the people of Mexico: "I welcome with pleasure the arrival of the day where I can walk the soil of my new and beautiful country and salute the people who have chosen me. May God grant that the goodwill that led me toward you may be advantageous to you, and that to all good Mexicans uniting to sustain me, there will be better days for Mexico."

The new leader introduced his wife to the people of Mexico. She was a tall woman yet was delicate by nature. She spoke good Spanish but needed to take her time to speak it. She was always careful to pronounce things as they should be. Her countenance was fair, and her demeanor was kind yet firm. She carried herself with great importance but was gentle to the smile. It was aggression in its most sophisticated form. Instantly, people knew she would not tolerate foolishness, and she was treated as someone who commanded that respect. She was embraced with Mexican fabric, which she was only mildly fond of. Carlota was not at a complete lack of regard for the fact that she had to assimilate to customs that were considerably different from what she had learned in Belgium.

The people of Mexico seemed to have taken to Carlota's persona rather quickly, and she was addressed with the respect of a true leader. The new secretary of state Joaquin Velasquez de Leon was the first to do so. "The Mexicans, Madam, who expect so much from the good influence of your majesty in favor of all that is noble and great, of all that bears relation to the elevated sentiments of religion and of country, bless the moment in which your majesty reached the soil and proclaim in one voice, 'Long live the Empress!'"

The following day, Maximilian and Carlota would journey through Mexico to look at their new country. With them, they brought a considerable number of documents to pass out to the people, gifts from Austria and France, and some food supply for areas that most needed it. Their journey was by carriage, which was most difficult when they encountered muddy roads, mountains, and rain forest. The area near Chiquihuite in the mountainous region of Paso del Macho proved to be thick and difficult. By 2:00 a.m., they had arrived in Cordoba. They were exhausted and quite hungry.

For Maximilian and Carlota, the part of the trip with the highest degree of uncertainty was the time they spent in Orizaba. Because this area was known for their loyalty to Benito Juarez, the new leaders did not know what kind of response they would get from the people. To their astonishment, they were greeted with a great deal of veneration and cheer. The women presented Carlota with a ring they said had been handed down from the family of Montezuma. Maximilian, in return, gave to the women a crate filled with all kinds of French and Austrian artifacts. The large crate was heavy and took several men to move it along through the crowd. Among the gifts was the ring of Napoleon Bonaparte.

Boy took out a cigarette and lit it. He didn't seem too interested in any more Modesto had to say.

"Boy, ain't you buying into any of this?"

"Come on, Curtis, he's fooling with us because he knows we just ain't learned in all this history stuff. He can tell us whatever the hell he wants and thinks we'll be taken in by it." This was said where Modesto could hear.

"Gentleman, I am not lying to either of you. I can give you the address to my professor's house. You can see the glass box from the street."

Boy threw his cigarette on the floor and crushed it with the heel of his boot. "Okay, Modesto, tell me why the hell the ring is still there and not with you?"

"That is easy, my friends. My professor gave me the ring to take with me."

"He just let you take it for nothing?"

"Damn it, Boy, let the man finish."

"No, that is okay, Curtis. Like Boy, I was surprised the professor would just let me have something of such value. Perhaps he knew me as an honest man and that any wealth obtained as a result of the ring would be split equally between us. I would be dishonest if I told you I was not interested in making money, but to me, the history behind the ring was of equal value. I accepted the professor's gift graciously, but I need to find a way to take it. It is a heavy box, and I cannot simply walk on the streets with it. So, on that evening, I left the professor's house without it until I could acquire the use of a truck. I found one to borrow, but when I returned to my professor's house, I was greeted by his maid. I said 'hello,' and she responded."

"Oh, Desto, I am so sorry for your loss."

"My loss?"

"Yes, I know you were very close to the professor."

"What are you telling me?" I asked her.

"Don't you know, child? The professor passed away last night."

"The professor has died?"

"Yes, I am sorry, I thought you knew. It is to be expected when you refuse the cartel's offer to purchase your land. I surely wish he had just accepted."

"I tell you, my friends, I had no idea the professor was being approached by drug cartels. He never mentioned anything to me, but you could imagine how hard his death hit me. He had been my good friend since I was ten years old. I did not think to take the ring with me at that time. I figured the more respectful thing to do was to go retrieve it after the funeral. His funeral was godawful. No one attended but his maid and the man who tended to his yard, for the professor had no living family. I waited for a few days before going back to his house, but when I arrived, I was greeted by members of the drug cartel. They guarded the outside of the house with machine guns and told me that they have taken claim to the professor's property and that everything inside belongs to them."

"Can they do that?"

"Yes, Curtis. In Mexico, the drug cartel has a lot of power with few authorities to stop them. In fact, in most cases, the authorities are on their side."

"Well, they don't sound like people to be reckoned with!"

"No, Boy, they are not. This is why I found it a terrible mistake for me to go back to the house and plead with them to allow me to get my belongings. I did not reveal to them the possible worth of the ring because they would be certain to keep it for themselves. They became annoyed with my efforts and captured me. It is then they sent me to the camp on the American side under the leadership of the boss who forced me to fight for my freedom. I understand he was the owner of the house. He found great amusement in watching me lose my battle. He did not fulfill his promise to set me free if I fought, but when he was not looking, I snuck away down a farm road to a neighboring ranch. It was there that Cotton saw me among a group of immigrants he was picking up and brought me here."

Boy and I were becoming more convinced of the legend of the ring. I wasn't ever known at any point in my life for being an intelligent person nor was I ever the impressive type in school, but I do remember my history teacher speaking of a man named Napoleon Bonaparte. Without Modesto, I never would have remembered where he was from. He could have been from Tomball as far as I was concerned. But he jarred my memory a bit, and the point I wanted to make to Boy was that in our predicament, what would it hurt to believe him?

"Boy, we're on the run. We were just talking about not being able to earn enough for a pair of rusty horseshoes. What would it hurt us any to pin our hopes in something that can get us some good money to live off of in Mexico?"

"Well, you tell me this, cowboy. How are we supposed to walk so casually past drug cartels into the professor's house, get the ring, and just walk out?"

"We ain't gonna do it like that, Boy. We're gonna use smarts about it. We need to get there first."

Boy called me over to the side of the shed to where Modesto could not hear us. "Look, Curtis, you ain't gonna like this, but if we're gonna get to Mexico, we're gonna have to take Cotton's truck."

"You mean steal from these nice folks?"

"Now, don't get all Christian on me now. We aren't gonna walk from here to Mexico. We have to have ourselves a way to drive out. Did you wanna walk or what?"

"I reckon that wouldn't be the way to do it."

"You're damn right it ain't. Look, you let me work out those details, and you need to speak to Lorena."

"About what?"

"Well, you just ain't gonna leave her without letting her know we might be moving on soon, are ya?"

"Don't you think it's best? I mean we're taking the truck and all. It's best we keep our intentions roped."

"Yeah, you're right."

We walked back to Modesto. He looked as if he had used every ounce of life he had left to tell us his story. He was ready to pass out again. "Okay, Desto, give us the address, and we'll help you out when you get better."

"It is in my wallet," he said slowly. He suddenly fell back asleep. He was in obvious pain and had blood coming out of his mouth.

A few hours later, the doctor arrived to visit with Modesto and some of the other immigrants. Boy was nowhere to be found, and by the time he emerged, the doctor had left the farm.

"Where the hell were ya, Boy? The doctor left already."

"Shhh, quiet, Curtis, I was trying to see where Cotton kept the keys to the trucks around here."

"Well, the doctor left already and didn't even get to look at your leg."

"I ain't died after all this time, have I? My leg is fine. Hey, how's Modesto doing? I was thinking we could wait to bring him with us."

"You can forget about that, Boy. The doctor said he needs to get to a hospital. He thinks he's bleeding from the inside or something like that."

"Bleeding from the inside? Who the hell ain't bleeding on the inside? We're all bloody on the inside. What kind of doctoring is that?"

"Hell, I don't know! Don't quiz me. I'm just telling you what he said. He said one of his broken ribs may have punched a hole in his lung."

"That don't sound good at all, does it?"

"No, it doesn't. We have to go at this alone. We have the address, and we have your plan for the truck."

That evening I spent with Lorena walking along the white fence surrounding the farm. It was always keep freshly painted, making the grass look even green than what it actually was. We rode around on horseback for a while and spoke about insignificant things. She had no way of knowing that she was looking at me for the last time. Her beautiful caramel complexion stood out against the light sun rays bouncing off her face. She looked like an angel, and I knew I was going to miss her. Boy and I had our well-being to consider, and we no longer had lives that allowed us to carry on romances the way other folks could.

The night came quickly, and Boy once again had been out of view for several hours. I hoped that whatever he was doing, it was not something that would hurt anyone else. The hours moved fast and before I knew it, midnight had arrived. I still had not seen Boy anywhere and began to get nervous. If he got caught without me knowing, someone would certainly be coming for me as a conspirator without much time for me to react. While I waited for Boy, I reflected on my last moments with Lorena.

"You know I love ya, don't ya, girl?"

"Yes, I know. I love you too."

"If something ever happens that you won't see me no more, please don't ever think I don't love ya."

"Don't say that to me, Curtis. Don't ever say that to me again!" She embraced me.

I snapped out of my thoughts and was overcome with a sense of calm when I saw Boy coming at a short distance. Everyone on the farm was asleep and recharging for a new day of work.

"Damn it, where the hell have you been?" I whispered loudly.

"Shit on me, cowboy! If you're going to whisper that loud, you may as well talk to me through a bullhorn."

"Well where have you been?"

"I wanted to get some last-minute details from Modesto."

"Did he tell you anything useful?"

"Nope. He's dead!"

Chapter 14

A New Journey

"It is worthy to note that a cowboy's heart breaks into many more pieces than it does for anyone else."

The vibrations on the seat of our pants from the gravel beneath the tires felt like we were reacquainting ourselves with a familiar stranger. The feeling that consumed me was confusing to my mind; I felt like two different set of emotions were pulling in different directions on my brain. On one hand, there was a sense of loss in leaving the ranch. Had Boy and I not been in such a predicament, I could see myself spending the rest of my life there. The simplicity of life, the tranquility of being lost in the woods, and the desolation that was more inviting than repelling were qualities of life I had always worked toward in Tomball. At another level, being confined to the ranch with such limited mobility gave me insight on what it would be like to go to prison. If being restricted to such a pleasant way of life was burdensome after a while, what would confinement to a less attractive environment do to me? It was then I realized that the loss of freedom is the worst thing any man could experience in his life. I knew then that I'd rather die.

There was also the emotional torture of having no closure with Lorena. I couldn't help but wonder if she would hurt with my absence or if there was a relief that I was gone. As angry as she must be with me, I couldn't help but hope that she did love me. Regardless, it is worthy to note that a cowboy's heart breaks into many more pieces than it does for anyone else, and at that time, I could not be reassured that I would ever feel any different than a setting sun whose light was forever extinguished.

"So, where you driving us to?"

"Just driving," I said.

Boy lowered the passenger window halfway to allow his smoke to escape the inside of the stolen truck. "Where to?"

"Does it even matter, Boy?"

"Hell yeah, it matters, idiot. We can't be driving along the main road like two lovers on vacation."

"Well, I can't get to the nearest town with back roads."

"What's the nearest town?"

"Goliad."

"Alright then, but we best find a way around the main roads to Mexico." The word "Mexico" alone provoked thoughts of Lorena that I could not support in my mind. I couldn't hear that word without smelling *menudo* or hearing *chicharas* buzz in my ear to welcome the rising sun. The broken English accent slept in my ear like a baby cradled by my lobes, and the vision of her golden-brown hair waved before my eyes like the Mexican flag. My heart was no longer my own: it belonged to Mexico. "Hey, Boy."

"What?" He had already finished his cigarette and pushed his cowboy hat over his eyes to sleep the rest of the way.

"You reckon we can go somewhere else besides Mexico?" I asked him point-blank.

"Like where?"

"I don't know. Don't you have a sister in North Dakota? I have always wanted to go there."

"Dakota? Hell, Curtis we ain't gonna make it without getting caught to no Dakota."

"What about that ole' friend of yours?"

"What friend?"

"That fella who lost his thumbs in a bar fight in Oklahoma City?"

"Oh yeah, poor old fella couldn't hitch a ride from Oklahoma City to Fort Worth cause he had no thumbs."

"What was his name?"

"Slim McGraw—but he ain't no good to us in Oklahoma City. He moved to Memphis to open up some barbeque place with his grandfather."

I quickly ran out of people to suggest, and it was then I was inclined to believe that there was no logical place other than Mexico. Cotton's truck had some money in an envelope in the glove compartment but had only enough to get us so far and for provisions worth only about three days of travel. By way of the main highway, getting to the border of Mexico in Laredo, Texas was only a day trip; however, this plan was countered by the fact that we could not use the main road and by Boy's stubborn persistence to cross into Juarez by way of El Paso.

"Boy, why on God's green earth do ya wanna cross in El Paso?"

"There's a girl I wanna see there."

"For a girl?"

"That's right."

"You're risking us being caught for a girl?"

"Sure, why not? You were gonna do the same thing, weren't ya?"

"Yeah, I reckon I was."

I don't imagine it was intentional, but he made me think of Lorena to the point of a heartache. I didn't even ask him what girl he could possibly be interested in seeing. We had lived in seclusion for the previous two years, and he was with Mary Beth before that time. I suppose that information did not matter, and my main focus was on getting out of Texas.

The night began to prevail over the bright, pink South Texas sky. It didn't take us long to realize that the lights in the truck didn't work and driving at night was no longer an option. We pulled into a private road looking for any abandoned building or barn we could set up camp at. Instead, we drove upon a dead end to a beautiful white house with a picket fence and a freshly painted red barn. A beautiful woman was leading two horses into a corral and apparently calling it a day. She took quick notice of us, and her face instantly revealed her dissatisfaction of our presence.

"You gentlemen best be moving on. I ain't buying nothing today, and I don't need no ranch hands."

Boy was busy lighting a cigarette, so I had to be the first to answer. "Actually, ma'am, we'd be much obliged if you'd let us park our truck here overnight so that we could get some sleep."

"Like I said, you boys best be gettin'. Ain't no reason in the world to choose here to station that tin can you call a truck."

"Now, you're surely right about that, ma'am, but you see we done stumbled across this road here, and we ain't got no sun to drive by and well . . ."

"Well, what? You thought you'd come here looking to get into my horses?"

"No, ma'am, not at all. Our head lights don't work proper-like. We can't see the road."

She seemed to show some sign of sympathy for our predicament as she paused to brush her golden blonde hair behind her ears with her own hands. "How do I know you boys ain't here to rob me blind?"

I could understand her believing that about two strangers, but in our case we were being honest. The lights on Cotton's truck gave out minutes after we turned them on. "Lady, I can assure you that our interest rests on nothing more than getting some shut-eye."

Boy still hadn't said anything. It was most likely fear of saying something he shouldn't. The night sky was getting darker and getting back to the highway would be a difficult task. "Well, I suppose there ain't no harm. You boys can bunk in the barn over there. But if I see so much as a tip of your boots poking out of there, you're both gonna get real familiar with my shotgun."

"Thank you, ma'am. Come on, Boy."

Boy still remained silent and followed me to the barn. I reached for the envelope with money that was left in the truck and took it with us. There wasn't much left inside it except for some Mexican candy, matches, and some playing cards. There was less than a hundred dollars in it as far as money goes. We went inside the barn and couldn't help noticing how neatly it was maintained. Boy searched his shirt pocket for another cigarette but couldn't find one. He surveyed the area closely, and his attention was drawn quickly to the corner of the barn. "Looks like we found ourselves some dinner." He reached into a small coupe where hens slept and from it pulled out a few eggs.

"I don't know that we ought to be taking that nice lady's food, Boy."

"Nice? She was a bitch."

"Well, what do ya expect, Sherlock? We're strangers. Now, she let us bunk out in her barn, and I don't think we ought to be taking her food without her knowing."

"So, what ya going to eat, cowboy? How about some fried Mexican candy with a side of playing cards?" His sarcasm put things into a different perspective. It had been some time since we had eaten, and there was nothing certain for the following day.

"Let's just take what we need, alright?" I suggested.

Boy was always good at making fires and could start a spark with two sticks ever since he was a young child. We wanted to preserve the matches for if we ever got caught in a rain when rubbing two sticks would be pointless. We didn't have a pan, so he dug a small hole and let it get hot. He used the tin surface of an old tin fence that was just leaning against the barn wall and made some of the finest eggs I had eaten in quite some time.

"You know, Boy? You could have been a cook."

"You're just a hungry man talking." By this time, it had become darker outside, and a light drizzle fell upon the top of the barn. "Hey, Curtis?"

"Yeah."

"Don't the smell of wet barn wood remind you of my old place?"

"Yeah, it sure does do that. It sure would rain like mayhem out in Tomball, wouldn't it?"

"You know it. We'd have a spell of tornadoes every season down there."

"You ever get to thinking about Tomball, Boy?"

"Yeah, all the time, but that place is a long way from me now."

"A long way from me too, partner." We got quiet for a moment, and my eyes rested on the dancing shadows off the barn being created by the small fire still burning.

"You know, Curtis, I could make us some fried chicken."

"Funny, Boy."

He pushed the rim of his hat over his brow and leaned against the hay.

"Hey, cowboy, you think you can promise me something?"

"Yeah. The way a doctor can promise a little boy that it ain't gonna hurt." He lifted the rim of his hat a little and saw I was serious. "Yeah, Curtis, I can promise you something . . . what is it?"

"If one of us ever gets out of this alive and safe, we tell the story of the other to our grandchildren."

"Yeah, why not? I can do that."

"You gotta promise me something too."

"Oh yeah? What's that?"

"If your ass gets out of this a free man, you won't die without getting to know North Dakota."

"You bet!" After a few more minutes of watching the flames dance, we were both asleep.

Chapter 15

Dolly

"Oh, don't mind Buck. He's always got this look in his eye like he's sitting on a porcupine."

The night was eerily silent. I could feel the tender warmth of the fire pressing against my face. It felt like I was in Tomball on my own bed. I thought hard about returning to Tomball and let happen whatever was destined to happen to me. To this day, the only evidence I had done anything was the assault on a deputy. Even for that, I wasn't rightly sure Dawson even knew I had a hand in that. Boy hit him so hard, he may have lost recollection of anything else. I didn't anticipate any serious time for that. The thought of returning home and facing minimal charges became recurrent in my thoughts, and the idea would not abandon me. After an hour, the gentle warmth on my face began to intensify in heat. Moments later, my entire body was hot. I opened my weary eyes, and the scene was evil in every sense of the word. The barn was on fire!

"Oh shit. Boy, get up!"

"Damn it, Curtis! What the hell?"

"What do ya think it is, cowboy?" The fire spread like a den of vipers racing toward injured rabbits. The beautiful dancing flames had turned the inside of the barn into an inferno. Chickens ran crazy with their wings on fire, and the golden color of the hay transformed quickly into charcoal. We could not exit through the front doors as the flames had enclosed the barn. We started to kick the older boards with our boots until one finally gave way. It was smaller than what we needed to get through, but the fire was spreading so quickly that we had no time to negotiate with the flames. I told Boy to force himself through first, but he wouldn't hear of it and pushed me forward. I managed to get through the tight squeeze without any damage to my skin or limbs. Boy had no such luck as the sharper edge of one of the broken boards scratched over the surface of the skin where he was shot. It had been some time since the wound bothered him; however, never having had adequate medical attention to the area left that part of his leg in a rather delicate state.

Boy's leg was further compromised by the possibility of being shot again. Over the loud cracking of burning wood, I could hear the lady from the house screaming and firing shots in our direction.

"Oh shit, Boy. Come on!"

I tried to assist my friend as much as I could, but his inability to use both legs mandated extra strength from me that I was not sure I had. I felt it was a miracle that the barn was less than a football field away from a railroad track. The true miracle was that a train was passing at a snail's pace, and I thought Boy and I could jump on it if we hurried. He started limping and began to bleed more than he had since being treated by that strange man at the hotel. Another shot landed just in front of Boy's boot, and this made him jump just a bit faster.

"Come on, Boy. We can get to this train if we move on it."

We both held on to the side ladder. One more shot could be heard at a distance, but I was feeling better about the gap the train had put between us and the fire. One final pull of Boy's arm took us both into the boxcar, and we dropped on our backs to catch our breath.

After a few minutes of heavy breathing, Boy finally spoke. "What the hell happened back there? Were you trying to kill me?"

"I don't know. Maybe it was a cigarette or something."

"Oh, so it's my fault now?"

"I didn't say that at all. I'm just using reasoning."

"Well, why don't ya reason that the fire was still burning from what I cooked for the both of us?"

"Alright, Boy! Alright!"

The night got very quiet. All that could be heard is the rattling of the moving boxcar. It was not a pleasant ride. There was no way to find comfort in the moving car, and the ride was nowhere as smooth as it seems to be when one sees the train moving from a distance. The train moved through Texas woodlands. The night's darkness refused to reveal anything about the environment, and the inside of the car was even darker. "You know Boy, I just thought of something."

"What?"

"I'm sure that crazy lady is going to call the cops and fire department."

"So?"

"Well, they're going to figure out that truck was stolen."

"So?"

"Damn it. You like to make things hard. Do you need everything explained to you?"

"Well, the way you get to things at a snail's pace . . . yeah, I do."

"If she tells the cops we got on this train, it ain't going to take much for them to figure out where it's going to stop."

"Come on, Curtis, do you think that illegal immigrants are going to call in their truck stolen?"

"It don't matter about the truck, partner. All they need is that crazy lady to point the direction of this train, and we're done for."

Boy leaned back against a stack of boxes to think things out a minute. We both looked out the boxcar probably thinking the same thing. These thoughts escaped our minds quickly as the speed of the train was much too fast to jump without risking further injury to Boy's leg. It had gained momentum from the time we jumped into it. Minutes later, Boy and I fell asleep.

The boxcar didn't offer much comfort to sleep in. My bones were aching so much that I could hardly adjust my body. My muscles felt like chicken feed. I saw the sun piercing the dark morning clouds and thought it was a good time for Boy to wake up.

"Hey Boy, get up."

He moved around trying to reposition his body. I could tell that his bones had become as fragile as mine. "Where are we?" he asked.

"I don't know, but I imagine this thing is going to stop soon and when it does, I'll bet there will be a shit load of cops waiting for us as we get off."

"Well, the train's gotta slow down before it stops, don't it?"

"I imagine it will . . . it's got to."

"We can jump then."

"Okay, stuntman. That's a good idea."

Half an hour expired, and the train had not slowed down. An hour more elapsed, and it had still not slowed down. Boy and I had lost our intent to leap from the train when it slowed down as it became a consideration buried in the back of our minds. In fact, we lost so much focus on that intent that the train came to a complete stop eight hours later without us realizing it had come to a rest. It took us a few minutes to realize that the train was no longer moving, and we had to quickly snap out of it. "Come on, Boy. The train stopped!"

"Stopped? Shit!"

We both jumped out like two wanted men would and ran into ranch land without much thought to who could see us there. We ran as far as our lungs would allow and began to walk at an even pace shortly after. Boy's leg couldn't take much stress as it would begin to bleed through the jean. We kept walking toward a ranch house that was visible from about a half mile away. We didn't know for sure that it would be abandoned, but our thirst and hunger forced us to look past that.

When we arrived at the front of the house, the first thing we noticed was that it was much too neatly kept to be abandoned. Bales of hay were neatly rolled and lined against one another. The roosters appeared to be fed well, and the overall grounds-keeping of the house was approached with a great deal of care. The land appeared to have everything, except for people.

"What should we do, Curtis?"

"I don't know, really. Let's take a look around the barn in the back for some water."

"Hell, cowboy, the house is empty. Why do we gotta go on and share water that horses drink out of?"

"Don't you think we've drawn enough attention to ourselves without breaking into a house to add to our troubles?"

To this, he had no reply. We walked toward the barn and circled around the back. To our amazement, we walked into a circle of people with their heads bowed down to the ground. Boy and I both froze like two hens that had been plucked and placed in a freezer.

"What was that you were saying, Curtis, about drawing attention?"

"Shhh, quiet. Pretend you're in church or something."

We looked on and from the circle of people a preacher of some kind emerged to say some words about death. We had walked into a private family funeral service. The preacher went on: "Why is it that we fear death? Why we are so religiously passionate about heaven, yet fail to see that the pathway to heaven goes through dying from this world? Are we hypocrites? Do we cry because we sincerely believe there is no heaven? And if you do believe there is a heaven, why are you crying? Do not be an unbeliever. Do not be a hypocrite. Believe in the Lord and believe in the life after someone leaves this world. It is our destiny, as human beings, not to live forever here on Earth but to embrace our journey into heaven. Death is part of that journey."

The preacher went on for a bit longer, but my attention span had gone with the wind some minutes before his last statement. The preacher stopped speaking, and the group of people began to walk past us as if we were ghosts. No one seemed to mind us being there, and no one was curious enough to ask who we were. Only one older lady remained behind sobbing over the plot of who was probably her husband. Now that the people had moved on indoors, I could clearly read the name on the plot: BRYAN D. TUCKER 1882-1980. I could only hope to live to such a fruitful age myself. Under the circumstances, I wouldn't bet a wooden horseshoe on that ever happening.

Perhaps it was the stress of having lost her husband, but the old lady walked up to me and Boy as if she had known us for longer than we've known ourselves. "I'm so sorry, boys. I meant to phone y'all not to come. Daddy's death happened rather suddenly."

Boy and I both looked at one another, thinking the other had met this lady sometime in the past. They must have money if Tucker passed suddenly, and they already had a plot for him. I just went along with it, realizing the old man was certainly old enough to have a lady her age as a daughter. "Don't worry yourself, ma'am. We understand."

"Well, come on inside for some food at least. I haven't had time to work out the details of the ranch. I will talk to you boys as soon as I tend to my guests."

"Uh, ma'am, we'd be kinder to let you grieve and be on our way," I suggested.

"Oh, nonsense, boys. I wouldn't hear of you coming all the way down here from Wyoming just to have you leave. We'll have time to talk in a while. Now, come on in and have some food."

It was an offer we could not refuse. Boy and I had worked up quite an appetite. We both felt out of place among the well-dressed cowboys. Our boots looked like they'd been stolen from the Civil War museum and our hats older than Bryan D. Tucker himself. People were grieving; however, few turned their attention to the two strangers who had no business being there.

The setup was quite fancy. They had wild pig ribs in homemade sauce, deer jerky, fried rattle snake, and sirloin tips. They had some other sides that Boy and I didn't pay much mind to. We thought we'd leave those provisions to members of society with weaker teeth. It didn't take long before we noticed they didn't have any beer, which might be why Tucker lived to be so old. We settled for freshly squeezed lemonade and iced tea and mingled with only each other until we were finally approached by one of the guests.

"So, you boys from Wyoming, huh?"

Boy and I looked at one another to be certain that we both agreed to play along with the previous notion that we were from somewhere in Wyoming. "Yeah-yeah, that's right."

The girl asking was a beautiful young woman with eyes bluer than the Pacific and mysterious like a child alone in the woods. She was to some extent out of place when compared to her robotic company and didn't at all seem to be grieving. This lack of emotion prompted me to ask: "You family to Mr. Tucker, are ya?"

"No, not really. My daddy and him are old friends, but since Daddy passed away three years ago, I just figured he'd want me to come on his behalf. So, what did Tucker hire you boys for?"

"Oh, you know, the usual ranch hand stuff," is what I answered. For some reason unknown to me, this statement seemed to have gained the attention of one of the men standing within arm's length to Boy and me. He gave me a nasty look like if the job had been promised to someone he knew.

The young lady noticed the inhospitable look from the cowboy and tried to mediate. "Oh, don't mind Buck. He's always got this look in his eye like he's sitting on a porcupine."

"Buck?" I asked wondering if there was a story to the name.

Boy thought he'd contribute to the theory. "Yeah, Curtis, that's probably how much they spent on the room where he was conceived."

The young lady let out such a beautiful laugh, and I could tell that she had been looking at Boy quite carefully throughout our dialogue. Boy had been just as intrigued by the beautiful girl. "So, what's your name, cowgirl?"

"Dolly."

"Well, Dolly, you're just about the prettiest thing we've seen since getting here from Wyoming."

"I'll take that as the most charming compliment I've ever gotten, considering there's so much to see between Wyoming and Oklahoma. Now, if you boys excuse me for just a moment, I'll be back in a spell."

Boy and I went into a deep thought as we turned to look at one another. "Shit, Curtis. We're in Oklahoma."

"That's a long way from the border, ain't it?"

"So, what do we do?"

"Just play it out for now. We're just lucky no one's asked about your leg. Maybe Dolly can help us get you patched up." I knew Boy liked the sound of that.

Boy and I spent most of the reception outside on the porch where we could stay away from people who might start asking questions. I leaned against the rail of the porch deck, and Boy sat on the first step to take some of the pressure off his leg. "So how about that, Boy? They think we're from Wyoming."

"Yeah, my grandfather is from Wyoming. It's beautiful out there."

"I reckon it is."

"You mean you've never been?"

"Nope."

"Damn it, Curtis. You ain't been to the Dakotas, and you ain't been to Wyoming! You gotta get out there some time and see the beautiful Dakota lands."

"I already promised ya I'd go, didn't I?"

"I'll tell you what, Curtis Cash. The first chance I see myself not being wanted for murder and trying to get to a country in the opposite direction, I'll be sure to take you there."

"Shh, quiet, bullhorn. Don't be saying shit like that so loudly."

"I'm sorry, okay? Just making conversation, that's all."

From nowhere, a hound walked from around the back of the house. It walked right up to Boy and began to sniff his boots. It was a beautiful hound with long floppy ears and three shades of brown on its face. His back had one large blob of black with freckles of red around it. It appeared to be quite interested in Boy.

Out of nowhere, emerged a voice, "Don't mind Chesney. He's got that natural gift as a hound." It was Buck.

"Oh, yeah? What gift is that?" Boy asked.

"You know, stranger, that gift of sniffing out an asshole no matter how covered in crap it is."

This was not a tone I was used to someone taking with Boy. His short fuse couldn't allow him to stay quiet, and Boy stood up mostly on one leg to face him. "Do you have a problem with me, you jerk?"

"Let's just say I find it coincidental that two drifters show up the day of the funeral of a wealthy man."

"Is that what you think? You think we're here for money?"

"Well, aren't ya?"

Before Boy could answer, Dolly came back out with a pitcher of lemonade and some plastic cups. "You boys want another drink?"

"No, thank you, ma'am," Buck replied. He looked at Boy in the eyes and spit chewing tobacco near his boot. Chesney followed Buck reluctantly, and the two disappeared around the house.

"Is Buck still eyeing you boys?"

"Yeah. What's his problem, anyway?" As he was sitting down, Dolly noticed his leg. She sat the pitcher of lemonade on the rail of the porch deck. "My heavens, what happened to your leg?"

I felt the need to interfere since Boy was often a slower thinker in these matters. "Um, it's stupid, Dolly. We was hunting quail and the damn gun just went off on him most awkward-like, but he'll be alright."

"Well ain't you going to have it looked at by a doctor?"

"Yeah, of course, first chance we get. Listen Dolly, we need to be getting on. I think we're here at the wrong time and with Tucker gone, I'm sure the job is no longer on the table."

"Don't be silly. Ms. Tucker will need you boys now more than ever. Aside from that, it's getting late and you need somewhere to sleep, don't ya?"

"That'd be nice, but I don't reckon Buck will let us sleep anywhere near this house."

"Well that's not for Buck to decide. You cowboys just take the barn for the night, and we can all talk about your jobs in the morning."

The last time Boy and I slept in a barn, things didn't work out so well. Considering how late it was getting, we needed to stay in one place. Dolly's relationship to Ms. Tucker was still unclear to me, but she must have been close enough to her that she was allowed to make decisions. The guests began to leave the house, and the sun began to set. Once again, Boy and I found ourselves inside the barn. A few family members were staying the night, including Buck. Something in the way Buck paid careful mind to us got me nervous. We settled into the barn, and sometime before midnight, Dolly came outside to give us some blankets and coffee.

"Thank you, Dolly. You really are kind."

"Think nothing of it, strangers. We'll see you at sun-up for fried eggs and potatoes."

It didn't take long for us to get comfortable, and just before I lost myself for the night, Boy thought he would apologize in his own masculine manner. "So, you really think you'll get to go to the Dakotas some day?"

"Yeah, Boy, I really do."

"It's beautiful, ya know?"

"Yeah, I reckon it is."

"You bet."

"Okay, I'm promising ya.

"I'll be sure to make time for it."

"You promise?"

"I said I would, didn't I?"

Chapter 16

The Buck-Toothed Mule

*Freedom didn't mean anything to me before
being a wanted man.*

We made it through the morning without burning down the barn. Boy woke up with Chesney snugged tight against his boot.

"Looks like the hound has taken quite a liking to ya."

"Yeah, well maybe Buck is right about Chesney knowing how to sniff out an asshole, so that's why he won't stay with him."

We both laughed and greeted the morning with a sense of tranquility that I hadn't felt in a long time. Throughout the entire process of trying to remain free men, I had encountered a sense of never having been free before. My entire life had revolved around trying to maintain a relationship, working, and paying bills. It is one of my life's mysterious ironies that in the process of protecting my freedom, I have discovered how beautiful it was to be free. Freedom didn't mean anything to me before being a wanted man. Being out of Texas was also reassuring, but there was no escaping going back if we wanted to get to Mexico. Arizona was too far.

Dolly brightened the morning with her glowing smile. She walked in with a picnic basket. We had fried eggs, deer sausage, biscuits, gravy, and fried potatoes. We spent a large portion of the morning getting to know each other and laughing. It was during the course of this exchange that we learned the most about Dolly. She grew up a cowgirl. Her parents did well for themselves in Amarillo, Texas, having inherited land blessed with oil. From how she related her story, I arrived at the idea she had never had to do anything to get anything in her life. All she had to do was ask her father, and it became hers. I can't remember ever knowing anyone in Tomball who had a life that required such minimal effort to get anything. One part of me was happy for her—another part was envious.

The conversation became more difficult to maintain when she began to inquire about our story. Neither Boy nor I cared to relate the truth, but a lie was difficult to invent on such short notice.

"So how long are you cowboys thinking of staying?"

Boy didn't want any part in this exchange and began to toy with trying to get some more tobacco out of a cigarette he had already smoked earlier.

"Well, I don't know exactly. We're just two guys who can't stay put very long."

"Afraid of commitment, huh?"

"Something like that."

"So how did two good looking men like you end up with such luck as to arrive in Oklahoma?"

Boy wasn't taking a liking to the sudden interrogation. I thought I would answer Dolly in a manner that may end all questions and hoped it would work.

"Look, Dolly, we're two cowboys who go where the work is. All these questions you're asking us ain't got no place for people like Boy and me. Them questions are for common folk who have direction in their life, you know? All our answers to your questions will be different by tomorrow, you understand?"

She laughed a little. "Okay, cowboys, you're entitled to y'alls secrets, I reckon. Well anyway, I thought this might help." She was holding a small box that I hadn't noticed before. She opened it, and it contained some first aid material. "Drop your pants, cowboy."

"Pardon me?" Boy jumped.

"Well, you don't expect me to patch you up on the outside of that pant, do ya?"

I didn't believe for a minute that Boy was too shy to pull down his pants in front of a beautiful woman. I do believe he was most concerned with what dropping his pants would reveal to Dolly. In the past two years or so, Boy and I had changed jeans maybe once or twice. We had hand-washed the same two pair of underwear over and over at a nearby river at the immigrant compound. By no means did Boy and I carry a stench, but our appearance told a story of more than just two men who worked hard. There was simply no way of explaining why we allowed our clothes to get so old.

"You ain't shy of a young lady now, are ya, cowboy?"

"Well no, ma'am, but Curtis and I came dressed under the assumption we were going to be laboring in the sun. I ain't exactly presentable underneath."

I knew exactly what Boy was trying to avoid. Our appearance at the compound made sense around hardworking immigrants. It had no place among wealthy ranch folk.

"Oh, don't be silly, cowboy. Come on."

Boy did not argue anymore and walked around a stack of hay. He took his pants off all the way and walked out from behind the hay completely naked. Dolly wasn't able to conceal her slight blush.

"Well, I didn't mean you had to go on and display yourself like that."

"Well, are you gonna patch me up, or ain't ya?"

"I told you I would. Come over here."

"Don't be going on and patching up what doesn't need fixin', you hear?"

"Hang on a minute and just sit still." It looked as if it was something Dolly had done before. She took good care to sterilize everything and did her patching with grace.

I couldn't help but ask her. "You done this kind of caring before, Miss Dolly?"

"Sure have. I went to nursing school and was quite the nurse for a spell."

"Why'd you give up something like that?"

"Daddy always thought it was beneath me. He wanted me to be a doctor."

"You would have made a fine one, Miss Dolly."

"Well, thank you, stranger. Now I want you to answer me something."

I regretted having asked her any questions. I was afraid she had it in her mind that I owed her an answer to one of hers. I was hoping it wasn't too personal. "What's that?"

"How come you boys are so cruel as to shoot at little quails with a twelve-gage shotgun?" She opened her hand: in her palm, we could see the small pellets from Old Man Winters's shotgun.

"Damn it, Boy. You've been carrying those things around for more than two years. It's a damn miracle you ain't got no poisoning or something." It was too late for me to retrieve the words that had already escaped my mouth. Boy looked at me as if I was the biggest fool there ever was. "Two years! You were shot more than two years ago, and it's still bleeding like that?"

"You know, Curtis? You have a jaw wider than a buck-toothed mule."

I've never had a naked man tell me off before, but he was right to be angry. Dolly just kept looking back and forth at us, and Boy put his jeans on.

"Okay, cowboys. I ain't messing with y'all no more. What's going on?"

"Could you give me a minute to talk to Boy alone, please?" She seemed reluctant to comply with the favor. "Come on, lady, we ain't going nowhere. Just give me a few minutes."

"Alright, but I'm coming back in five minutes." She put the first aid material together and looked back at us as she walked out of the barn.

"I don't like this, Curtis. I don't like it one bit."

"Look, we might need her along the way."

"In what way, Curtis, to turn us in? You didn't kill nobody, alright?

It's easy for you to take risks."

"We don't have to tell her everything, Boy. We can just tell her a tick's worth. A tick's worth can be enough, don't ya think?"

"I don't like it!"

He walked around the barn a few steps thinking. Boy picked up his jeans and looked in every pocket he had for a cigarette but couldn't find one. He turned and walked directly to my face. "You tell her what you want, Curtis, but don't make me a mule for trusting you. It won't do me any worse off to kill one more person."

I wasn't sure if he was talking about me or Dolly, but I didn't want to know. "Just relax a minute, okay? We're going to be fine."

We could hear Dolly's boot steps getting closer. "Well, I leave ya to her. I'm going for a walk."

"Alright, but do me a favor."

"What do ya want now?"

"Put your clothes back on."

"Where's he going?" Dolly entered.

"To be honest with ya, Dolly, he ain't too taken by the idea of me saying much about who we are."

"Are you boys in some kind of trouble?"

I had to quickly decide how far I was going with my story. I immediately backed away from the truth. "The thing is, Dolly, that we owe some dangerous men some serious money that we just ain't got."

"Is that all?"

"What do you mean is that all? Maybe to a rich girl like you that ain't much of a bind, but to two ranch boys like Boy and me that makes for something tough to get out of."

"That's not what I meant. I just thought you boys were some escaped convicts or something."

I laughed genuinely. I wasn't sure what one would call two cowboys on the run before they went to prison.

"So where you boys really heading on to?"

"Mexico."

"You got some time to go before Mexico."

"Well, it's a long story, but we were actually closer at one point. We gave it a thought to play the role with widow Tucker there, but if the actual ranch hands she was expecting arrive, we could run into problems—especially with that Buck character."

"No, I don't suppose that would be a good idea. I'll tell ya what. Why don't I drive you boys to Mexico?"

"Drive us? Oh shit, Ms. Dolly, we can't ask you to do that."

"And why not? I can use some adventure in my life, and hell, Texas is the next state. We can be there in less than two days."

The offer was appealing, but I wasn't sure what Dolly's intentions were. I was not even certain she believed the story I told her. Owing dangerous men money was not a complete explanation for why Boy had been shot. She did not ask me what we owed money, which was a question that most people who believed the story would have asked. "Let me talk to Boy for a minute."

I went around the side of the barn. I did not see Boy anywhere. I thought he would have found a cigarette by the time I was done talking to Dolly and that I would find him out back smoking it. I walked a little further out near a patch of woods to the rear of the Tucker ranch. There was not much in the form of concealment in the area, and I could not see Boy as far as my eye could go. My search reached an hour and worry transformed to panic. Boy did not take a liking to filling in Dolly on our predicament. It did not take me long to realize that Boy had left me!

Chapter 17

Where is Peter "Boy" Jenkins?

One would think that after more than two years, a cowboy would feel quite settled in his boots, but this was not the case.

I had never felt so alone in my life. I never before considered how much different it felt to be on the run from the law alone. Boy had no way of knowing I had decided not to tell Dolly the truth. Not knowing what method he used to leave was also a burden to the decision I would make. I could have Dolly drive me to the border, but I could not help but wonder if Boy was close enough for me to catch him. Another perspective had me think that he could have hitched a ride with a trucker and was already some miles ahead of me. Either way, it was time for me to think of myself. I began to get curious about Dolly as well. She hadn't returned the entire time I had been looking for Boy. The guests had gone with only Buck rocking back and forth on a rocking chair on Ms. Tucker's porch.

I was ashamed of myself for thinking that Boy and Dolly decided to run off without me. Boy wouldn't have done that to me—or would he? I never considered Boy to be all that bright, but it didn't take much smarts to know that the law would be looking for two men and not a man and a woman. Perhaps he was feeling desperate and was ready to take a new course with our endeavor to get to Mexico. One would think that after more than two years, a cowboy would feel quite settled in his boots, but this was not the case. The more time expired, the more it felt that the time for our capture was near. It was an odd feeling. There was a sense of my freedom already being stripped even if I had not been found yet.

The day was fading, and Dolly had gone with Boy nowhere to be seen. Whether they were together or not was no longer an issue to ponder over. I needed to get moving and had to go at it alone. Boy's company was all I had to that point,. Now I had nothing. I walked along the farm road for about seven miles, and by this time, it was pitch black outside. There was no choice at that time but to keep walking. Sleeping out in the wild like that was not an option. It was so dark that I could hardly see my boots. The moon wasn't out, and the Oklahoma stars didn't seem nearly as bright as those in Texas. Less than a mile later, I saw a very dark shadow in front of me. I was not certain if it was something my mind had designed on its own or if there was really something there. If it was something, it was big. I proceeded with caution as I got closer. I hoped it was an abandoned shed or farmhouse but was not close enough to see it well yet.

I stopped short of the large shadow and stared at it. I bent down to pick up a rock and threw it at the large figure. It was the sound of a metal and not so much a wooden structure. I got curious and got the courage to get closer. It was a heaven-sent sight. I'd just thrown a stone and hit a boxcar to a train. The train was not moving, and the doors were opened. It didn't look like the train was going anywhere, but my main concern was finding a safe place to sleep. I jumped into the boxcar. It was filled with bags of some kind of grain. I was hoping it was rice so that I could take some with me to cook later. I went to the very back where I could not be seen and used a sack of grain as a pillow. It was the hardest pillow I had ever slept on, but it was pre-ferred over the floorboard of the boxcar.

Aside from having been woken up once by howling coyotes, I had a very pleasant sleep. I had a dream that night of fishing in Conroe Lake just down the road from Tomball. I doubted I would ever get back to those days, but I had expectations of making a new home somewhere I could establish those kinds of memories. It was very early in the morning when I heard some men talking at a distance. I was certain they were railroad workers as I could feel the jerk to my body as they attached new boxcars to the train. I wasn't sure if there were border patrol in Oklahoma or not, but I didn't see anyone paying much mind to securing the boxcars. I had to choose between getting off unseen and staying where I was in hopes that the train would begin to move. I just didn't know how much more walking the soles to my boots could take.

After about an hour wait, the train pulled and began to move at a turtle's pace for a few minutes. I was excited the train was going in the direction I hoped. Within minutes, it had gained momentum and was going quite fast. The speed of the train told me it was going far. This too was a pleasing thought. Part of me was hoping it would head north. Going back to the state that wants me the most made me nervous. Boy had been a great companion for me, but there was something peaceful about having the night to myself. Perhaps it was something we should had done a long time ago. Authorities were looking for two men to-gether and not just one. Perhaps I was just telling myself this to not think about not having him around anymore. There was nothing smoother about the tracks in Oklahoma than those in Texas, but I was able to fall into a deep sleep rather quickly.

There was a time when I depended on a rooster to wake me in the mornings, but I had not heard one in a long time. I was shocked to have heard one singing while I was inside a boxcar. It seemed as if the rooster sound came from a different part of the train. The train was at a complete stop, and the sun had risen completely. I heard a noise inside my own boxcar. I quickly took a defensive stance in preparation for what may come out of the sacks of corn stacked on the opposite end of the car. I was nervous at first, but I saw a child slowly emerge from behind the sacks. He looked Mexican but spoke near perfect English to me.

"I don't mean to intrude, sir. I thought the car was empty."

"You been here all night?"

"Yes."

"Are you alone?" To this he had no reply. He looked behind the sacks of corn as if he was trying to reveal there was someone there he did not want me to know about. I walked over to the sacks and saw a woman sitting with her knees to her chest.

"Please don't hurt me, sir."

"Hurt you? Hell, I ain't got no cause to hurt ya. What are you doing down there?" She raised herself slowly to her feet. She was barefoot, and her clothes were dirty.

"My son and I were trying to get away from my boss."

"Your boss?"

"I brought my son to America for a better life, but it didn't work out."

"You guys are from Mexico?"

"Yes."

"Hell, you guys don't speak like no Mexicans."

"I always told my son that good English would make things easier for him in America."

"Well, hell, lady, I speak English, and America ain't done shit for me. So where is this boss of yours?"

"He had been following us for some time, but we managed to get on the train before he caught us."

I could only imagine what her boss had done to her. I preferred to speculate based on her clothing and the bruises on both the woman and her child. It wasn't that I didn't care, but time was of the essence, and I didn't want to be caught storytelling on government property. "Well, it was nice meeting you kind folks, but I gotta be moving on."

"Sir, can you please help us?"

"Help ya? Shit, lady, I can't even help myself. I ain't got but a few dollars and the clothes I'm wearing."

"We just need some food. You don't have to find enough for both of us. Just for my son."

It was difficult for me to turn my back on such a noble gesture. I hated myself for not being able to just leave. I was compromising the time I had to push on, but the thought of the kid going hungry wouldn't let me put the first boot forward. It was also safe to say that it was nearly impossible to see a Mexican girl without thinking of Lorena.

"Alright, then, come on. The first thing we gotta do is find out where the hell we're at."

Chapter 18

The Snotty Grin

"Shake and break a cowboy three times, gentlemen.
And slap a pig silly on the side, will y'all?"

It took some asking for me to learn that I was in Hartley County somewhere named Channing in the northern part of Texas. It is a small town that housed under 400 people. The welcome sign confirmed this information for me, and I knew quickly I would stick out like a snake in an eagle's nest. Now I had two hungry companions that I couldn't allow myself to let go hungry. We walked about half a mile before coming to a place called *The Messy Chef*, but it didn't appear to be open. A few paces later we came to another place called *The Cowgirl Café*.

I didn't think I had enough money to feed all of us, but I designed a plan in my head that some would argue lacked in good taste. I figured on slipping out of the café once we had eaten by excusing myself to go to the bathroom. What would happen to the two illegals was not a concern to me. I just wanted to make sure they ate. Leaving them behind may hold them accountable for the tab, but certainly they would not go hungry. I made myself feel better by convincing my conscience that they were better off being deported. They would never survive in America.

The café had only a few people in it. The place was quiet, and most of the conversations that could be heard were coming from the kitchen. The waitress took a few minutes to come to our table. "Howdy! You guys new in town?"

"Just passing through," I said without showing my face too much. I was well aware of how far my body had traveled in the past two and a half years, but I had no idea how far my face had gone. My new companions didn't seem too willing to show themselves either. They both buried their face in the menu and kept to themselves a bit. We didn't converse much on the walk from the tracks, and I still knew nothing about them aside from the fact they were hungry.

"So how far you guys coming from?"

Once again, I found myself confronted by someone asking too many questions. My only reaction was to ignore it. "What are your specials today, lady?"

"Well, we got the Southwestern omelet."

"Just bring us three with toast and extra bacon."

"Want some coffee with that?"

"Just a pitcher of water and three glasses."

She turned to face the cooks in the back and called out the order. "Shake and break a cowboy three times, gentlemen. And slap a pig silly on the side, will y'all?"

The next few minutes were quiet. It was frustrating not to have anything to say. "So, what's your name, lady? Ain't no sense in staying quiet."

"My name is Yolanda. This is my son Enrique."

"Where are you guys going?"

"We hear a truck comes through here to pick up workers. I am hoping we find something like that." For a brief moment, I thought of Lorena. I went back in my mind to the wonderful days at the immigrant compound. It seemed like a distant memory now, and I wouldn't know how to get back to it even if I could return. When occupied, my mind made no time to remorse over what had transpired, but in those brief moments when thoughts of Lorena got past my defenses, my heart reminded me just how much I hurt for her. "So which way do these trucks go?"

"Mostly up north to Minnesota. They have turkey farms there that need a lot of help, especially before the holiday seasons."

I could not help but to briefly entertain the thought of changing directions and getting a ride north toward Canada. Having to get through just one state to get to Mexico, however, was much more appealing. The irony is that I was further away from the border than when I was in Tomball. The breakfast came, and my two companions ate as if they hadn't eaten in weeks. I was quite hungry myself and whether it was owed to that or the talents of the chef was not as relevant to me as it being the best breakfast I had experienced in a long time. My two new friends were quiet as they ate. This was preferred over them asking too many questions about me.

As the time to pay for the meal approached, I thought it would be best if I excused myself for the bathroom and leave from there. To most, it may seem pointless to invite people to lunch when one does not have the means to pay for them, but my logic was that if I could teach them the frame of mind that is required for them to make it out here, then I would have done them a world of good.

I excused myself to the bathroom, and to my surprise, it had a window. I thought it would be the logical exit from the business, but I had my doubts as to whether or not I could force myself through it. The window was more rectangular than it was square, and I wasn't sure if I could even get a boot through it. I decided to use that method of escape as an alternative to walking out through the front. I opened the bathroom door slightly to get a better understanding of what kind of view the employees would have as I walked out. The first thing that grabbed my attention was the waitress setting the bill down on an empty table and looking around. The lady and her kid were nowhere to be found!

My alternative method of leaving very quickly became the primary, and the question of whether or not I fit through the window was replaced by the concern of how much it would hurt when I forced myself through it. I ran to the bathroom window, and as I looked outside saw a 1962 pickup driving off with a bed filled with immigrants. I could see both the lady and her boy within the crowded group. I needed to get out quickly and pushed off the toilet seat to secure myself at the window's pane. The push to the outside had to be done in one singular motion because giving it too much thought would do me no justice. I pushed myself up and forced my entire body through the rectangular window. I got bug-eyed trying to squeeze through. It was not nearly as painful as I expected, but it was just as tight as I imagined. It was so tight, in fact, that my jeans were lowered to my ankles—belt and all.

I was prepared to endure the embarrassment of running into the countryside while exposing myself. This scenario was preferred over having a boot slip off my foot and having it land on the inside of the building. The Texas landscape was not suited for walking barefoot, and I was not sure how far I would get on one boot before being caught. As it turned out, both boots stayed on just fine, but I found myself running while trying to pull my pants up to my waist. I took a glance back and could see the cook looking through the window at me. He may have been ordering the waitress to call the sheriff, but he was not doing anything himself to run me down. I did not have many options as far as places where I could conceal myself. The town was small, and businesses were few. I ran alongside what appeared to be an abandoned gas station and caught my breath.

I left a good distance between me and the café, but its proximity was still too close for me to remain in that area. Without many places to hide, I was sure the sheriff would consider circling the abandoned gas station. The only option I had was risky, but it appeared to be the only choice I had at the time. I needed to make my way back to the main highway and try to hitchhike in any direction that was offered. There did not seem to be a lot of traffic, but a car or two would speed by every ten seconds or so.

I remained hidden behind the wall of the abandoned building and thought it would be a better strategy to remain there until I could hear a car coming. Once I heard the distant tires on the Texas highway, I began to trot slowly toward the highway in hopes of scoring a ride the first time. As the car got closer, I began to wave my hand as if I needed help. The car was a Chevy convertible with two people inside. It began to pull over, and a male in the car began to wave his cowboy hat at me as if he knew me. I was confused and thought maybe they were there to pick up someone else. But as they got closer, I adjusted my eyes and could see Boy's snotty little grin with Dolly at the wheel. "Hey cowboy, where the hell you been?"

"Oh, shut up, Boy, and get me the hell outta here!" I jumped into the car and saw something that was more pleasing to me than seeing Boy again.

"Hey, Chesney! You guys brought Chesney. How are ya, boy?"

He jumped up toward my face and began to lick me recklessly. Dolly and Boy looked as if they were in good spirits, but I was confused by her being with him.

"So, Dolly, whatcha doing leaving the ranch like that?"

"Well, your friend here can be very persuasive."

"Can he now? You know we ain't going back to Oklahoma?"

"Then, a reckon I ain't either. I told you boys I needed some adventure in my life, didn't I? I didn't need much convincing."

"And where the hell were you, Boy? What do you mean disappearing on me like that?"

"Damn it, Curtis. You should be glad I'm even alive. I took my walk like I told ya but then got forced up an oak by some wild coyotes. Them there coyotes had no intentions of letting me go either. I saw you at a distance calling for me, too, but just wasn't close enough for you to hear me."

"How on God's name did you guys find me?"

"Pure luck, my friend . . . pure luck."

Chapter 19

Melon Juice

*"Curtis, this better be damn good, or I'm slapping
your ass with a cactus."*

We drove for hours before we had to stop and fuel. Dolly had
fallen asleep in the front and Chesney used my lap as a pillow.
Boy seemed tired and looked at me through the rearview mirror. "You
wanna root beer?"

"Yeah, man, I do."

He reached into Dolly's purse with a great deal of confidence. I
was not sure at that point what kind of arrangement the two had or if
she had at some point agreed to finance any part of the trip. I did not
ask because, in all honesty, I did not want to know. Boy asked Dolly if
she wanted anything, and she said Virginia Slims and just went back to
sleep. Neither one of us knew much exactly what that was, but when
we asked the clerk, he handed us a pack of cigarettes that must have
been new on the market. Boy pulled out one out of the pack for himself
and lid it. "So how far you think we oughta go tonight?"

"Damn it, Boy, if you're leaving it up to me . . . let's go all the way
to Mexico. I'm tired of all this running all the time. I don't even know
if they're looking for us."

"There ain't no way they ain't looking, Curtis. A missing girl. A beat-up cop."

"Yeah, partner, but how do you know they just don't think Mary Beth is with you? What if they think you guys run off together or something?"

"Curtis, you're talking as if you and I exchanged our smarts. Mary Beth was tight with her family. She ain't just leaving her family for over two years without calling on them. Besides, didn't you see them sketches of our face at that diner some time back?"

"So why don't we just get Dolly to call and pretend she's Mary Beth?"

"Now, that's a thought, Cowboy. But what if they recognize the voice as not being her?"

"It's been a while. They might come to expect she should sound different."

"I don't know, Curtis . . . shit, this cigarette sucks!" He flicked it to the floor and crushed it with the tip of his boot.

"Okay, then, how about we have Dolly call as an old friend just to see what they tell her?"

"What excuse do we give her? We can't tell her why we're looking into her."

"Tell her she's an old girlfriend and just curious on whether she got married or not."

"Alright, then. It's risky, though."

"I know, Boy, but I'm so tired of running. I'd at least like to know there's cause for it."

"I'm tired too – believe me – and I do appreciate ya, you know?"

"What do you mean?"

"Well, shit, Curtis, give me some credit. I know I ain't got so much smarts, but I'm alright to know that I don't even know if you need to be here with me."

"What are you saying to me?"

"Look here. You ain't done nothing wrong, cowboy, at least, nothing that will send you to prison. I hurt Mary Beth, not you. All the other shit you've done they don't even know about or ain't even worth probation."

"So, what do you reckon I do?"

"Go home, Curtis. I think you'll be alright. Tell them you saw me kill Mary Beth, and I forced you to come with me to keep you from talking. Tell them you escaped me just outside Amarillo."

"I don't know about that. I mean, we've been together a spell and . . ."

"Don't get all emotional on me right now. I ain't gonna cry for no man. Now I ain't alone anymore. Dolly is really into me, and I can do this without ya."

"I don't know, Boy. Maybe they want me just as bad. I ought to wait for what they tell Dolly."

"Alright, let's go wake her." We went to the car, and she wasn't there. Boy and I looked at each other. "She didn't hear us, did she?"

"Hell, I don't know."

We walked around the filling station and knocked on the door to the girl's bathroom. "Dolly?"

There was no answer. Boy and I were more silent than we had been since our reunion. We made our way back to the car, and there was Dolly with Chesney.

"Where were you, girl?" Boy asked.

"Chesney had to go for a walk. You don't want him pissing inside the car, do ya?"

Boy didn't have an answer for this. He handed Dolly her Virginia Slims and got in the car. "Come on, guys. We'll rest in Killeen."

The drive was long, but it was made much shorter by all the thinking I had to do. I decided not to involve Dolly and call Angela myself. That night we bunked in a cheap hotel right off the highway. Having Dolly made it easy to rent rooms. Boy and I were able to keep our names out of the registration desk. I was forced to take a longer than usual shower. I could hear through the walls that Dolly and Boy had gotten much closer to each other than I had previously suspected. I had no intentions of interrupting my friend seeing that he never interrupted me with Lorena. If anything, they made me miss Lorena or at least the sexual part of her. Whether or not her full intentions were to have a long and lasting life together I'll never know. I left much too quickly to ever learn much about the scenario. Somewhere in my heart, I still sheltered the hope that she would find me and explain that she loved me and didn't care whether I was wanted or not. At that moment, I could not entertain this thought any further. I had a phone call to make.

The noise stopped. I came out of the shower carefully and noticed they had both fallen sound asleep. Dolly was completely nude on top of Boy as if she fell asleep on the job. Boy didn't seem to mind much. The road has a way of taking all the energy out of a person, and both were done for the night.

I walked to a nearby pay phone and reluctantly pulled a coin from my pocket. I inserted it and waited a few minutes before I dialed. After so much time, I would not have remembered the number if it weren't for the fact that part of it was my birthday. It made me think for a minute that I had not even thought of my own birthday in a while. I dialed the number, and the ring sounded loud and angry. The nerves in my body jolted my blood as if electricity was running through my veins. I almost hung up and was semi-relieved that no one answered. But as I was returning the receiver, I heard the sleepy voice on the other end.

"Hello."

"Um . . . Angela?"

"Who is this?"

I stayed quiet not knowing whether or not I should initiate any dialogue between us. This appeared to be a much bigger risk than I had previously believed. But there was something beautiful in the sound of Angela's voice, and I wanted to hear more. The sound of her voice alone seemed to have returned me to Tomball. I returned to a point in my life that was very special to me and that I missed being a part of. For a minute, I thought I could smell the Tomball air and taste the sweetness of the homemade barbeque sauce.

"Hello, is anybody there?" she continued.

"Hey, it's me."

"Me who? Dalton, is this you?"

I had no idea who Dalton was. "It's Curtis, Angela."

There was a brief silence on the other end. I could not see what she was doing, but I could feel her getting herself up out of bed, turning on the lamp that stood on her nightstand and sitting up to hear better.

"Curtis Cash? Don't tell me this is really you?"

"Yeah, Angela, it is."

"Well, where are you?" She sounded pleasant and not nearly as angry or unreceptive as I had expected her to be. Her tone was worried and nourishing to some extent.

"I'm in Tennessee, Angela." She seemed to have believed this.

"What are you doing there? Is Boy with you?"

"Yeah."

"Curtis?"

"Yeah?"

149

"Is Mary Beth alive?"

I stayed quiet and did not believe she would jump into this topic so quickly or so abruptly. "What do the police say?"

"They think Mary Beth is dead and that Boy had something to do with it. They figured that's why he killed poor ole' Dawson."

"What? No, no, Angela. Boy didn't kill Dawson. It was just a fight."

"Well, he can tell that to a Texas judge if he wants, but Dawson's frail head got some kind of clot or something after a couple of days, and he just fell asleep because of it. He never woke up."

"Angela, it ain't right for you to be messing with me like that."

"I ain't playin', Curtis. Now why don't ya tell me where you're really at?"

I hung up instantly and ran back into the room. "Boy, Boy . . . get up." He was completely unclothed but still had his cowboy hat on. Dolly's face was still buried in his chest with her tangled dirty blonde hair covering most of Boy's upper body. Her pearly white nude backside was completely exposed with one of her legs hanging off the bed. Her pink heals moved slightly as if she was unconsciously disturbed by my intrusion.

"Boy, get up!"

He began to move slowly and reached down to scratch a part of the body that was covered by the bed sheet. It took him a few minutes to come out of it, but he finally adjusted. "Damn it, Curtis. What is it?"

"It's not good, partner. Come on, let's talk outside," I whispered.

"Curtis, this better be damn good, or I'm slapping your ass with a cactus."

"Just put something on and come on."

I went outside and waited for him. He did indeed put something on. He came outside in his underwear and cowboy boots. He was lighting a cigarette.

"What do you mean coming out dressed like that, Boy?"

"Should I have put on my hat?"

"Never mind, damn it. I just got off the phone with Angela."

This got Boy's attention. He did not bother to continue the process of lighting his cigarette. He placed it in his ear and walked over to me. His nut sack was peeking out of the edge of his underwear, but he didn't seem to care. "What'd she tell ya?"

"Boy, it ain't good."

"Stop the stallin', will ya, man? What the hell did she say?"

"You know that ass kicking we gave Dawson?"

"What about it? He's lucky that's all he got." He went for his cigarette again and walked to a part of the parking lot where the hotel lights gave him enough light to see what he was doing as he lit his cigarette. Boy's scar from where he was shot was visible under the light and seemed to have gotten quite ugly over time.

"We couldn't have given it to him any worse, Boy. We put him to sleep for good."

"The hell you say?"

"I ain't playing with ya, Boy. Dawson had a head weak as a melon. We made juice of it."

He took one long drag from his cigarette and flicked it to the floor as he walked back toward me. His testicles had made their way back into his underwear somehow. "You mean to tell me that Dawson is dead?"

"Yeah, Boy. He's dead, and that's on both of us. I gotta keep running with you now." This was not entirely true. Angela had made no mention of Dawson's death being on me, but I was more afraid to go back than I was willing to admit to Boy.

Chapter 20

Highway to Hail

"I'll lay my balls down under a bull's hoof if I'm lying to you."

The next morning was restless. I had not slept most of the night. I kept having those dreams that seem like I was falling from a very high place. I always woke up before I hit the ground, but my grandmother once shared the theory that if you sleep through the part when one hits the ground, the person dreaming it would die in their sleep. I hoped never to find out since I had yet to make it that far. Life was getting more stressful than it had ever been. Boy was quiet and wasn't saying much to me or Dolly. I was still nervous about having Dolly around. We didn't know much about her, and we both got to know her outside much better before knowing her inside.

We had some dried beef jerky and leftover root beer for breakfast, and we were off once again. "How far are we from Mexico?"

"I reckon eight hours," Boy said. He appeared a little annoyed and didn't seem to want Dolly's company anymore. I was beginning to wonder whether at some point we needed to abandon her. I was not certain what Boy's position would be on that, but I knew I would have to at least hint at it soon enough. We had not been on the road two hours before we experienced our first interruption.

"Honey, I gotta pee," Dolly said to Boy.

"Hold it."

"I can't. Please pull over at the next station."

"Damn, girl, we ain't drank anything. What are you about to piss?"

"Is it that much trouble that we can't stop to pee?"

Boy made eye contact with me through the rearview mirror. I gestured that maybe there would be no harm in it. I had to go myself, and Chesney had not had a snack yet. We pulled over to a busy establishment. We had been stopping at the smallest towns possible, but as the road went on, we were running out of those options. The highway was getting busier and towns bigger.

I waited for Dolly to leave before speaking to Boy. "Why didn't you want to stop, Boy?"

"Hell, I don't know. I'm just a little anxious, I guess."

"You don't trust Dolly, do ya?"

"I don't trust anyone."

"Why did ya give her the time of day, then? We should be alone."

"Because she had a car, and I needed sex. You know how good it felt to be with a woman after all this time?" He must have forgotten that I had fallen in love at one point along the way.

"Yeah, I do know all too well."

"People can downright judge me as much as they want, and maybe I hauled off unexpected-like on Mary Beth, but she wasn't no angel either, Curtis. She never talked to me when I got home from work. She never wanted to have sex with me—not even on my birthday, Curtis. She always had something better to do than to give me a minute."

"You're shittin' me?"

"I ain't at all. I'll lay my balls down under a bull's hoof if I'm lying to you. We got home from a night of celebrating my birthday one time. She hardly said a word to me. When we got home, she took to her reading her romance novels, and I went to be alone."

"Well that ain't proper-like for a couple."

"You ain't kidding, partner. It ain't proper at all. Now, I ain't thinking she ought to die for it, but something goes on inside a man when his woman doesn't want him no more. It kinda takes the man's inside away, you know?"

"Yeah."

"Now, I ain't gonna sit here and play the victim either because it ain't proper. I done something wrong–real wrong–but I also think that if I had been taken care of like a man, I wouldn't be so God damn angry all the fuckin' time. When a man doesn't take care of his woman, the world mourns for her, but when it's the other way around, ain't nobody gonna think twice about it at all. I've got feelings, too, and for her to deprive me of being a man and feeling together-like, well that's just not alright."

I had never heard Boy express himself in this manner about intimate matters. I felt badly for him regardless of what he had done. I understood where he was coming from. It had not been long since I felt something so strong for Lorena that how she would treat me mattered a great deal. One thing I had learned with my experience with women is that one sure way for a woman to get a man to fall out of love, is to deprive him of feeling like a man. One of the reasons for having a woman is because we are men. What is the point if I could not feel like one? Dolly came around and filled a void for Boy. I could understand why he would take the risk of having involved someone in our travels, but after having learned what we had from Angela, I was not sure that the risk was the same. Who was Dolly? How much did she really know?

"So why don't you trust her? She doesn't seem off or anything."

"Not sure, really. She just seems awful smart to be a drifter or hanging around funerals of people she wasn't emotionally attached to."

We got some items and snacks at the store and were on our way. The clouds began to cover the light emitted by the sun. We were on the road about another hour before we heard that familiar tune from Dolly.

"Boy, I gotta go pee again."

"Woman, you can't be serious?"

"Golly, Boy, I'm sorry. I wouldn't ask ya if I didn't really have to."

This time was different from where I was sitting. I was in the back seat behind the driver's side where Boy was. Chesney was in the back with me. Dolly was in the front passenger seat. Her hair was getting tangled in the wind, but she didn't seem to mind. She looked a little pale from the face and was thinning around the cheek bone. We stopped at a truck stop, and she pretty much ran inside to make it. "Boy, do you think our friend here is on drugs or something?"

"You think?"

"Yeah, maybe. She sure is looking awfully different in the short time we've known her."

"Oh, come on now. We ain't kept her company long enough to know if she's looking different."

"Maybe you're right. I think that maybe we're just a little paranoid."

"You think she's a cop?"

"Nah, that would be one weird way of trying get us."

"I reckon things aren't done that way, but she has been stopping us a lot."

"Ya think she's trying to slow us down, Boy?"

"Don't know. Maybe we should just let her pee in the car next time."

"Damn, not even Chesney has to go so much."

We were on our way once again. Dolly looked much better and had even gotten some color back in her face. I think that she was on drugs but did not want to admit it. It wasn't any of my business, and as long as she was not with law enforcement, that was just fine with me. The dark clouds blanketed the sky even darker, and every minute or so, I could feel a droplet of water on my face. "Boy, ain't ya gonna stop to put the top on?"

"No can do, Curtis."

"The top doesn't go up, honey," Dolly intervened. "Yeah, it got stuck some place back in Oklahoma, and we haven't been able to get it up anymore. We're gonna have to find a roof to park under."

I had a good joke about Boy not being able to 'get it up,' but I saved it for later. Boy drove for another ten minutes, and the occasional droplet worked itself into a constant drizzle. I could see Boy was looking more toward the back roads off the main highway. We drove another ten minutes.

"Guys, Chesney is getting all wet and so is the inside of my car," Dolly pleaded.

"Hang on, I think I found a place," Boy said.

There was an old house near a dirt road off I-35 South. It was a small little town, and we could not see a single person anywhere around. It was the perfect place to wait for the rain.

The house had a carport we parked under. We did not consider going into the home, but the rain was getting heavier and heavier by the minute. Chesney's fur was flat on his skin and began to look like an oversized rat after a while. "Hey, Boy, I think we should try to get inside somehow. That wind is really picking up."

"Alright, then, let's have a look."

The town was so quiet I could hear the passing cars on the main highway two miles away. I was afraid to walk in on some old man with a shotgun who just did not take care of his property, but I was happy to see that it was just a vacant house that no one had lived in for probably years. The floors were dirt, and the corners were filling with small puddles of water. It wasn't the ideal place to live, but it was a perfect place to stay out of the rain. The lightning got louder, and the winds picked up violently.

I began to fear a Texas-sized tornado. There was no way the feeble structure we sheltered ourselves in could withstand any winds faster than what they already were. Chesney didn't seem to care too much for the loud thunder. He found a loose pile of broken floorboards and sniffed his way through until he was completely buried under them. I peeked out with one eye in anticipation of the next loud bang. I thought Dolly would be the most scared being she was a woman, but she didn't seem to fret much over the violent storm.

"We should all just get some sleep. It will all be gone in the morning," she said.

I wasn't exactly certain where it was we could get some sleep. The floor was getting muddy, and the house was filled with old boards and trash. We figured the best way would be to find a dry area on the floor where we could sit with our backs against the wall. None of us said much to the other with the exception of an occasional comment about the storm getting weaker. I think we all knew that it was not getting any slower. An hour later, hail began to fall.

"Shit, what the hell is that, Curtis?"

"Sounds like hail."

"Hail? That sounds more like asteroids or something."

"It'll be alright soon. It's not like it never hailed in Tomball."

"Tomball?" asked Dolly. "Where is that?"

Boy looked at me as if he wanted to brand my tongue. He quickly changed the topic. "Is hail anything like ice?" He asked as he put his head out the window frame. There was no glass there, so it was easy enough to do. The next we heard was Boy screaming out. "Shit!"

I pulled his head back into the house, and his head was covered in blood. "Good God, Boy, you're just as sharp as a fox sticking your head out in a hailstorm like that."

"Is it bad?" He wondered as I looked at it.

Dolly was examining him as well. Her opinion was more valid than mine. "It looks pretty deep," she said.

"Damn it, cowboy, you beat everything, you know that? We ain't even got a manner of patching you up right now."

"Well, who asked ya, anyway? You ain't gotta tend to me. Just let me be."

"Nonsense," Dolly interjected. "We'll think of something. Now you boys stop your fussing at one another. This ain't no time for us to create our own storm."

I knew she was right, so I stayed quiet until her duties were performed. She used some hand cream to moisten a cloth. I am not exactly sure how, but she did a miraculous job in cleaning Boy up. His cut was visible and looked something awful, but it was not bleeding, and that was a good thing. It was good to see Boy in good spirits and not on the brink of death or anything like that, but the most unusual thing happened after he was tended to. Dolly fainted.

"What the hell, Curtis? I didn't lay a hand on her. Honest."

"Shut up a minute, will ya now? Poor girl went on and fainted."

"Why in hell did she go on to do that?"

"Don't know. Come on, help get her up."

We lifted her to a dry part of the floor and leaned her against the wall. I tried talking to her, but I was not convinced she could hear me. "Miss Dolly? Miss Dolly? You alright?" She mumbled some words and then slowly started coming around. "Miss Dolly, can you hear me?"

"What happened?"

"Don't know, really. You just went on and fell asleep on us while you were standing. Are you alright?"

"Yeah, I'm just tired, I guess."

"Shit, you must be, woman," Boy said in amazement. "I've never known a single animal on Earth that could fall asleep on its feet."

"Come here a minute, Boy."

We assembled in a corner of a different room. "I think there's something wrong with Miss Dolly. Maybe we ought to take her to the hospital."

"Nah, I don't think so. My Uncle Bud used to fall asleep on his feet all the time."

"He did? Why'd he do a thing like that?"

"Well, he had Alzheimer's. Maybe he'd forget to lay down."

"That ain't it with Dolly, Boy."

"What do you think she has?"

"I don't know, really. Do you remember those goats we saw on television once? Remember the ones that used to faint when they were standing?"

"You think she went on and caught what they have?"

"Maybe."

"Maybe she ate some of that goat meat."

"Hell, I don't know, she's your girl, but I've never heard of any other creature to do that only to claim they were sleeping. She fainted, you know, and that ain't correct with the body. We just don't do that."

"Should we just talk to her then?"

"Yeah come on." We went back to the room. Dolly was awake and leaning against the wall with what appeared to be little energy.

"Dolly, are you alright?"

"Oh, I'll be fine."

"Dolly, please tell us. What's going on with you?"

"What do you boys mean?"

"Well Boy and I have noticed you been quite peculiar lately."

"How so?"

"You go to the bathroom a lot, we thought we saw you throwing up once, and now you're fainting. And a person never ought to faint for no reason like that."

For some reason, Boy thought it was a good time to interject with foolishness. "Girl, you been around any goats lately?"

"Goats?"

"Come on, Boy. Don't mind him, Dolly, just tell us."

She repositioned herself against the wall to get more comfortable. The rain didn't stop, but the hail seemed to have come to an end. "Just let me begin by telling you boys that I know who you are." Boy and I were paralyzed by these remarks. She continued. "You boys don't have the smarts enough to go on the run under different names. How far did you expect to get like that without getting figured out?"

I had never given it much thought, but there was some sense to what she was saying. I just never figured me being anyone else but Curtis. Boy was more interested in what that had to do with her than whether or not we were intelligent people. "What does our not using other names have to do with you?"

"I thought you boys would've killed me by now, but you ain't killers at all, are ya?"

"Kill you? Why would we do that, Miss Dolly?" I asked.

"Because I'd just as soon die than live with cancer."

Boy got very serious. "You got cancer, woman?"

"Yeah, and I ain't doing all too good either. I overheard you guys talking over your problems, which is why I know who you are."

"So, you thought we would just kill you?"

"Yeah, Boy I did, but you guys just turned out to be the nicest fellas I've ever known."

"So how sick are ya, Dolly? I mean really?" I asked. I think she understood well what I wanted to know.

"I'm four months past a six-month expiration date if that's what ya want to know."

"I'm so sorry, Dolly. I thought you were on drugs or something."

"Hell, I'm on plenty of drugs, they just don't do a damn thing for me. So, I just stopped taking them."

"Well you came to the wrong place, Miss Dolly. We ain't gonna kill ya."

Boy said while foolishly sticking his head out the window again: "Looks like it's finally letting up." He pulled out a cigarette and did a terrible job concealing the fact that what he just heard from Dolly was troubling to him. I had for the first time, based on his demeanor, felt that Boy had developed a special liking to Miss Dolly. I suddenly felt ashamed for having felt so heart-broken with Lorena being gone. When someone you care for dies, that's just something awful. Boy didn't even excuse himself when he stepped outside to what was now a light drizzle. Dolly had closed her eyes, so I thought I'd go talk to Boy.

I stepped out into the broken-down porch. The smell of wet dirt took me back to Tomball on an August evening. Boy hadn't finished his cigarette and was already looking for a new one. "You alright, Boy?"

"No, I ain't alright at all, you know–all this is on me."

"On you?"

"Yeah, on me. Dolly has cancer because of what I went and done to Mary Beth."

"Boy, you've said some things in your day, but this beats them all. Now what the hell are you talking about?"

"Come on, now, don't tell me you ain't never heard of karma."

"Oh, so you think God is striking down a girl you hardly know because of Mary Beth?"

"That's right. He doesn't want me falling in love anymore."

"You telling me you're falling in love with her?"

He got shy. He may not have realized what had come out of his mouth. "I don't know, Curtis. But she's alright. That's all I'm saying."

"Well don't be acting all bashful about it. There ain't nothing wrong with taking a liking to such a beautiful woman. But now that we got this bit of information on her, what are we gonna do about it?"

"I don't know, really. Do you have a cigarette?"

"No but you better stop smoking them things, or you'll be next to get cancer."

"I may as well have it, partner. I've really messed up my life." He found a cigarette somewhere on his body and put it in his mouth with nothing to light it with. He leaned on a rusted wooden pillar holding up a tin roof on the porch. Chesney came out and sniffed at Boy's boots as if he was looking for something.

"Boy, I'm gonna feel like a snake slithering under your skin, but you must be thinking what I am about Miss Dolly."

"Yeah I know, Curtis. I know that plain well already. You don't have to tell me like I'm dumb."

"You ain't dumb, but I'm glad we're on the same saddle here cause you know it's gonna be a burden something awful getting to Mexico with a sickly girl."

"What are we supposed to do about her? Just leave her here?"

"Hell, I don't know. We can talk to her, I guess. She's gotta go get some treatment or something."

"Curtis, are you a deaf cowboy or something? She's done told you she wants to die. Why in hell would she agree to treatment?"

"Look, we ain't talking about what she wants or doesn't want. The idea is get rid of her!"

Boy rubbed his face with both hands and put the unlit cigarette on his ear lobe. He leaned against the wooden pillar again and crossed his arms. "Where's the gun?" he asked.

"In the car, I guess. Why?"

He did not answer and walked over to the car. The interior was flooded and began to develop a stench from the wet fabric. The top wouldn't raise, and there was no way to protect it from the rain. He reached around the floorboard until he found the gun. He walked back inside the house, and all went quiet. I came to my senses as to what Boy might be thinking, so I ran inside the house. Boy went and stood over Dolly's body with the gun pointed directly over her head.

"Boy, are you crazy? Put that thing down!"

"It's the only way, Curtis."

"No, it ain't! Now, put that thing down."

"She said it herself to the both of us. She went on and told us she knew who we were."

"So? If she wanted to turn us in, don't you think she would've done it a long time ago?"

"How do we know she's telling the truth?"

"You mean about being sick?"

"Yeah about being sick . . . Get up, Dolly," he told her.

"Why would she lie about something like that to two strangers? Besides, she ain't been looking well . . . you know that."

"She didn't look sick-like to me when we first met."

"Come on, now, Boy. We ain't known this girl nearly enough to know what she'd been through before we met her. We have no idea!"

"You two been talking, Curtis?"

"What?" He took the gun off Dolly and lifted his arm toward me.

"Why are you protecting her? You two been talking?"

"Hey, cut that shit out! Stop pointing that thing at me, and what the hell are you talking about?"

"Angela told you that you weren't in the kind of trouble like me, and you cut some kinda deal with the cops, didn't ya?"

"You're outta your mind, you idiot. Now, put that thing down!"

"Why are you defending her, then?"

"I ain't defending her, Boy. She just looks sick to me, that's all. We don't know her well enough to know if she'd been sick before us. Just cause you fucked her don't make you an authority on her—that's all I'm saying. Now, put that thing down before it goes off."

He threw the gun angrily at the floor toward a pile of wet wood. "I ain't got no bullets." He gave me the nastiest look I had ever seen him give anyone. I wasn't sure how much Boy trusted me anymore, but the mere thought that he would think I'd betray him in that way tells me he was on the edge. From this point on, anything could happen.

The car stench was overwhelming, but that was not the most serious problem with it. When Boy turned the ignition, it made an awful sound I had never heard come out of a vehicle. That car is done for," I told him. "Ain't no way something sounding that silly is gonna start."

"Now what are we supposed to do?"

"Hell, I don't know. I ain't no mechanic, and I'm not knowing these parts too well to get us out of here on foot."

"Damn it! Is that woman still asleep?"

"Hey, come on, now. She's sick."

His demeanor changed as he obviously regretted complaining about Dolly needing so much rest.

"Well, go get her, will ya? We have to get out of here."

I got the feeling he put me in charge of Dolly from that point on. He didn't want to seem to want to deal with a dying woman after what occurred with Mary Beth. I went into the old house and saw Dolly had found a comfortable manner of positioning herself against a dry corner. She looked so comfortable I did not want to wake her. It was getting late, however, and we needed to get moving much faster than we did when we had a form of transportation.

"Miss Dolly? We gotta go, honey. Come on." Chesney came to assist my efforts. He got close enough to lick her cheek and sniff at her blonde curls. I had to nudge her a little. "Dolly, come on, sweetheart, we gotta be getting. I've got some bad news about your car."

There was something mysterious about the entire dialogue I was having with myself. Dolly's color had changed too, and there was no movement from her breathing. I knew exactly what I was looking at, and it scared me something awful.

Boy came in with his usual attitude. "You guys coming, or do I need to slap y'all with a porcupine?"

I walked right past him having shouldered him a bit. I was annoyed at his constant fussing. "One of us is coming." I told him sarcastically and went outside to lean on the same pillar Boy was at earlier. It wasn't until about fifteen minutes later Boy came out to join me.

"What do we do with her?"

"Shit, I don't know, partner. I really don't." I knew exactly what he wanted me to confirm. I was aware the sad reality was that we couldn't bring her with us. There were too many questions to answer to too many people. We stayed silent for a good twenty minutes. Without saying a word, we both started walking down the long muddy road and did not look back. Chesney stayed to mourn.

Chapter 21

Maxwell Conner

"You're about as sharp as a fly using a spider's
web for a hammock, ain't ya?"

The road seemed much lonelier walking than it felt in the car. It began to drizzle again, and our soaked cowboy hats were getting heavy. We walked for about an hour without saying anything to each other. I think we were both feeling guilty, but I didn't see anything healthy about keeping it all inside. "You know, Boy, I ain't been this bad my entire life. I used to be a pretty nice guy you know."

"I reckon I've never been nice, but I ain't never been this bad either."

"Man, I wish we could turn back the clock a spell."

"Where would ya want to turn it back to?"

"Hell, I don't know." He made me think about it for a minute. I finally had an answer for him. "You remember that barbeque place called Vera's?"

"Yeah, I remember. Somewhere out there by Lake Conroe."

"That's the one. The food there was surely good."

"Yeah, it was. It was worth the ride from Tomball, wasn't it?"

"Sure was. Remember that beautiful girl up front?"

"Oh, yeah. I can't forget a girl like that. She was something beautiful, wasn't she?" I stayed quiet for a minute remembering her beautiful smile. Her hair was somewhere between brown and red, but strands of a lighter color would sometimes come out. "She sure was pretty. She always had this beautiful smile when tending to ya."

"Curtis, you mean to tell me there was a girl in front of you who could fill a pair of jeans the way she did, and you were looking at her smile?"

"Damn it, there's more to women than just tits and ass all the time. That girl was genuine. I loved her hair in a ponytail."

"Yeah, she sure made the food taste better, didn't she?" At that point I regretted the direction our conversation had taken. I reminded myself how hungry I was. "We still got some money?"

"We got a bit. You hungry too?"

"Yeah, I am."

"What we don't have is a place to buy any food." We had walked for some time without coming across a main road. I was beginning to question our route. "Are you sure we drove in from this direction? I know we came through in a car, but even so, we didn't drive all that long for us to have been walking so long."

"I don't rightly know for sure. I was so messed up about Dolly. I just started walking."

I kept looking back hoping Chesney was somewhere at a short distance trying to catch up. Boy and I walked for another hour, confirming my fear that we were walking in a completely different direction than we intended to go. A much more critical concern was the closing of the sky. It appeared as if there were signs that the rain was returning, and Boy and I were nowhere near a roof to get under. After another fifteen minutes, a new drizzle began to fall. The land around us was becoming greener, and the possibility of a farmhouse or a store was looking more promising. We never came across a strong structure, but we did stumble upon an old carport. It looked as if it was once a garage or a place where cars were repaired.

"This will have to do." Boy said, appearing unimpressed with the environment.

"Hey, anything out of the rain is fine with me right about now. I already got a cold coming on."

The inside was just as dirty as the previous shelter we found. Boy didn't have much to say. He quickly chose a spot on the ground to sit and lean against the aluminum structure. Only two sides were open, so the breeze from the rain would run right through us. But it did have a tin rooftop that kept us dry. There were rusted tools throughout the ground and an old motorcycle that looked as if it had been discarded years ago. Boy lowered the rim to his hat and kept to himself for a while. I knew he had Dolly on his mind, and I wasn't sure how to bring it up.

"You alright there, partner?"

He raised himself up to be flat on his back side and lifted the rim of his hat. "Well, I've done made up my mind."

"To do what?"

"I'm taking the few bucks we have left and getting a bus back to Tomball."

"The bus? Boy you know that's the first place they put pictures of us?"

"You ain't getting me, are you, smart guy? You're about as sharp as a fly using a spider's web for a hammock, ain't ya? I'm going back to Tomball. This is it. I quit."

I could tell on his face he was serious. I thought there was more he wanted to say, so I stayed quiet.

"You know, Curtis, I can't imagine prison is much worse than what we've been living. I lost one girl because I didn't fuckin' get ketchup and lost another cause God didn't think I should have any more . . . hell, I even lost the dog."

I wasn't sure how sincere Boy was about what he wanted to do, but I had to decide whether or not it was wise for me to do the same. He was more emotional than I had ever seen him before and thought for a minute that there was something more specific than being tired upsetting him so much. "Now, do you think maybe it ain't running you're tired of?"

"What are you talking about?" The rain got a little louder, so I had to get closer. "Well, I thought maybe it was becoming too much for you to be around other people."

"What? You think I need to get rid of ya to feel better?"

"Maybe."

"Curtis, this ain't about you. It's about me and this running all the time. I'm getting sick. I just can't imagine my life going on any further like this. I haven't had work to earn some money, I haven't seen family, friends, or been fishing in a while. Is this how's it's gonna be 'til we get old and die?"

I wasn't sure how to answer that. I really didn't know how things were going to be. Somewhere inside me, I knew how Boy was feeling. I was beginning to miss some of the subtler comforts that life had to offer. Most take these things for granted, but I felt like taking the walk down Fish Road to check the mailbox just before Sunday breakfast.

"I should've believed her, Curtis."

"Believed who?"

"Dolly. I should have believed she was sick."

"Now, there ain't nothing you can do about Dolly. You didn't kill her."

"I could have believer her, though." He took off his hat completely and tossed it on the ground. "Do you know I went in there to say good-bye and leaned over to kiss her head, and her damn hair went on and fell off her head."

"What the hell you saying?"

"No joke. Dolly's beautiful blonde hair was a wig! Girl was sick. She was bald as an eagle."

"Damn, I never would've known, Boy. She wore it well."

"Anyway, I don't much like leaving her there anymore. I think we ought to just fetch her and call someone. I'm ready to face my punishment like a man. This is too much."

I gave it some thought. I didn't see the point in my running alone. I had nowhere to go and would probably die in a place like Mexico anyway. "Alright, Boy. I'm with ya. But let's take a load off before we make that walk back."

The rain weakened and there was a nice cool breeze running through the structure. We both found a nice place to nap for a couple of hours. The surroundings were very quiet and pleasant. The rain fell softly and played a big part in me getting to sleep. Aside from the dirt floor, the accommodations were more than favorable. Sleep, however, is the least pleasant when disturbed by a rude awakening. This is exactly what Boy and I got.

"Damn it! Mother fucker!"

"What the hell, Boy?"

"Shit, something just about gave me a nasty burn to my leg." He quickly removed his left boot and tossed it. He pulled up his jeans and exposed an opening on his calf muscle. I managed to see the culprit slither under some loose boards not far from where Boy was napping.

"Shit, you got bit by a rattlesnake!"

"The hell you say!"

"You did. Let me take a look at that thing." I got close, and sure enough, he had a snake bite I could put a finger in.

"I'm getting dizzy now. What do I do?"

"Well, I ain't got no snake kit. I'm gonna have to break the skin and take out the poison."

"Poison?"

"Well, yeah, what did ya think? This ain't a worm bite. Damn Rattler got to ya."

"How you going to break the skin?"

"With my teeth."

"What?"

"Just hang on, alright?"

This wasn't the first time I would have sucked out snake poison. I learned a long time ago that it isn't fatal if I were to swallow it accidentally. It can give a person nasty diarrhea, but I was not about to let that happen. I got down to Boy's calf and did what I could. He started moaning like a child getting a tetanus shot. It was then I heard a voice from behind me. Although it came in nice and clear, I couldn't let it distract me from saving my friend.

"What the hell are you two queers doing in my shed?"

I could just imagine what it looked like from behind being down on Boy like that and him moaning like a two-dollar whore. I extracted what I thought was enough and spit it out.

"You disgusting faggots, get the hell out of here!"

Boy tried to get up on his feet with the intentions of saving his manly honor. "I got bit by a snake, you fuckin' moron!"

"Yeah, this idiot let a snake bite get at him."

"I didn't let him, Curtis. He just went on and bit me. I would have defended myself, but I didn't happen to have a mongoose in my pocket I'm sorry to say."

The man looked around a bit and analyzed the situation. I imagine he understood after a minute what was happening. "Well, alright. Serves you boys well for being on private property."

"Just trying to get out of the rain," Boy said while bending over on one leg to get his hat from the floor. Suddenly, the atmosphere with the man changed.

"Peter? Peter Boy Jenkins, is that you?"

This caught us both by surprise, and Boy erected himself defensively thinking his face may have come out somewhere. But the case was much different than that. "Maxwell . . . Maxwell Conner, how the hell are ya?"

They both embraced. I never thought Boy could look like a small man next to anyone, but there he was standing next to a man twice his size. His hands were large and his chin firm. He had a slight shadow of a beard and cowboy boots we could all fit in should the weather cause any flooding. "What on earth are you doing in these parts?"

"Just looking for work, stranger. How about you?"

"I left Tomball years ago. Right after high school, I came out here with my uncle and took over some of his property when he died. Now, I got a good thing going here. Haven't been out to Tomball in more than ten years."

"Well, shake hands with my buddy Curtis." Both of my hands could fit in one of his palms. He shook my hand, and half my arm disappeared. I counted my fingers after he released just to make sure they were all there. His grip was firm and his bone structure massive.

"Curtis, now, this is Maxwell Conner. He and I used to spend quite some time together as children out in Huntsville during the summers. Our mamas hated us together. We'd always get into trouble in each other's company."

"Oh, that we did, Boy. Well, you look great, man." He looked around and was probably looking for a car. I am not sure if it was my own fears playing with me or if the suspicious look in his face was genuine. "Ain't you boys got a car or something?"

"Um no, Max, it broke down some hundred miles back, but we didn't see no point in stopping our job search," Boy replied quickly.

"So, do you boys need a ride somewhere? Hell, why don't ya come over to our ranch? We're fixin' to have us a cookout. You guys hungry?"

It was then I knew Maxwell was sent from God himself. We didn't give Dolly much of a thought, but she would come up again later. Maxwell's truck was rather impressive. It had a long back seat, and the inside was brand new. Boy took a great liking to it as well. "Woo wee, Maxwell. You got yourself quite a ride here."

"Yeah," he responded with a cocky smile. "Just a little bonus from some people I do business with."

"It must be some business."

"Yeah, you know, just some ranch stuff. Maybe I can interest you boys in a healthy living."

Boy was in the front seat and turned to the back to look at me. I knew right away he liked the idea of working again. I didn't mind the sound of it either. "You think you can set us up like that, Max?"

"Come on, Boy, I wouldn't have told ya if I couldn't, would I? I'll tell you all about it at the ranch. Let's not talk business now . . . let's have us some fun tonight." He let out a whistle and Chesney came out of nowhere and jumped onto the bed of Max's pickup.

Boy and I just looked at each other curiously. "Nice dog, Max," Boy said, fishing for a response.

"Oh, yeah. He was just running around here. He'll be even nicer once I clean him up." We had no idea whether Max saw Dolly or not.

Chapter 22

The Peculiar Type

"You boys know that when you ride a horse drunk,
the ride is much smoother?"

Maxwell's ranch was personalized with a large letter "M" on the front gate. It would split right down the middle when the gates opened to let the truck through. Most ranchers put both initials on their gates, but Maxwell had a serious falling out with his father and did not care to use his last name unless he absolutely had to. The ranch land was green and well-groomed. The drive into the ranch house was another ten miles, so the property was large and functional for ranching.

The land was nowhere near as dry as it was at the ranch where I met Lorena, and it was much newer. A cobblestone driveway led to the front door with a white horse stable fence dividing the home's yard from the rest of the field. Less than a hundred yards from the front door, there was a beautiful pond that made home to wild ducks. Maxwell said that in the evenings, wild game would gather to drink water. The back yard had a long patio about the length of half of a football field. It was here where all the party tables were lined. Tables of endless food of all kinds were laid out. A separate table of desserts and drinks had been neatly organized to one side. To me and Boy, it looked like much more than a simple cookout.

"Wow, Maxwell, what the hell are you celebrating?"

"Prosperity, my friends."

He led us to the food and introduced us to a few kind people who quickly continued about their business and did not care to carry much of a conversation with a couple of strangers. This was the ideal scenario for Boy who despised having to talk about himself to people he didn't know. Maxwell got lost among the vast number of guests he had at his ranch while Boy and I ate until we were getting ready to burst.

"Some damn good eating, ain't it?" Boy said with food still in his mouth.

"Yeah, sure is. What does your guy Maxwell do, anyway?"

"Hell, I don't know. Haven't seen him in years, but whatever he's doing, he's doing it well."

"You ain't lying about that. Do you suppose we'll be able to borrow his barn?"

As it turned out, Maxwell was behind me and heard my question. "The barn? Are you kidding me? You guys are my guests. My friends. Hell, you're soon-to-be employees. You men are sleeping in my guest house."

"So, what will we be doing exactly, Maxwell?"

"Curtis, my friends call me Max, and you'll know soon enough. For now, it's time for you cowboys to enjoy the evening. I don't know if you boys have taken notice of the many single young ladies that are walking around here."

Once again, Maxwell was evasive about the nature of our employment, but the atmosphere was so festive, it was easy to put that out of our minds. Maxwell got lost once again in the large crowd of cowboys and cowgirls on the premises. I had lost Boy as well but found him after a while sitting away from the crowd near the pond on a larger rock. He was holding a palm full of breadcrumbs and tossing them one by one into the family of ducks that had assembled just below the soles of his boots.

"Where you at, Boy?"

He lifted the rim of his hat and looked back at the party behind us. "Just a lot of people, you know?"

"Yeah, we ain't been around this many in a long time."

"Not at the same time, anyway. I just got to thinking that out of all these people, how many may have heard of our case on the news or something?"

"Well, at least they ain't got no interest in speaking to us."

"Yeah, I reckon that's a big relief."

The evening went by with Boy and I having successfully prevented any kind of treatment that could bring attention to us. At about eleven that night, people began to slowly make their way home, but it wasn't until near 2 a.m. before the ranch was completely emptied out. All the ranch lights went out, but there was an unusual amount of light because of the bright stars and full moon. I was jealous of such a beautiful ranch and wondered how it was that wealth was divided among people. All my life, I had been lectured about hard work. This is exactly what I had done since being a young one with little to show for it other than getting by.

"You know, Maxwell ain't any older than we are, and he's got all this shit." I brought to Boy's attention.

Boy took out a cigarette and looked around. "It sure is a nice piece of land."

"I could weld all my life and not get a ranch like this."

"Fuck, no! Not on our income. I'd put in sixteen hour shifts just to get what I needed."

"You ain't kidding, partner. You reckon Maxwell got some schooling?"

"Don't know. He doesn't speak like he's a learned man or anything like that."

We both stopped talking when we saw Maxwell galloping on a horse toward the pond. "You boys know that when you ride a horse drunk, the ride is much smoother?"

"Well that might be more because of the alcohol and not the horse," Boy responded.

I could sense that Boy was a little frustrated, but I didn't know why. I imagine knowing someone with the same background—yet who has so much more—can crawl into any cowboy's saddle.

"Come on, Peter, let me show you the guest house."

I had never known anyone refer to Boy as Peter. It may have been the sense of hospitality from Maxwell that made it more tolerable. Maxwell jumped off the horse and spanked it while making a clicking sound with his jaw. He allowed the horse to run around the ranch freely, and it galloped confidently as if it knew exactly where it was going. Our wealthy host then walked with us back to the main yard. "So how do you boys feel about earning a shit load of cash?"

"What'd you have in mind?" Boy inquired.

It wasn't the first time he asked, but Maxwell would never answer the question. That is, until now. "All you cowboys have to do is manage some of my help. You guys would be in charge, of course."

I let Boy do the talking since he knew Maxwell better. "Just like that?"

"Yeah, just like that."

"What are we gonna manage exactly?"

Once again, his explanation was interrupted by our arrival at the guest house.

"This here house is where you keep your guests?"

"Sure is, Curtis."

It was much larger than my own home I had back in Tomball. The walls were decorated with trophy game from Maxwell's hunting experiences. There was a beautiful fireplace and bar filled with liquor.

"Now, you boys don't worry about a thing. You'll know exactly what to do in the morning." He was gone before we could say good-night, and he disappeared into the dark wooded path that led back to the main house.

"You alright?" I asked Boy because he looked overly pensive.

"Just something ain't right here."

"Why do you say that?"

"I don't know, really. I reckon I just ain't used to people being so kind is all. I mean I never really knew Max all that well outside the summers in Huntsville to be tended to so kind-like."

"That don't mean he didn't like you, does it? Maybe he's just glad to see ya."

"Yeah. Maybe."

I admitted to myself as I was trying to get to sleep that Maxwell was a peculiar type. He didn't seem to hold a conversation for more than two minutes before moving on to someone else, and his clothes were neatly pressed and clean for someone working such a large piece of land. I didn't want to burden Boy with these minor details and fell asleep after a while.

I was only an hour into my sleep before I woke up to the sounds of a disturbance somewhere nearby. Boy was already awake just staring at the ceiling. I knew he was bothered by the abrupt manner we left Dolly where she was, but I didn't want to bring it up then.

"Ya hear that, Boy? What do you reckon that is?"

"Hell, I don't know. It sounds like cheering of some kind."

Neither one of us had taken off our boots. We looked out the window and noticed light coming from the inside of the oldest barn on the ranch. There was some kind of commotion taking place. Boy and I walked over to the barn and looked through a gap of a loose board. A circle of Mexicans–obviously illegals–were fighting roosters. They would tie flat blades to their talons, and the creatures would fight to the death. It was a horrible scene even for a cowboy who has seen almost every aspect of nature. Boy and I watched in silence. We didn't have much to say to each other having witnessed such brutality for the first time. After a few roosters fought, dogs were lined up to fight each other next. Money exchanged hands, and with every dollar that was made or lost, there was Maxwell involved in every dealing.

Two pit bulls were let loose on each other: one black and the other a dark gray. They went at each other for no other reason than having been taught to hate. Blood splattered everywhere until the black dog finally managed to take hold of a vital part of the gray dog's neck. A main artery must have been severed because it was too much blood to have been spilled from an ordinary cut. The gray dog finally dropped without an ounce of life left in it. The black dog stayed put looking over his victim with a look that advertised a sense of remorse. I don't know if the black dog even wanted to hurt the other, but he was trained to do so, and that is what he did.

The inhumane treatment of animals would have been enough, but Maxwell had much more to host. The Mexican men all got rowdy and cheered loudly in anticipation of what was coming next. Maxwell stood in the center of the man-made ring, and without taking the Cuban cigar he was smoking out of his mouth, announced two Mexicans that were scheduled to fight the next day. There appeared to be a scheduled fight at that time as well.

"Now remember, boys, those of you who lose don't work or eat tomorrow. Only winners are rewarded here."

Boy looked at me with a disturbed look. "What the hell is going on here, Curtis?"

"Shit, I don't know. Come on, let's go. We can't do nothing about it."

"Wait, I wanna see what happens."

The two Mexicans took the center of the circle. They were even in height, but one was most certainly heavier than the other. Maxwell had had taken the destitute Mexicans and used their poverty to fuel their human nature to survive. The fight began, but both fighters hit one another with obvious reluctance. Maxwell fired a shot in the air with a pistol to stop the fight. He walked into the crowd and pulled a child from the group. It was a little girl holding a dirty, handmade rag doll. The child was one of the fighter's daughter. "You mother fuckers are going to fight like men, or this little girl dies!"

Both fighters went at it with a greater deal of force. Money exchanged hands, and after five minutes without rest or rounds, both were so bloodied they could barely stand. Their bare feet were covered in blood, and each was fighting for nothing more than an opportunity to eat and work the next day.

Boy finally gave in. "I can't watch this shit no more. Let's go to bed."

We got back to the guest room quickly. I sat at the end of my bed and Boy went to the liquor cabinet. He pulled out an unopened bottle of Patron tequila and opened it. He took a drink right out of the bottle. "Is that what I am to you?" Boy caught me off guard with this question.

"What the hell are you talking about?"

"That animal in there."

"Maxwell?"

"Yeah, Maxwell. Do you think of me what I think of him right now?"

"What do you think of him?"

"He's a beast!" He took another drink from the bottle.

"No, Boy, I don't think no such thing of ya."

I reached out for him to give me a drink from the bottle. He took another drink before giving it to me. "I didn't mean to hurt her, Curtis. I didn't mean to hurt her. I ain't no killer–bad tempered, maybe–but I ain't no killer."

"I know you didn't, partner. I've never thought you meant to hurt Mary Beth."

"I haven't meant to hurt nobody at all, and now I've got Dolly pricking my brain like a cactus. I just left her there like a dead dog. I didn't want to hurt Old Man Winters or his gay boy either, but I was scared. I ain't like that now. Please tell me I ain't no beast."

"Look, we couldn't do nothing about those things. We couldn't bring Dolly with us either. I'm scared too. People do dumb ass things when they're scared."

"Well, I think we ought to just move on. I don't want to work for Maxwell no more. This is surely what killed that Modesto kid. Max was the boss he was talking about who made him fight."

"I thought about that too, but you sure you want to leave? You sure about that, Boy? We could really use the money."

"I'm just not feeling right about the whole thing. We don't even know how much he's gonna pay us, if he plans to pay us at all, or if he's gonna make us fight."

"What are you saying? You think he's playing us?"

"I don't know what to think right now. After what I saw tonight, who knows how Maxwell plans on treating us?"

"I don't know either. I think we ought to at least give him the benefit of the doubt."

"I thought I was the killer here, Curtis. How can you even trust this guy?"

"I reckon I don't trust him either, but what choice do we have? We've been running for almost three years and neither one of us has had to make a phone call. We haven't had to call a brother or a friend just to let them know we are okay. We haven't got folks or a cousin to ask if they can spare a few dollars. Hell no, Boy, we ain't got nothing but each other, and if Maxwell is offering a job, damn it, we gotta take the chance. We just got to."

I could see that Boy detected the frustration in my speech. I did not trust Maxwell any more than he did, but we had taken greater risks than the one I was requesting of him.

"We best hit the sack then, Curtis. We only have a couple more hours of sleep."

Chapter 23

The Sheep Herders

"I was born on a Friday, but it wasn't last Friday."

The following day began just after five o'clock in the a.m. With so many roosters in the yard, I was surprised not to have had them wake me up to their singing in the morning. Instead, we woke to sounds of a factory whistle that echoed throughout the early morning sky.

"Boy, get up." He was sound asleep and hadn't even removed his boots. "Come now, I think it's time to work."

He let out a short mumble beneath his breath. I pulled the cover off of him. "Did you get to drinking after I knocked off, or what?"

He did not say anything, but I noticed he was shaking like a rattle-snake tail. "What the hell?" I placed my palm on his head. "Damn it, Boy, you're burning up!"

Maxwell came into our guest house. "You boys ready for some breakfast?"

"Don't know about that, boss. Boy here is burning up."

"Oh hell, he'll be just fine." He walked over to Boy and forced him to sit up. "Come on, cowboy. I got some fried potatoes, eggs, and grits waiting for ya."

"I really don't think we ought to force him up, Max." I hated his lack of consideration for how Boy was feeling.

189

"What's this? Is he your boyfriend or something?" He looked back at Boy. "Now get your ass up, cowboy. We got a long day ahead of us."

"Hey, Maxwell, I said he ain't feeling up to it!" I stepped up to him. "Your asshole attitude might work well with these illegal immigrants you're shacking up, but I'll be damned if that shit is going to work with us!"

"Now that's where you're wrong, cowgirl. Neither of you got a choice in the matter. You work for me, or I'll have the sheriff here in less than a minute."

Boy looked up at me and spoke in a low voice. "Alright, Maxipad . . . what the hell do you know?"

"Maxi-pad? Now that's cute, cowgirl, but both of you are dumb asses if you don't think I know y'all left that pretty girl for dead back in Dilley."

This statement did not surprise me or even Boy at all. "She was sick already, you asshole."

"Still against the law to leave her like that."

"So, what do ya want?"

"Just need you to take some goats and sheep to Mexico for me."

"Mexico?" I asked. I looked over to Boy.

"I thought this would grab your attention. There's gotta be more to your story than just that girl. I was born on a Friday, but it wasn't last Friday. Come on, fellas, let's call a truce. All you gotta do for me is a little herding to the Mexican side. I get my animals across, and you boys get a free pass into Mexico. I'd say that's a good deal, don't ya?"

"What's the big deal with these animals getting over to Mexico?" I asked.

"Come on, Curtis, Mexicans gotta eat too. What do ya say?"

Boy and I looked at each other. Boy got up and straightened his shirt and got his hat. "Did you say fried potatoes?"

Maxwell's face lit up like a mongoose in a snake hole. "And the best bacon you've ever eaten, boys. Follow me." He escorted us to a part of the ranch we had not been to yet. We walked past a large pile of roosters victimized by the cock fighting the night before. I figured there weren't any roosters left to wake anyone in the morning. We walked past a long table of illegal immigrants eating canned beans and bread. Some were nursing the injuries from having fought the night before. One of them pleaded with me in Spanish, but I could not figure out what he was saying.

We walked over to the far end where the farmhands were eating a more proper breakfast. We had our suspicion that Maxwell knew much more about us than he was willing to tell. Boy and I didn't know how many of the men knew what Maxwell knew about us, and this was an unsettling fact. We had to rely on chance that no one there had any interest in seeing us go to prison. They seemed more obsessed with getting their animals into Mexico. Based on the ranch Maxwell had, it must be a more profitable business than I had expected. I didn't detect that any of the men were looking at us in any particular way. They all carried on and spoke to one another about their hunting adventures and the best whores they've ever had.

Boy was eating alright, but he still did not carry a healthy demeanor. "Hey, partner, what the hell is going on with you?"

"I don't know, man. I just woke up sick, that's all."

"You gotta get yourself together. We'll be in Mexico soon."

"I'm trying, Curtis. Now let me be."

I noticed Maxwell coming toward our end of the table with a plate filled with hotcakes, eggs, and bacon. It was piled high as if he were eating for more than one man. I was hoping he would inhale those portions somewhere else, but it was too much to wish for. He forced himself between me and Boy and continued pestering us. "So, tell me about that girl you guys left back there?"

We did not give Maxwell the satisfaction of surprised looks on our faces. "What do ya wanna know, Maxwell?" Boy asked him.

"Did ya kill her?"

"No, we didn't kill her, asshole. She was already sick when we met her. I done told you that."

"So, then do people just drop like flies around you boys?"

"If you don't shut the hell up, Maxwell, you'll be next," Boy lashed out.

"How is that, Boy? You can hardly move. What the hell is wrong with you, anyway? You look like a goose caught in a windmill."

"Just mind your own, Maxwell."

Maxwell stood up and called out to a woman. "Milly? Milly, come out here a minute." A beautiful young girl came out from somewhere. All the men continued to eat and talk undisturbed. She was a young, black girl who appeared reluctant to speak to Maxwell. He whispered something in her ear. She took Boy by the left wrist and escorted him into the direction she had emerged from.

"Where is she taking him?" I asked Maxwell.

"Don't worry about your boyfriend, cowgirl. Milly there knows a lot about medicine. She was a nurse just like that girl you left behind. She's just going to look him over. She actually has a few years of medical school under her boots."

"How do you know so much about that girl back there?"

"A good buddy of mine is the sheriff in this here town. They found her nurse license and I.D in her car. She'll be getting some science done to her to see what she died of. Hope you boys didn't do anything to her."

"We already told you, Maxwell. We didn't do shit to her. She done came to us already sick."

"Hey, I ain't judging. I just think it mighty peculiar having two grown men running around the backlands of Texas leaving dead girls behind."

"Why don't you just tell us what we're supposed to do?"

To this, Maxwell didn't say anything. He gave me a sinister smirk and got up waving his index finger as if to round everyone up. I waited a few minutes for Boy to get out. After a while, he came out with Milly.

"What's going on with you? What did she say?"

The young nurse interjected. "His leg went on and got infected. Do you know he's been shot and bit by a snake?"

"Yeah I knew that."

"How do either of you come to expect anyone would feel good after that? His leg is surely infected."

"What do we do?"

"I injected him with antibiotics and an anti-venom. But if he doesn't get some medical treatment soon, that infection is gonna start crawling up and down that leg."

It didn't sound like Boy wanted to hear any of that. "Come on, Curtis. I'll be fine. Much obliged to you, ma'am." He signaled me to follow him.

"Hey now, did you hear any of that?"

"Yeah, I heard. Now let's get this job done so we can get to Mexico."

"Alright then."

We got to the outside of that large mess hall and saw Maxwell giving the immigrant folks instructions. "What the hell kind of talking to is Maxwell giving them now?" Boy wondered.

"Hell, I don't know, maybe he's telling them what to do."

"What is there to herding sheep?"

193

"Lot's to it if you don't got the know-how. Come on, let's catch up."

There was a new face among the group who looked a lot cleaner and well-dressed compared to the other Mexicans. Maxwell walked him over to us. "Boys, this here is Pedro Garza. He is the tour guide who knows all these back woods into Mexico. With Mr. Garza here, none of you will go on and get lost with my animals."

I could see a curious look in Boy's eyes, but I didn't know what he was thinking. "These here are the sheep?"

"Them are it. Damn, you're smart, Boy. Here I thought you didn't know what a sheep was."

"You know, Maxwell, those teeth are only held by your gums, so you best cut your shit!"

"Oh, come on, Boy, you got a better idea of humor than that. Now, get going. You guys have a ways to go."

Boy eye-balled Maxwell as he walked past him. "Well, ain't Mr. Garza here coming with us?"

"Yeah, he likes to walk in the back."

"What kind of guide walks in the back?"

"Oh, don't you worry about it, cowboy. He'll steer you right."

We were three hours into our walk and Boy began to limp slightly again.

"Are the meds wearing off or something?"

"They might be. These damn Mexicans don't lose pace, do they?"

"No shit about that. It's like if the hotter it gets, the faster they walk."

"Well I'm fuckin' tired. How do you say, 'Let's rest' in Spanish?"

"Hell, I don't know."

But it wasn't long after this exchange that we saw the immigrants leading the sheep under the large shade of a family of trees. They all leaned against the large trunks and pulled out their canteens. The sheep grazed a little and sucked on cacti to get some water out of them. I cut a few cacti slabs myself, so Boy and I could suck on.

"Sure is beautiful out here, ain't it?" I asked to distract Boy from his pain.

"Sure as hell is. I wouldn't mind a little patch of land like this in Mexico."

"That's if we're even going the right way."

"Where the hell is that Garza character?"

"Shit if I know, Boy. He thinks he's in charge of the employees here and didn't see him do shit."

"Well let's go look for him. I've got some questions about where we're going right now."

We looked around and tried to ask the immigrants about Pedro Garza in Spanish, but we weren't very successful. We looked around and saw some ruffling of leaves from some nearby bushes. I could see a little lamb struggling. "Look, Boy, some lamb went on and got its head stuck."

"Damn, let's get the poor thing out. I don't want to give Maxwell any excuse for not paying us or getting us to Mexico."

We got a much closer look and realized it wasn't the lamb's head that was the problem. Boy and I looked at each other with a mixture of disgust and amusement. "Shit, looks like we found Pedro." Boy observed laughing.

"Damn it, Pedro, what the hell do you think you're doing?" Boy broke out in laughter. "Are you fuckin' that poor animal?"

Pedro was quick to back up off the lamb and pull his pants up. "N-no, I was taking a piss."

"Man, your English sure got good in just a spell," Boy said.

We both pulled new cigarettes out and lit them. We found a carton in Maxwell's guest house and took a few packs. We felt a sense of leverage on Pedro Garza. I was the first to take advantage of the situation. "You wanna tell us why these animals are being sent to Mexico this way?"

"I don't know what you're talking about."

"Come on, Pedro, aren't you like in charge here? The human resource guy to some degree?"

"I don't know," he said nervously while adjusting his belt.

Boy couldn't stop laughing. "Let me ask you, lamb lover," Boy said while still laughing. "How do you pick a lamb to fuck? I mean do you go for the fur? Their ears? How do you know which one is hot?"

"I don't know what you're talking about." He walked past us to meet up with the other men and called out that we should get moving again. Boy and I continued to laugh uncontrollably.

Chapter 24

The Slaughter

*The men walked past us as if we were desert ghosts
that could not be seen by other people.*

Three days later, we were extremely exhausted and only six miles from our destination. Aside from having invaded a few private ranch lakes, there wasn't much chance for a bath. Our food supply was running short, and after the first day, the lambs continued to look rather odd to us. On one occasion, Boy and I thought for sure that one had died. We approached it and caressed it, and it jumped back up like a jack rabbit and continued on its path. Boy joked about it being exhausted for having had too much fun with Garza, but there was something more than Garza's peculiar interests wrong with the animals. There was not much I could do with this suspicion, so we just kept marching on. Now we found ourselves much closer to where we were going to cross.

Matters got more confusing upon our arrival at where we were supposed to stop. We sat for another three hours before we saw Maxwell's truck approaching down a dirt road leading up to where we were. This also did not make sense to us, and Boy addressed him immediately.

"Damn it, Max, can you tell us what the hell is going on? If you drove your ass out here, why didn't you just haul a trailer with these tired animals in it?"

"Calm down now, Peter, we are both getting what we want, and that's all you need to know."

"No Maxi-pad, that ain't all I need to know. No one here has bathed, eaten, slept well, or received any pay. Most of the animals look sick, and Garza is sticking his cock in the healthy ones. I wanna know what's going on with you!"

At that moment, a caravan of trucks approached from a distance. Nothing could be seen from our point of view but the dust from the road rising like the ghost of a rattle snake.

"Looks like you're about to get your answers, Peter."

The trucks got closer, and the men walking with us all went toward the rear of Max's truck and climbed in the bed of it. Boy and I stood where we were. It seemed as if everything that was taking place was part of a routine that we had never been a part of.

The trucks parked carelessly in different directions and positions, and too many men to count began to get out. They were also Mexican, but there was no way they were Max's servants. Max spoke to them with a different level of respect, and these men's demeanor commanded that respect. They were too far for Boy or me to hear what was being said. In a sudden moment, the men returned to their truck and retrieved heavy artillery weapons. Boy and I looked at one another and got very curious. I didn't know what Boy was thinking, but I imagine it had to be something along the same lines as I was. These men could be collecting me and Boy for reward money. I would not put it past Max to give someone payment in this manner. Instead, the men walked past us as if we were desert ghosts that could not be seen by other people.

They rushed directly to the family of lambs grazing peacefully under the first shade and decent patch of grass they'd seen since we left Maxwell's ranch. The men positioned themselves at different angles and all began to brutally shoot the defenseless beasts. My first reaction was to stop the men, but this was only a thought. My better reasoning knew well that this wasn't the approach to take with what was unfolding in front of us. The actions of these men were so sudden and organized that it could not have been random. I just did not know what possible good could come out of this plan. Boy was just as shocked as I was, but he wasn't able to refrain his disapproval as much as I could.

"What the hell do ya mean by this, Maxwell?"

Maxwell lit a joint and just laughed as he walked up to Boy. "Come on now, Peter, some men who are going to have enough meat to feed their families for weeks are happy for this."

"There's a way about it, Maxwell, and it ain't slaughtering them like that."

"Cowboy, you mean to tell me that a man who leaves a dead girl in an abandoned house gives a shit about some useless animals?"

I was afraid of what was coming. Boy had already made it clear to me that he didn't care to talk anymore about Dolly. Before I could even think about reacting on his behalf, a right cross had laid Maxwell on the floor.

"Damn it, there you go with that uncontrollable temper again."

"I don't need you taking sides, Curtis."

He kicked him in the gut with the tip of his boot. Maxwell began to cough up a little blood. "That's enough, Boy. Let him be."

I turned back wondering if the Mexicans were going to shoot us. Most were gutting up the animals and not paying much mind to what was going on with Maxwell and Boy. Those who were watching didn't seem to care anything about it. They were more interested in hurrying their partners. They cut the animals down the center of their belly and pulled out small sacks.

Boy looked over to Maxwell and kicked him in the face. "This is about drugs?"

With a small gasp of breath, Maxwell whispered, "We have to get creative or get caught, right? At least I don't leave dead ladies in muddy houses!"

Boy kicked him again with the tip of his boot. This time Maxwell stopped moving.

"Damn it, Boy Jenkins, you beat everything, you know that? Shit, man, can't you take hold of your calm just once in your life?"

Boy didn't give me any attention. He got down to his knees, lifted Maxwell's head, and started to yell: "What's my name?"

Maxwell didn't answer, so Boy stuck the tip of his boot against his throat. "You better tell me my name, Maxi-pad, or I swear to God I'll kill ya!"

Maxwell was fading fast, but you could hear in a low whisper that the next words out of his mouth were, "Boy Jenkins."

"That's right!" And Boy took his boot to Maxwell's head even harder. This time, Max was out for good.

"Damn it, you crazy son of a bitch!"

"I don't need your crap right now."

The Mexican men calmly collected what they had gone for and proceeded to their truck. From a distance, another truck was approaching. My heart raced thinking it was some kind of authority, but no one else seemed to have had a reaction to it. The men went about their business and finished loading everything. Without ever even acknowledging that we were there or caring anything about Maxwell, they drove off.

"Now what, angry man? We were supposed to get a ride into Mexico, and those men probably didn't know that because Maxwell ain't awake to tell them!"

"You always gotta blame me for everything, don't ya?"

"That's cause you're always to blame!"

"So what, Curtis, you're perfect or what?"

"No, I ain't perfect, but ain't killing nobody either."

"Well, he ain't dead, is he?"

"I don't know if he is or ain't. I'd rather not know. Just leave him be. If we wake him, he ain't gonna be forgiving. He'll be acting nice just to turn our asses in."

The truck that was approaching had finally arrived. Men quickly loaded the dead animals into the truck, and they began to get in themselves. They were piled up on top of the animals, and I knew well they weren't going to invite us to go.

"Damn it. You fucked everything up, you know that?" Boy could sense how angry I was.

"Look, can you stop bitchin' for a minute? How are we getting to Mexico from here?"

I didn't know how to answer that, but while I pondered over the question, two Mexican men walked over to us. The others had already loaded the animals and themselves onto the old truck. They spoke to us in broken but clear English. "You boys want to get to Mexico, eh?"

"Yeah, what do you know about it, Jose?" Boy said sarcastically. I was about to get on to him again before the man's response eased my mind.

"No, he is Jose. I am Juan." Boy turned to me and smiled. "Yeah, we need to get to Mexico."

"You are very close, *hombre*. The river is low and ten miles further south."

"Can your men help us? I know you're tight, but we really need to get there. We're too damn tired to walk."

"We are not going to Mexico, *hombre*."

"Don't bullshit me, man. I know you're going home."

"Sir, I am so sorry, but we do not live in Mexico. Home is San Antonio."

"Oh, that's fuckin' great! Did you hear that, Curtis? Home is San Antonio. How the fuck are we supposed to get to where we're going?"

The Mexican men gestured with their head toward Maxwell's truck. I looked at Boy, and we exchanged smiles. Boy shook both of the men's hands and thanked them. "Thank you, men."

"You are welcome, *hombre*."

The men were on their way, and I got really curious about the entire scenario. Sometime earlier at the immigration camp, Cotton was talking about these new group of people calling themselves cartels. They were bringing marijuana illegally into the United States from Mexico. Modesto had made mention of them too. Boy and I understood they were dangerous and that Maxwell probably had something to do with them. Some things didn't make sense to me. I asked the men before they got too far.

"Hey, listen I have a question. Why would Maxwell be shipping drugs toward the border and to Mexicans? Don't drugs usually come the other way?"

"*Hombre,* I have always felt it better never to ask Mr. Maxwell his business. I do not know."

"Do they always use animals like that?"

"No, *hombre*, they usually use people." They hastened their step toward the truck. I believe they were a little frightened of Boy for having seen him take out someone Maxwell's size. I didn't blame them for a second; I was afraid of him too.

Chapter 25

Boom Boom Khalia

"I felt the bones in my rib cage rattle so hard it felt as if someone was rubbing them together to start a fire."

So off we were to Mexico in a beautiful truck with air conditioning and a couple of beers in an ice bucket in the center. Boy had a brand-new oversized wardrobe and was singing to country music we hadn't heard in years. "So, what do ya think of my new boots?"

"You look great, Boy. You didn't have to undress the guy."

"Oh, come on. You checked him. He had a pulse. What's gonna happen if he comes to? He'll go right to the cops. This will just slow him down a bit."

"Yeah, if he doesn't die from the cold tonight."

"You're just sore cause he wasn't your size."

"You're damn right, I am." I popped open a beer and we both started laughing. "The shirt looks a little big on you too."

"I just rolled up the sleeves, that's all."

"What about them boots?"

"Nah, they ain't that much bigger."

We weren't used to fast traveling, so when we found ourselves near the border in just minutes, we got nervous.

"So, what do you think, Curtis?"

"Well, I imagine they ain't gonna ask us anything on the U.S. side of the bridge."

"Do you reckon they gave any information on us to the other side?"

"It's been a while. I'm not sure, to be honest."

"I heard from an old buddy that they were big on bribes in Mexico."

"Oh yeah, smart guy . . . and what do you imagine we have to offer as a bribe? We have twelve bucks between us."

"I got something."

"Oh, yeah? What?"

"Just wait and see."

We drove past the American side without a problem. When we got to the Mexican side, we learned something rather quickly. The Mexicans didn't care much for having Maxwell return to their country. They ran the plates and figured Boy was Maxwell.

"*Señor* Maxwell, it is best if you turn back to your country."

"Shit! Listen to that, partner. The little man speaks English."

"Come on, Boy, don't fuck this up."

"Well, I ain't *Señor* Maxwell. I am a friend of the family."

The custom agent looked over the truck and at Boy suspiciously. "What business is yours here in Mexico?"

"What business is mine? Well, I need to pick up my wife and kids."

"You have wife who is Mexican?"

"Yes, I do. Her name is Maria."

"Maria what?"

"Maria *Tortilla*."

"Damn you, Boy!"

"What? That's gotta be a last name, doesn't it?"

I was ready to slap him before I saw the agent's reaction. He erupted into a hard laughter. He related what Boy said to the other agents, and they began to laugh together. Before long, Boy and I were laughing with them. The agent got serious again and asked Boy how much money he had. Boy pulled the keys out of the ignition and handed them to him. The agent was more pleased than I had ever seen anyone before.

Boy and I were now on foot, but we were in Mexico. I couldn't get angry at him for his decision. If Mexico wasn't too accepting of Maxwell, it was just a matter of time the truck would draw attention. Boy and I walked a block further south. We stopped at the corner and began to laugh uncontrollably. We embraced and shook hands.

"Now does this feel like freedom or what, Curtis?"

"You bet."

"So what do we do now?"

"Shit, I don't know, but one thing's for sure–we best get us some work."

"Well, let's get a drink first, alright? I'm tired as hell."

It seemed as if most of the bars in this area had garage doors that went up. The drinking area was exposed to the outside, and there was no real inside to the buildings. It was odd yet refreshing.

"Hey, look on that for a minute." Boy announced excitedly.

A woman who seemed to be a street walker walked into the bar. She seemed to have made great use of strings as a fashion statement. Most of her body was hanging out, but she wasn't anything to complain at.

"Now, is that a body or what? I reckon people down here don't cover up much, do they?" Boy observed.

"I reckon not, partner but hush up a minute. She's coming this way."

The woman sat between Boy and I at the bar without being invited. "I haven't seen many cowboys in this part of the country."

"Shit, she speaks English too." Boy was amused.

"What? Did you think we are all illiterate dumb asses out here or what?"

"Not at all, ma'am. I just figured being Mexico and all that most people spoke Spanish."

"Well, I speak that too. What's your name?"

"I'm Boy Jenkins. This here is my friend, Curtis."

"So, your mama named you Boy?"

"Something like that. What's your name?"

"Khalia."

"So, Khalia, I reckon a beautifully-shaped woman like yourself comes at a big price, no?"

"What the hell are you talking about?"

"The price, how much . . . wait, you are a whore, ain't ya?"

"You fuckin' bastard! I happen to be a dancer at *La Sombrilla*. Just cause I show my tits to feed my child don't make me a whore!"

Boy removed his hat. "I'm surely sorry, ma'am. I just . . . ." He was not finished with what he had to say before Khalia had walked off without ever ordering anything. I imagine we ruined her mood for a drink.

"Damn it, Curtis, we done gone and made an enemy in Mexico already."

"What the hell are you talking about 'we' for? I didn't say nothing."

"Alright, alright I fucked up, okay? Can we just finish our drink and get moving? We ain't even got a single wit about where we're gonna sleep tonight."

"I reckon in a strange place we might have some trouble figuring that out."

We drank a Mexican beer that had a watered-down taste compared to American beer, but with a little salt and lime, the taste was refreshing. Small bowls of popcorn were on the bar top and people squeezed lime and sprinkled chili powder on them. I had not seen this practice before, but I figured it was worth trying some other time. The side of a taxi said *Tamaulipas* on it. Boy and I looked at each other.

"You ever heard of that?" Boy was curious.

"Sure haven't, partner, but I imagine we're a long ways from Tomball."

"You like your beer, Curtis?"

"I wouldn't trade my used boots for it, but it was alright."

"Listen up, I've been studying over something in my head."

"You have a cigarette?"

"Yeah, there was a pack in Maxi-pad's truck." He pulled out a cigarette and gave it to me. He lit it for me and continued to tell me what it was he had been thinking about. At the time, I didn't think it was anything too worthy. After all, it was Boy's thought.

"I've been thinking that maybe that we're here in Mexico already, you might want to call your girl back."

"Angela?"

"Yeah."

"What the hell for?"

"Look, Curtis, there ain't no need for you to live your life out here in Mexico. You didn't do nothing worthy of throwing your life away."

"And what am I supposed to say, Boy? Hello everyone, I'm back–did ya'll miss me?"

"It ain't like that at all. You can tell them I brought you along by force as a hostage or something."

"And what proof do I have that's the case?"

"What proof would they have that it ain't?"

"Hell, I don't know really. But I'm not so sure I want to go back."

"Don't you want your life back?"

"I didn't have no life back there, Boy. I was working all the damn time. I never could find a good girl. Living paycheck to paycheck. The most exciting thing that ever happened to me was riding the mechanical bull at Gilly's. I don't rightly know. I'm scared to go, and I'm scared to stay."

"Well, just think on it for a minute alright?"

"What will you do if I got to steppin'?"

"I don't know really. Learn the ways around here I guess."

We walked a good way without saying much after that. I didn't want to share with Boy that I was feeling scared being in a new country and all. What I really did was hint that maybe we needed to create a more secure plan.

"Boy, I don't know if I have the smarts to make it out here."

"I reckon if you don't have them, neither do I."

"What should we do? It's getting dark."

"Hey, look there." Boy pointed at the large sign on top of an old building. It read: *La Sombrilla.*

"Ain't that where that girl we met works?"

"Sounds like it to me, but I don't think we ought to be going out there. She don't like us much."

"Come on, Curtis. I have to apologize to her. Besides, who else have we conversed with here that could possibly give us any direction or an idea of what to do?" I hated when Boy did that. He always seemed to bring his smarts with him at the worst possible time. But there was truth in what he was saying. We didn't know a single soul in Mexico, and Khalia had been the only person we had even conversed with that we knew for sure spoke English.

We entered the club. The first thing I noticed was the popcorn on the bar. It must be a recurring theme throughout the bars in Mexico. It was still early, so the place had not filled completely. We sat down to a beer, and the waitress came to us immediately. It was Khalia.

"Damn girl, I thought you was a dancer," Boy said instantly.

"Yeah, well I do this too. Are you boys sampling all the beer in Mexico or what?"

"Look, Khalia, I'm really sorry about earlier. I reckon it's too much to ask you to forget all about that."

"I suppose I've been accused of worse." She smiled and once again went about her business. "So, what'll you boys have to drink?"

"Just beer, sweetheart, and listen, do you think you can talk to us for a spell when you have a few minutes?"

She smiled curiously. "Maybe for a minute. I'll be back with your beers."

There was something old about the environment, yet it was very comfortable. It felt that way at least until three men entered the club and sat at the bar. They seemed to have taken a specific interest in me and Boy.

"Hey Boy, don't you think it's odd those men keep looking at us?"

"Are you going back to that paranoid shit again? Every time you do that crap, you pass it on to me. Give that bull a rest, will ya?"

"I just think it's odd, that's all. Ain't no need to act like fire ants got in your boots."

"Well, tell me this, cowboy, who the hell do we know in Mexico that would care anything about us being here?"

There he went again making comments that were far beyond his intelligence. Khalia arrived with the beer and a drink for herself. She sat down.

"So, what can I do you for, cowboy?"

"Listen Khalia, I know I stepped with the wrong boot with ya before, but Curtis and I could really use some know-how here in Mexico."

"So, what, you boys just came out here on a whim?"

"Well, we can't say it was in our lifelong plans or anything. We just kind of came across it."

Khalia laughed. "You just came across an entire country, huh? Like a little rabbit coming across a vegetable patch?"

"More like a rat comes across a copperhead's nest!" I said.

"Okay, so what do you want me to do?"

"We just need to know where we can rest a spell tonight and maybe get some jobs tomorrow."

Khalia thought for a minute. Before she could provide an answer, the MC announced her in Spanish as the next dancer. We couldn't tell much what the MC was saying, but we did hear the stage name being "Boom Boom Khalia." Both Boy and I looked over to her and almost simultaneously repeated, "Boom Boom?"

"You haven't seen me dance yet!" She smiled and walked over to the platform to perform. We learned quickly that her name was quite appropriate for her presence on stage. She did two songs and disappeared into the back. It took her some time, but she reemerged with new beers.

"I gave it some thought, boys. I imagine you can stay with me for a couple of days. It'd be nice to have some company for a minute. But jobs? I wouldn't know where to begin to help you with that. You guys came to the wrong country to start a new life. Now, I don't know what

214

you boys are up to or if you're running from something, but you gotta promise me I ain't in any trouble by helping you out."

"You ain't getting in any trouble, Khalia. We're just down on our luck right now."

"Alright, then, but you guys have to wait for me for a couple more hours. I can't just leave work like that. The boss won't like it."

"Fair enough. Hey, Curtis and I were wondering if you would know how to get to this address." Boy showed her the address that Modesto had provided to us.

"Oh yeah, that isn't more than three blocks west down *El General Ave.*"

"We're gonna visit some friends up there and be back by the time you get out."

She looked at us curiously. No one would believe that two cowboys from Tomball would have any one they knew in Mexico. She didn't ask anything and went about her business.

"Come on." I told Boy. The less we spoke, the better.

He followed with a more noticeable limp now. For a time, it looked like his leg was going to heal just fine, but we had been putting our bodies through quite a strain. It made sense to me that his leg continued to get worse after all this time.

The walk west to *El General Ave.* was dark, silent, and intimidating. The quiet night reminded me of the old west when people expecting a gun fight would retire to the inside of their homes. I could hear dogs barking at a distance. I hoped they could sense us strangers coming and were barking at us. If they weren't, that meant they could be barking at something else waiting for us just around the corner. Boy and I didn't say anything to each other. The still night encouraged silence. It was so quiet. It was almost as if something evil would wake with the slightest noise.

So far, there was nothing impressive about Mexico. All the brochures I had ever seen always showed women in string bikinis drinking margaritas and basking under the sun overlooking Cancun. Men with exaggerated abdomens walked around drinking Corona beer. I took this as a well-learned lesson about how people advertise. My impression of Mexico in the few short hours I was there was a million miles away from whatever place those pamphlets took photos of. The pavement on the street had cracks the size of bowling alley gutters. The sidewalk was no different. Homeless slept against the wall with heads resting on each other. They were weak and hungry, but for some strange reason, I was afraid of them. I felt more out of place at that moment than a snake at a mongoose conference. The homeless in the United States looked like they had just come back from a square dance compared to the homeless in Mexico.

From one block to the next, the character of the streets began to change. The houses would not by any means be classified as wealthy, but they were certainly in much better shape than the row of houses we had just passed. Boy removed his hat and reached on the inside of the rim. He took out a small piece of paper that had the address Modesto had provided.

"Hey, it's that house over there across the street." Boy appeared certain.

"Are you sure about that?"

"I have the address here, don't I?"

We walked a little closer and cracked the silence of the night with the rough heels of our dusty boots. We got to the front gate and looked up to all the windows. The paint on the house was falling off. It was a light olive green with specks of white in some places. It was coming off, revealing the water-logged wood underneath. The windows were covered in a film of dirt, but we found just the right angle to see on the top right-hand corner window.

"Look, Boy, that's gotta be the glass case! That's gotta be what's holding the ring!" I could see a shiny glass on the edge of the window. Modesto had made mention that it could be seen from the street, but I never imagined it would be possible with such little effort. "What do we do, Boy?"

"Well, I don't see no one. Let's go inside."

I don't know what gave us such blind courage. Modesto made it clear the house was now under the command of the Mexican drug cartel. The earning potential of the ring made us forget all about that, and we went up to the front door as if we were stopping by the house to visit our grandmother. In Tomball, it would not have been believable, but something about the area kept me from wondering why the front door wasn't locked. We went into the house as if we knew exactly where we were going.

We caught a glimpse of the glass case, so we already knew where to go once we got upstairs. "Hey, maybe one of us should wait down here." Boy was showing signs of reluctance.

"You heard what Modesto said about the case holding the ring. It's heavy."

We thought for a moment about our next move. No mention was made of it, but I know we were both thinking the same thing. There was just no way of knowing who was upstairs sleeping. The glass case was probably sealed, so simply removing the ring was something to do later. The house smelled like wet wood and one step was all it took for a loud creaking sound to penetrate the walls. I don't know if it was the still silence of the night or the volume of the sound that made it echo throughout the home so loudly, but either way, it was enough to worry us about waking someone up. Boy and I stood still with blank stares in each other's direction.

"I didn't hear anything." Boy whispered.

We surveyed the area like two night-cats looking for prey. "Ya think the house is empty?"

No sooner had I asked than a bright flash penetrated my eyes with a loud *boom* vibrating my bones. I felt the bones in my rib cage rattle so hard it felt as if someone was rubbing them together to start a fire. I began to hear one *boom* after another, and nothing between those booms and where I was next would become a mystery to me.

I was being dragged down the same path we had taken to get to the house. I didn't understand why Boy was now dragging me in the opposite direction. "Where are we going? What happened? What were those sounds?"

"You just keep quiet, Curtis. You've been shot, buddy, but I'm going to get you some help."

What he said sounded muffled to my ears, but I understood what he told me clearly. My vision was limited by what felt like cobwebs over my eyes. This was not enough to keep me from seeing my blood all over Boy's boots. I didn't think it was going well for me. I don't even know how Boy was getting me to move. We made our way back to where Khalia worked. Boy helped me to a small alley between two buildings.

"Now, Curtis, I need to go inside and get Khalia. You don't move one muscle. I don't know if them Mexicans are following us."

"Boy, tell me the truth–how bad am I?"

"To be honest with you, partner, it's just a flesh wound. It just hurts like hell."

"How do you know it hurts?"

"I've got a shotgun hole in my leg, don't I?"

A few minutes later, Boy came out with Khalia. "Oh, my goodness, what happened to Curtis?"

"We got into it with some men, and he was shot. You got something at your place for him?"

"Yeah, I should have a first aid kit that will help. It doesn't look like more than a nasty cut. He should be okay.

Chapter 26

The Revelation

"I don't know how to be Mexican, Curtis. Hell, I don't even know how to be American. The only thing I know how to be is Texan, and that's done been lost."

We left the bar late that night. The men who gave me a bad feeling earlier were surely to be among the group inside the house. I anticipated for some reason they would be waiting around the corner, but I was wrong. We walked for some time before Boy finally inquired. "So how far is your place?"

"About five more blocks. You tired, cowboy?" Khalia was calm as if seeing people get shot was common in her world.

"No, honey, Curtis and I've been walking for a spell and getting shot at. Now, I'm just missing a horse to take a load off."

We walked a little while longer and finally got to a house that seemed much larger than I expected to find. "Damn girl," I couldn't help but respond. "How much does dancing and waitressing pay out here?"

Khalia laughed. "I'm house sitting, honey. I go back to my broken apartment in a month or so. The owner of the bar I work at went to Cancun on business. He hates leaving his place without no one to tend to it."

"I reckon if your boss comes back early, he'd want to blow our heads off, will he?"

"Nothing like that," Khalia laughed. "He's a good man."

I was the first to cross a sore spot with Khalia. "So, you said something about a child. Is he here?"

She got awfully pensive. "No, Curtis, *she* ain't. Now come on in, boys."

The place was as beautiful as one might expect of a businessman in such a crippled country. Exotic birds flew freely throughout a glass atrium built in the center of the living room as one walked into the house. The staircase to the second floor was made of marble, and the first floor was Santa Fe tile.

"Damn, partner, have you ever set sore eyes on anything like this?" Boy was amazed.

"No, I ain't never."

"Khalia, how well is that bar doing?"

"It does alright for itself. It's rarely any busier than what you guys saw tonight, but he has other bars throughout Mexico."

She continued to walk us through the house until we got to the area where she meant for us to sleep. "You can have this room. It's the only one with two beds in it, so I imagine you two boys would want separate beds unless there's something you haven't told me."

"You put me in the same bed with Curtis, young lady, and he'll wake up with a boot in his ass. Two beds are best."

Khalia chuckled at Boy's masculine humor. "Alright then, you boys get some sleep. I can't have you guys running around loose in the house all day while I get to work, so you have to get moving until I come back later in the evening."

"Damn, girl, how early does that bar open?"

"Boy, if you think a girl can make a living in this country working in one place, then you need to do some reading about Mexico. Now, you guys sit still, and I'll bring Curtis a first aid kit. It looks like he just needs a bandage for that one."

She closed the door partially behind her and vanished into the dark hallway that led to the many different areas of the house. Boy was looking around the room at the expensive-looking artwork on the wall and satin curtains hanging loosely over the window.

"Are you thinking what I'm thinking?" I asked.

"God, I hope not."

"Well, Boy, that poor girl may not have the sense God gave a jack-rabbit going into a cougar's bed, but we know better than to think that raunchy bar makes this kind of money."

"Does it scare ya?"

"Hell, I ain't scared of nothing, but if coincidence ain't at all our friend, the owner of this house could be somehow connected to Maxwell."

"Shit, you had to go on and say it, didn't ya?"

"Well, just cause it ain't said don't mean it ain't so. We gotta know." I said honestly.

"And you didn't want me to kill 'em."

"Hell, you can't just go on killin' people. Besides, you don't even know if he ain't already dead yet. His eyes looked like a stomped-on bullfrog when you were done with him. You just can't do things like that, partner."

"I can if that person is Maxwell Conner. We can't shake him off, and he knows too damn much."

"He knows about us having left Dolly back there in that abandoned house, Boy, and do you know what that means?"

"What, smart ass?"

"It means many other people know what he knows. Hell, Boy, Khalia speaks perfect English. For all we know, she's an American who knows about us and showed kindness to keep us here, and we'll wake up to a mess of Mexican cops just waiting for our ass or even holding us for Maxwell."

"You had to give me something else to worry about, didn't ya?"

"I don't mean to do that to ya, but we gotta have smarts about it all."

Boy stayed quiet for a while. He took off his boots and pulled out a cigarette. He quickly tossed it inside one of his boots without lighting it. Then, he threw his hat across the room in frustration and ran both hands over his dusty hair. "So, have you given any thought to what I told ya about calling Angela?"

"Not much, but I'll tell ya in the morning."

"Look, you got to. You ain't got a hand in any of this and you surely don't need this crap. Ain't ya scared?"

"Hell, yeah I'm scared, Boy. What are we gonna do when we get hungry again?"

"Well, I wouldn't mind eating Boom Boom Khalia over there!"

"Really, cowboy? You're funning about this right now?"

"What do ya want me to do? Die of a heart attack? Yeah, I'm scared. You wanna hear me say it? I'm scared too. I don't know how to be Mexican, Curtis. Hell, I don't even know how to be American. The only thing I know how to be is Texan, and that's done been lost. There's good cause for it for me, but you are one dumb son of a bitch if you think there's cause for it for you. You need to get your ass back to Tomball and go on with yourself. There is a way for you to tell the story for it to all fall on me. What difference would those years of prison make, anyway? Killing Mary Beth is enough to end my life!"

Boy was getting passionate on me again, but this time there were tears in his eyes. I gave it some serious thought, and I'd be as dishonest as an armadillo—who'd say he could see in front of him—if I told Boy that what he was saying didn't sound appealing. His eyes were fixed on me as if he had waited long enough for an answer and wanted one immediately. This one moment was the most critical since we began to run, but Boy wanted an answer. So, I gave him one.

"I'll call Angela in the morning."

He had a look of relief on his face but didn't say anything. He pushed his boots under the bed and dropped back on his pillow. We both knew I wasn't going to call. Khalia came into the room holding what looked more like a tool-box than a first aid kit.

"Everything you need is here. The bandages are clean."

Boy helped me bandage myself up. There were two shirts inside the large first aid kit. Khalia had given us more attention than we deserved from her. I helped Boy get cleaned up with new bandages as well. I can't say that the pain stopped, rather that area just below my rib cage became numb. I was sure to feel like the devil licked me in the morning.

I don't know what time it was, but it didn't feel as if I had gotten much sleep before waking to the sounds of moaning. It sounded distant at first, but once I woke up more completely, I realized the sounds were coming from Boy. I turned the lamp on and walked over to him. I thought he was having a nightmare at first but, instead, noticed he was sweating like a mule with no water. I placed my hand on his head.

"Hey, Boy . . . wake up! Boy, get up. You got some nasty fever again."

He barely moved. I turned him over, and even in his dazed condition, he reached for his leg. I turned him back to his original position and pulled his jeans down to take a look at his leg. It was the most grotesque thing I had ever seen since I was a child, and I once saw an owl eating the insides of a raccoon. I must have woken Khalia because she burst into the room without knocking.

"Don't you boys sleep?" She then got a good look at Boy's leg. "What the hell is wrong with your friend?"

"Not sure, girl. He's been shot, bitten by a snake, and bombarded by hail, so take your pick. All I know is that this doesn't look good."

Boy's leg had turned black from his ankle to almost the edge of the sore.

"We need to get a doctor, Curtis."

"Hell, I ain't going to argue with that girl, but we ain't gonna move Boy. He's heavier than a dairy cow with horseshoes. The doctor has to come here."

"Okay, I will see what I can do."

She vanished with a great deal of concern for Boy. One would think she knew him for a long time. I was trying to keep him awake. I really wasn't sure what harm there was in just letting him sleep, but I've seen it before when someone's health was in question, people would always try to keep them awake.

"Boy, try to keep your eyes open. Just talk to me, alright? Try and focus. Hey, did I ever tell you what I really wanted to do with my life? I wanted to be a country singer. Yeah, I know. I never really mentioned it, but I actually know how to play the guitar a little and do some singing too."

I don't think he was paying much mind. Almost two hours passed before Khalia returned with a doctor. "Damn, girl, did you go all the way to Harvard Medical School to find a doctor?"

"Give me a break, will ya? I went as fast as I could."

"Well as long as you ain't running any races any time soon."

"I'm here, ain't I?"

The doctor asked us both to stop our bickering, so he could look into Boy's condition. He asked us to leave the room. I didn't count on Boy's treatment being fast, so I figured on speaking to him in English there in front of the doctor. "Boy, I think we should just forget about this ring."

"You think?"

"These drug people aren't gonna let that property be. We just ain't enough with the two of us."

"Curtis, there ain't no way on earth I'm going back to that house. There ain't no need to even talk about this. Those people are danger-ous, they have lots of weapons and have a hell of a lot more manpower than two cowboys that ain't ever been out of their own country."

"So, now what?"

"I've been telling ya to call home, haven't I? Find out how safe it is for you and just go home. There ain't no need for both of us to die of hunger out here in Mexico."

The doctor kept working on Boy's leg. He finished his treatment and casually began to open my shirt and treat my injury. There was no real need to ask him how he knew I was hurt. Blood was seeping through the shirt. He never looked up when he transitioned from Boy to me and interjected in our conversation with an accent but in good English.

"There is no need for either of you to go hungry in Mexico. What is it that you want from this house?"

"Some money that's owed to us." Boy answered so quickly it sounded like the truth.

"Gentleman, the cartel are very dangerous people. The only way through the cartel is within the cartel themselves. I have a man on the inside who can help you, but you will have to share your money with him."

Boy and I made eye contact. We did not know whether anyone in Mexico could be trusted, but we also didn't have much of a choice. Our escape from serious prison time relied heavily on whether or not we could survive in Mexico, and to do that, we would need a way to get ourselves started.

"What do you think, Boy?"

"What choice do we have?"

"Not much. We have to find a way to get started here. All we need is to get going. Once we are settled, keeping it going shouldn't be too bad."

"And what do you want out of this, doctor?" Boy wanted to know exactly how deep we were getting.

"Very simply, gentlemen, I do not want my name to ever be mentioned."

"I don't think that would be a problem," I remember thinking to myself. "We don't know your name."

"No mention should be made about a doctor having come to see you either."

"No problem, doctor. How are we supposed to know who this person is?" I inquired hoping to learn more. Boy was not a big fan of mystery, and I have to admit that it didn't make me feel comfortable either.

"You won't know. He will contact you."

The next couple of days were spent in simple fashion. Khalia moved us over to her apartment before her boss came home. We got a hold of a box of cards, played a little poker, sipped whiskey, and played a guitar missing a string we found in Khalia's closet. We didn't mind her apartment was a long way from being the mansion we stayed in the first two nights. Her boss would be returning from his business trip, and she didn't think he would be in favor of allowing two strangers stay at his house. She previously claimed he wouldn't mind and that he was a kind man, but she may have thought about it a little longer and felt differently about it. We waited for almost a week before we heard a knock at the door.

"Listen, Khalia ain't due home for another three hours." Boy said.

"Keep it down a minute," I whispered. "Let's take a look to see who it is."

The door did not have a peep hole in it, so I had to try and look through the gaps between the door and the door frame. This was a common thing in the building where Khalia lived. None of the doors in the building looked like they belonged on their frame. I moved as carefully as I could to not make any noise on the old wood. I saw a man who was consistently looking to both sides of him. He did not appear to be intimidating at all but was awfully anxious to get out of the hallway. I opened the door slowly, and he walked in without being invited.

"Gentlemen, are you the two who need assistance in retrieving your money?" He had a thick Mexican accent.

"Are you gonna help us?"

"You must promise me half of what you receive, and you must further agree to leave Tamaulipas and never return."

"Okay, so what do we do?"

"Neither of you will do nothing. You will wait here for no more than two days. I will return with what you are asking for. I need you to never leave this apartment until you are ready to leave Tamaulipas. Exactly how much is owed to you?"

Boy and I looked at each other with a great deal of confusion. We were not prepared for that question since it was the ring of Napoleon Bonaparte we were after and not actual money. I tried to answer as convincingly as possible. "We don't know exactly, but it is quite a lot."

"Very well, gentlemen, I will try to recover for you what I am sure will be adequate compensation."

The man left quickly and left the door open behind him. I closed it and looked back at Boy curiously. He had a big smile on his face. "Damn it, Curtis, forget the ring. We may just get ourselves paid money we ain't owed and can start with that."

"I don't know. It's all curious-like to me."

"There you go again. You always have to ruin the moment with your thoughts and suspicions of everything. Why can't ya just feel good about something once?"

"Well, ya can't be all trusting either, Boy. Don't it seem the least bit odd to have some Mexican willing to help two cowboys he ain't never met before get money that is supposedly owed to them from a drug cartel? Why in hell would he risk his own neck like that? It doesn't make sense, partner."

"He don't owe us, but maybe he owes the doctor."

"Maybe you're right, but what does the doctor owe us?"

"Okay, I suppose there's some smarts to that way of thinking," Boy admitted. "But what do ya want to do?"

"I think we should speak to Khalia about it."

"Khalia? Why do ya want to bring her into this? Ya know how much I hate telling people about us."

"We don't have to tell her everything. We just need to tell her what has been happening here in Mexico and what we're trying to do. She knows the culture, and she would be able to tell us what would be in it for that man to take money from a drug cartel that can chop him up like cattle and ask us for only a percentage of the entire amount he can leave Mexico with."

"Fine, Curtis, we'll do this your way, but if it fails and if you say too much, I'm gonna chop you up like cattle and mail your ass in a box back to Tomball."

"Fair enough."

Khalia arrived. She had a small fresh bruise below her left eye. Boy and I both took notice of it, but we didn't bring it up. She took off her shoes and threw herself on the sofa and rested her feet on a small handmade coffee table.

"Listen, Khalia, Boy and I would like to talk to ya about something."

"What about?"

"Well, being from here and all, I reckon you've got some good smarts about how things work."

"I suppose I have to know."

"I was just wondering what a man taking drug money from a drug cartel would have to gain by getting money for a couple of guys he doesn't even have a care in the world for?"

Khalia stood up from her resting position and became more attentive. "Curtis, what are you talking about? What are you and Boy into?"

"Nothing, really. We just went to a house to collect on something that's owed to a friend of ours. His name was Modesto, but his friends would call him Desto. He was a good kid, and we just wanted to honor his memory by delivering on something owed to him."

"Modesto?"

"Yes, we met him out at an illegal immigration camp somewhere between Tomball and Dilley. I can't say for sure. Boy and I were mighty disoriented with all those back roads."

"And you say he is dead?"

"Yeah, the poor fella had a drugged bull for a boss who made him fight. His own rib bone went on and poked his lung."

Khalia got very serious and her eyes began to tear up. My curiosity could not keep me from asking. "Khalia, did you know him?"

"I knew him once as a child. I have always wondered about him."

"Wait a minute!" Boy interjected. "Girl, your real name is Jimena, isn't it?" This caught Khalia completely by surprise. "Desto spoke of me?"

"Spoke of you? The man was crazy about you. He wondered a great deal about you as well. He sure would be happy to know you're alive and well."

"It would have been nice to see him."

"So, Miss Khalia, or Jimena—what happened to you?"

Chapter 27
Jimena's Story

The faster one has experiences like mine, the older you get regardless of how young numerically you really are.

Modesto and I had always been good friends. He never showed any kind of hatred for anyone in his heart, but he had always had a poor relationship with his father. There was a rumor within our part of Mexico that he was sexually abused by him. I never knew if this was true or not because I never thought to ask him. If he wanted me to know, I am certain he would tell me. I was like a comfort zone for him. He came into my father's bakery where I would often provide him with sweet bread. This is what I was doing the morning I went to go see him. We took a walk along the riverbank, and it was there we saw a group of local *federales* disposing of a body in the river.

I couldn't help but let out a sneeze within all that wet brush, and we were quickly discovered and compromised what the *federales* were doing. The man who appeared to be in charge was a frightening man I would later learn to be Pasqual Torres. His followers called him "Pasca" and followed his orders to run after us. He had a large scar that ran down the length of the right side of his face. Each of his eyes were a different shade of blue, but his skin was dark and sweaty. I could not run nearly as fast as Modesto. My legs were cut from the tall brush and were much shorter. I cannot blame him. He waited for me and pushed me to keep up with him. We finally found a good opening that led to a house at the end of a dirt road. Modesto pleaded with me to go with him, but I was eager to get home and thought I could do so safely. It was my fault that we parted at that time. I did not get far before I was scooped up like an animal by Pasca's men and thrown into a vehicle.

I was blindfolded and taped at the mouth. I didn't see a purpose in this, for in Mexico, people do not react to someone yelling. We drove for a very long time to a small town just outside Mexico City. I was taken to a house and placed in a room with locks on the outside of the door. The room appeared to be made of some kind of clay or brick. It did not have the feel of the usual structure of a house. There was a round window carved into the clay wall, but it didn't have glass or curtains. It exposed me to the outside world with no concerns by my captors of me escaping. This would be an impossible task anyway. I realized early when I looked outside. I was on a high floor. The room had a thin, smelly mattress laid out on the floor on top of a thin layer of grass and a small blanket. There was no other kind of furniture and no other way to occupy my time. I remained in this room all day and did nothing but cry. Every day, they would bring me a meal in the evening. This was the best part of the day because the food was really good. I was quite scared because I had heard people talk about how many prisoners or people who are taken are fed poorly. I was pleasantly surprised even at that young age with the quality of food I was getting.

This process repeated itself for about three days before I finally had interaction with a beautiful young lady. She walked into my room wearing a pretty red dress. She smelled like flowers and had the most pleasant smile. I instantly felt safe with her and knew she would not hurt me.

"Hello there, my little Angel. My name is Magdalena." She introduced herself to me. She took me by the hand and led me to a room in a different floor. The rest of the building was a miraculous thing to see. I didn't know a lot about the Mexican mafia at that point in my life, but in Mexico, one does not get to be very old before understanding that they are evil and extremely wealthy. The drug trade was just beginning to be brought up in meetings at that time. I never said or asked anything, but knew I was among them. I was scared. I had read in the papers how they take people's heads off. I was afraid Magdalena was a trap to have my head taken off as well.

She took me to a pool and told me to take off all my clothes. She took her clothes off too. We got into the pool and played a while in the water. She walked on her toes like a ballerina and did various pool exercises. She had me do this with her every day for about three weeks. This was my only recreation. Magdalena would not speak much, but when she did, she was polite. After three weeks of this, she started to teach me how to style my hair, do my makeup, and how to dress nicely. This part I enjoyed because my mother would never allow me to wear makeup. She would always tell me she thought I was still too young to do so. Even at that age, I was confused by the kindness these people were showing me, despite being at the mercy of their imprisonment. I couldn't understand why they did not let me go home. I was no longer afraid, but I missed my parents a great deal. Still, I was happy that my abduction was nothing like I had heard people talk about or read in the papers. I was even given a job serving party guests when they came to the house for gatherings. I began to wonder whether it was all a lie about kidnappers being bad people. Maybe they were groups of men who captured little girls to make their life better. This manner of thinking stopped when I turned fifteen years old. It is true that time travel is possible. The faster one has experiences like mine, the older you get regardless of how young numerically you really are.

I realized why Magdalena had trained me in the art of walking in the pool, maintaining my hair and appearance, and how to socialize and serve guests. She was developing my skills of eloquence so that I could be of profitable service to the head boss. By the time I reached my eighteenth birthday, I had been with hundreds of men and was the most coveted whore among the drug dealers who came to the mansion. Security remained strict with me and not once did I ever encounter Pasca or any of the head men. My dealings were with Magdalena, who warned me from the beginning that I should not resist the men who waited for me in the rooms I was taken to. Resisting could cost me my life.

The first man I had to be with was old. He smelled like old tequila and tobacco. I didn't know what to do, but he was forceful and specific about what he wanted. He did not treat me like someone he paid to have sex with. He treated me like a rape victim. It was a horrible experience, and I was so scared for what the future held for me. I cannot say that some experiences were pleasant because being used as a prostitute at that age has no way of being pleasurable, but it is safe to say that some men were much kinder and gentler than others. At the age of eighteen, I met such a man. He was handsome, gentle, and kind. I became his habit after a while, and there were times when he would come visit me for free service. I didn't mind. There was a natural feeling about being with a man without it having been paid for. It felt real even though it was a mere illusion of reality. He was an American by birth, and dreams of someday earning his trust enough that he would take me to America would plague my mind as I went to sleep. I only had to wait two more years for that very thing to happen. He spoke to Pasca's boss, who agreed to sell me to him for the price of $100,000.

Inside, I hoped I was worth much more to him than that, but that is what they asked for, and that is what he paid.

Of course, as is the case with many young vulnerable women, I had misjudged my new owner. His intentions were not to marry me or to provide me a beautiful escape into a life of love and family. His intentions were for me to dance topless and sleep with men here in the clubs he opened near the border. I tried to remain positive with the exchange. I was now closer to my family, who I still have been unable to locate. The bakery is now closed–they must have lost all hope of ever finding me. Finding victims of abduction still alive after this much time is extremely rare. In this part of Mexico, I feel closer to them and do much more dancing than sleeping with men. I am thankful to be alive.

I am afraid that Modesto may have been looking for me and was somehow directed to my boss for the beating you say he took. His boss that you speak of is the same man who bought me from Pasca's superior. His name is Maxwell.

Chapter 28
The Plan

"I can't understand you any more than a man with no fingers playing the fiddle."

Boy and I looked at each other and neither gave a hint at our prior experience with Max. We also understood why being called a whore offended her so much. We both must have been thinking along the same lines. If Khalia feared Max was after us, she may have to give us up for her own safety or ask us to leave her place. Our conversation went a different direction.

"So why do you have your own apartment? Why doesn't this Max character have you living in his mansion?" I asked.

"I'm just property to Max. I am not someone he cares about. Besides, I like being by myself. I hope to someday have enough money to leave here."

Boy was still curious about her story. "I thought you said your boss was a kind man."

"I don't know you boys. What did you want me to do, stranger? Tell you I work for men associated to the drug cartel?"

"So, what do we call you?" I interjected.

She thought about it for a good while and responded softly. "My name is Jimena."

"Well Jimena, finish telling me and Boy here about what a man has to gain by helping us get our money."

"He has nothing to gain, gentlemen. You boys are in serious trouble, and I'm not sure how to get you out."

"So, why offer help in the first place? Why not just let us be? Why did the doctor interfere?"

"Because, Curtis, you boys are strangers in town, and the cartel has tabs on any American coming here out of nowhere. They think you boys are with this American organization that call themselves the DEA. There are many street level workers trying to gain higher positions within the drug cartels. If they can impress their boss by delivering someone trying to take their money, that is a good thing for them."

"Well, now we've done it, Curtis. We're wanted on both sides of the border. The bad guys on one side and the good guys on the other."

"Alright, then, let's just think on it a moment. We've gotten this far. Let's just think a moment."

"How are two cowboys from the American side even owed money by the cartel?"

"It's not really money, Jimena. There was just something inside that house we wanted."

"You boys can just forget about that. There ain't no need for you guys to get shot for any reason."

"What do you reckon we do?"

"Well, if you and Curtis are asking me to choose for you, I would say you need to go home. I don't care if you go to your actual home, but you need to go back to your country."

It was sound advice but not one we could take. Boy and I were two men without a country, and coming up with a plan on how to repair everything that had taken place was not going to be easy. My flesh wound was burning a little, but I was in considerably good health compared to Boy. For some reason, his leg never healed completely. He was a tough man, so he wasn't about to complain. The expressions on his face did not lie; I knew he was in pain at some points. At the moment, it had stopped bleeding, but when we found streams to wash up in, I could see that his leg was taking on an unusual color. I had no education in medicine, but I didn't think it was proper for the human skin to turn into colors if you weren't a reptile. I kept those sentiments to myself for the moment and figured the sooner we found a safer way to remain in Mexico, the sooner we could get him real attention for his leg.

There were so many approaches to consider in our situation and so many problems to overcome. First, we had limited financial resources to start over anywhere. Secondly, we had to smooth things over with the cartel, which for the moment did not know who we were. The more obvious liability was having Maxwell come around and pointing us out. He would never forgive us for what Boy did to him nor would I trust him if he said he did.

"Jimena, we can't go back to America right now. We need you to help us find a way deeper into Mexico, so we can start over."

"Curtis, you keep saying 'we' like you're coming along for the ride. I already told you to go home."

"Damn it, I ain't leaving ya. I don't friend like that, and you know it."

"Well, I don't friend like this–taking people down with me. How do you reckon you get your way?"

"What do you mean my way? If I had my way, I'd be fishing in Humble, Texas right now, drinking cold beer from the can with a carton of Winston cigarettes by my side. How in hell can either one of us get our way? If I leave you here, I'll go the rest of my life wondering if you're alive, and you'll be wondering if I'm in prison."

"Okay then, what are we gonna do?" Boy asked.

Jimena looked pensive. I knew she had something on her mind but was not sure if it was something she should share. I couldn't wait for her to finish thinking.

"What's on your mind, girl?"

"There is only one solution to this."

"What solution is that?" I was curious and suspicious at the same time. Her tone expressed a glimmer of hope. Her demeanor advertised a disaster. I wasn't sure which one I should obey the most.

"Look, guys, you don't have to tell me what you did in America, but you boys aren't out here on vacation with no money. So, if you got this far doing something in a country where the police actually arrest you, then maybe you should consider doing more of the same here in Mexico."

"Where are you getting at, Miss Jimena?" Boy asked with the same curiosity I had.

"I can get you boys some weapons my boss keeps in the bar."

"Damn it, girl, you're speaking in riddle. I can't understand you any more than a man with no fingers playing the fiddle. What the hell would we need weapons for? We already lost one gun."

I didn't like it when Boy's temper would slowly escalate. I tried to calm him down. "Give her a chance, Boy. Let her speak her mind."

"I think you boys should rob a bank."

Boy threw his hat against the wall. I sunk down on a chair made of tree bark Jimena kept more as decoration than as furniture. Boy and I were both equally frustrated with the suggestion, but I would do my best to not hurt her feelings. At the moment, Jimena was the only friend we had in Mexico. I was trying to tell Boy this with my eyes, but he wasn't looking. He had his face to the corner lighting a cigarette.

"Look, Jimena, that would be a great way to get some money and all, but don't you think Boy and I have enough problems without having the police on both sides after us?"

"That's the thing, Curtis. There ain't no police. Everything that happens here is in one way or another connected to the cartel. Do you think the few honest police we have here are going to invest their time or risk their safety to find two bank robbers they feel are connected to the cartel?"

"Okay, little lady," Boy turned to intervene. "That huge mansion you're house sitting for is a strong indication that the drug cartel has no need to rob no banks."

"Look, Boy, you and Curtis asked me for information about Mexico, right? I'm telling you that if it is an act of mischief, it will be associated to the drug cartel. Sometimes lower level street thugs are trying to prove themselves. Sometimes they are given tasks as initiation. Sometimes they are sending a message to certain businesses if they are not paying the fees enforced by the cartels. Whatever the reason, Boy, damn it–just listen!" She was yelling by this point.

"Okay, little lady, Okay. Calm down. There ain't no harm in asking about such a dangerous suggestion, alright?"

"Guys, let's just relax, okay?" I thought about what Jimena was saying. It was a desperate move, but it could be exactly what we needed. "You know, Boy, we ought to do some thinking on it."

"Taking out a bank, Curtis?"

"We need money, don't we? What are we gonna do for it here in Mexico?"

"I will be back in an hour, boys. You guys talk about it while I am gone. You need to decide if we are going to do this job before this man who is supposed to help you comes back."

"Wait one minute, girl." Boy erupted. "What do you mean 'we'?"

"Yes, boys. You are taking me with you when you leave here!" She said those words with conviction before closing the door. Boy looked at me like if it was all my fault. He took his cigarette out of his mouth and threw it on the floor.

"You best take a boot to that cigarette, cowboy. We don't need to be starting any new fires."

"This shit is all your fault, Curtis."

"Oh, really. All this is because of me? Clear back to when we left Tomball, all this is because of me?"

"You're going to go there, aren't you, shithead? You're really going to go there?"

"Well, I'm sick of all your hissing like a little bitch, Boy. You ain't got the smarts God gave a brass monkey if you think we're gonna make it out here without some form of money."

"Maybe not, but he gave me something else made of brass!" He punched me hard to my face. It was quite the assault. I think my late granddaddy felt it. I had too much cowboy in me to show Boy just how afraid I was of him, so I took my boot to his gut as I was getting up. He went flying back and crashed into the wall like a wild mustang slamming against his cage. It didn't take him long to get up and charge me like a bull that just got kicked in the nuts. He slammed me to the ground and punched my lower body repeatedly. I hammer-fisted his injured leg, and he let out a loud yell.

"You son of a bitch!" He fell on his back and immediately stopped his assault. I stayed on my back as well and began to feel guilty for attacking his injured leg. We didn't say anything to each other for a few moments before Boy spoke.

"You think Jimena has beer in her fridge?"

"I don't even see a fridge."

"Okay, Curtis. You wanna be a stubborn mule–that's fine. Let's rob the damn bank but on one condition."

"What's that?"

"If we get us enough money that you're comfortable with, you get your ass back to Tomball and try to live normal-like."

It took me a minute, but I did like the idea of going home. Maybe Boy was right about the level of trouble I could be in. I had no reason for hurting Mary Beth and was sure I could get Angela to help me think of a story that would exonerate me. She was never very fond of Boy. She would love nothing more than to see him get punished for Mary Beth's death. "Alright, Boy. I'll do it."

"You ain't foolin' now. You're really going home?"

"I'll call Angela right after our job."

He got up looking as if he was in the serious pain I was feeling myself. I tried to hide it. "You know, partner, I only want ya to go home because I love ya. I don't wanna feel responsible for you having a messed-up life out here." Boy said.

"I know that, and you know I'm only being stubborn because it's hard to leave ya. You know it's all together possible we won't see each other ever again."

To this, he just looked down without saying anything. He paused a minute before breaking the silence. "You know, Curtis, you hit like a little girl."

"Yeah, I know."

"Well since there ain't no fridge here, let's go get a beer across the street."

Chapter 29

The Job

I needed to come to my senses and realize we were in Mexico, and people got by quite differently than most folks in Tomball.

Boy and I went for our beer and found Jimena in her apartment when we returned. We had a chance to reflect on her proposal for a while. We decided that it was an extreme idea to hit a bank and that such a scenario had no place in the story of our lives. It was too romantic, it was too unreal, and more than anything, it was too dangerous. "So, how do you reckon Jimena is going to react to our decision?" Boy asked.

"I imagine there ain't much she can do about it."

"Do you think that maybe we ought to tell her about that French guy's ring?"

"What good would that do anybody?"

"Well, if this woman was so willing to pull a bank job, who's to say she wouldn't go into a house she probably has access to and get us the ring?" There was serious truth to what Boy was saying. I wasn't sure if the ring was even worth anything because we didn't get to know Modesto long enough to understand him as a wishful thinker or as realistic.

"I suppose we could mention it to her at some point. Maybe she knows something about it already."

"I don't see that we have much of a choice. We're in another country with no money." Boy always made sense at the worst possible time. It was only a while longer before we met with Jimena back at her place. "Where have you boys been?" She wondered curiously. It was almost as if there was a sense of fear in demeanor that we had abandoned her. Her light brown eyes looked tired and child-like. "I thought you boys had left me."

"Well, Miss Jimena," Boy lit a cigarette again. "We ain't left ya, but we decided we ain't doing no bank job either."

She sat pensively and placed her milk chocolate palms on her own lap. "I know, boys, it was a dumb idea. I was just thinking randomly out of desperation."

I could sense for some time now that there was something more to Jimena. There was a burden she carried with her that she unsuccessfully tried to conceal behind her jovial smile. It was not my business, but I wanted to know.

"What are you so desperate for, girl?" I signaled with my hand to Boy to pass me a cigarette. He handed me one but did not give me a match, so I pinned it on my ear for later and waited for Jimena to answer.

"I thought you boys may be wanted for robbing banks in America and came here to escape. I thought by suggesting a bank job you would stop thinking about going for your money in that house you went to."

Boy looked at me with a curious eye. Jimena became more mysterious than ever. "Now, little lady, why would you concern yourself so much with whether Curtis and I went back to that house?"

She looked specifically at me and stood from her seat. She walked over to a ceramic rooster she kept on and end table and lifted the top off it and reached in. She pulled out a match and gave it to me. "Curtis, do you remember you asked me about a child?"

"I do."

"I have a daughter. Her name is Esperanza. She is often held there by Max's men to ensure I don't leave when Max is in America. But he has been gone so long that I have not seen her in months. He was due to return sometime this week, but I was told by one of his men that he was attacked or something by some men who stole his truck. Now he's recovering before he comes back."

Boy looked as if he felt responsible for yet another calamity in someone's life. I avoided eye contact with him for fear it might be too obvious that we were the very men Jimena was talking about. I quickly took the conversation in a different direction.

"But what does our staying away from the house have anything to do with Max?"

"You boys were shot at. I don't want bullets flying inside that house with Esperanza in there. I was trying to think of a different way to get you your money so that you wouldn't go back. That is why I came up with that dumb idea about the bank. I thought about it some more and don't think Mexican banks even have the kind of money you boys are probably owed."

"We're sorry to say, Miss Jimena, but Curtis and I ain't no bank robbers. We'd be sitting pretty as we speak and further down the line in your country if we had money."

Boy and I exchanged looks and made a nonverbal agreement to share with Jimena what we were really looking for. Boy occupied his mouth with a pinch of Copenhagen, leading me to believe he wanted me to tell her. I don't even know where he got the snuff, but it did not matter.

"You know you can't spit that snuff out indoors, don't ya?"

Boy knew I was stalling and looked at me with half a smile. "Go on and tell her now."

"Tell me what?" she asked.

"We ain't owed no money, Jimena. Our business in that house was something of a promise to your friend Modesto."

"Desto?"

"Yeah, you don't have to feel guilty about him having been abused for having been looking for ya. He wasn't looking for ya. He probably thought you were dead."

"Then what was he doing?"

"He told us of a historic ring that's inside the house. He said it could be worth millions of dollars."

"A ring?"

"Yeah, he knew the entire history of it. I hope you don't make me repeat it because I can't hardly remember a word of it, but it sounded all real-like. I think he had some pretty good smarts about it."

Jimena became pensive. I believe she was taking a tour of the house with her memory to see if she could find the ring in her head.

"Of course, boys. Of course."

"Of course, what?"

"At the time that Desto and I were being chased, that area where the house is was undeveloped. It was at the end of dirt road that did not make much sense to anyone. That is where Desto and I split up. He must have found refuge in that house and acquainted himself with the professor who lived in it."

"You know about the professor?"

"Oh yes. Everyone did. He was a fine man, but he was a private man. Rumors of witches living at the end of that road spread. But new things have been built over the years, and the house wasn't mysterious anymore at the time of the professor's death."

"So, you mean to say that Modesto may be on to something?"

"If the professor told Desto the history of it, then it must be true."

"So, do you think you can help us get it?"

"Boys, that will be immensely difficult. You see, I am not allowed to see my daughter while Max is gone. The problem is that when he is here, there are more men who stay in that house."

"Do you know people on the inside who might help?"

"Yes, but they should not know they are helping."

"How can you do that?"

"With man's greatest weakness," she said this with a confident smile.

Her plan was not difficult but was risky. She relied heavily on her looks, outgoing personality, and wit to convince the man who said would help me and Boy that she was interested in more than just friendship. After all, man's greatest weakness is women. His name was Alfonso Calderon, and he was more of a thug than anything else. He was a street level dealer always trying to get in good with the cartel in one way or another. Most of his efforts tended to consist of making someone else look guilty about something he plotted himself. Boy and I learned all this from Jimena, who knew of Alfonso for some time. For years, he been nothing more than an errand boy who would go get the beer before a big meeting. He wasn't even allowed into the meetings on most occasions unless he was carrying the food the cartel members ordered. He was the perfect person for Jimena to use to carry out her plan.

She went to him crying and pleaded with him to help her. He wasn't sure what it was she needed at first. He was confused, mostly because her beauty and charm wouldn't allow him to listen clearly.

"I need your help," she told him. "I've done something horrible."
Jimena told him she had put some money aside for her daughter. She

kept it in the safe that was in the house that once belonged to the professor. She explained that Max had promised she could leave her small apartment and move into that house when he returned. Now, Max had been delayed, and her money was trapped inside the house. Thinking she could repay it, she took the money out of the safe from the club where she worked. Max, however, had not returned, and the main boss would be visiting soon to account for all the money that had been made.

Alfonso was curious and asked her, "What did you do with all the money you took?"

"Put it in an American bank so it can earn interest for my daughter. I called to ask, but there is no way to get the money back without penalty. But you know very well, Alfonso, that the big boss will not like one dime missing from his money. Can you help me?"

"What do you want me to do?"

"I need you to get my money from the house, so I can put it back into the safe at the club."

"How much is it?"

"It is $300,000."

"*Señora*, you will be in big trouble if you do not replace that money. I can help you, but what will I receive in return?"

"The drug cartel will not allow penalties, but I don't mind taking a penalty to take out $100,000 for you from my American account. On top of that, Alfonso, you may call on me any time you want."

Boy and I knew exactly what she meant by this. As she told us her story, we still weren't quite sure how it would work out, but the offer of that kind of money and a girl like Jimena whenever you wanted her was too much for Alfonso to reject.

Alfonso went to the house as he usually did. There was no way for him to appear out of place there. He waited for it to get late and went to the safe. By three o'clock the next morning, he was at Jimena's door. He looked around for Boy and I before going in. It was nice of him not to forget about us. "What happened to those two *gringos*?"

"They went back to America. They gave up on getting their money."

"Good, I almost had them set up nicely with the boss, but I had to do other things."

"Well, never mind them. Do you have the money?"

"Yes, Khalia. But no one must learn of this, or I will surely be killed."

"Don't worry, if anyone asks, I will blame it on the *gringos.*"

"So, Khalia, how about you giving me my first payment tonight?"

"I will not be able to get to the bank until tomorrow, Alfonso."

"I mean the other thing. It was, after all, part of the deal."

"Yes, and I will comply with it, Alfonso. Can we please do this tomorrow? I am still so worried. Tomorrow when the money is returned before the boss gets here, I will feel so much better. I will get your money and we can get together." She added to this by stroking his hair lightly.

"Very well, Khalia. I look forward to tomorrow night then." During Jimena's carrying out her plan, Boy and I had to do the Texas thing and look for a place to sleep. It wasn't safe to return to Jimena's apartment. There wasn't much in the form of farms or barns in the area, but we did find an old empty house about three blocks from where Jimena's apartment was. It had furniture on the inside, but it appeared to be abandoned. The sofas were old and damp as if they had gotten wet with the rain. This meant the roof leaked, so Boy and I were just hoping it wouldn't start pouring. The furniture was placed in odd spots. There were two small beds in what appeared to be the dining area and fold-up beds against the walls in the living room. Whoever was living there seemed to have left in an awful hurry.

By nine o'clock the next morning, Jimena had taken $300,000 from the safe in the club, placed it in a large suitcase and made arrangements to have Alfonso bring her daughter over for a visit. Considering what was at stake for Alfonso, he was quick to comply. Jimena was so excited to see her daughter. She rolled out the suitcase and told Alfonso that she was going to send Esperanza with nearby friends so that she could see her more often and explain to Max later why she took her.

"Alfonso, please wait for me here, and be sure to watch the money. It is in the same bag you brought it to me in under my bed. I am leaving it so that you have no doubts I will return." Alfonso was satisfied with this and waited for who was to him Khalia's return.

Jimena's next move was to meet us at the bar where we had first met her. "Boom Boom" Khalia was who she was when Boy and I first entered the country. But our plan was seriously delayed by an unexpected event. Earlier that morning, Boy and I woke to a family of roosters singing as loud as they could. We could not see any of them, but the Lord knows we could hear them. Boy already had in mind how he wanted to start his day.

"You know what today is, don't ya, Curtis?"

"I don't rightfully know what you're talking about."

He pulled out a cigarette for breakfast. "Damn it, Boy, do you have a cigarette dispenser in that shirt pocket of yours?"

"Don't you try to avoid the topic. You promised."

"I promised I would call Angela if we hit a bank. I didn't say nothing about no plan from Jimena."

Boy had no response, but he looked at me like he was about to brand his initials on my eyelids with a cattle branding iron.

"Are you gonna be alright if I go?"

"I'm gonna be fine, just fine. I promise you. I'll see ya again."

"Let's go."

"Go make your call, partner. I trust ya. My leg is hurting again." I hadn't noticed, but Boy was getting pale again at the face.

"I'll be right back, then."

It took me some time to figure out how to call to the United States, but once I got a hold of the right operator, I managed to get a ring.

"Hello."

"Angela?"

"Hey, Curtis, is this you?"

"Yeah, I'm sorry to wake ya. I just wanted to–"

"Never mind that, Curtis, I owe you and Boy an apology. Is he with you?"

"He ain't feeling well right now. Well, what do ya owe us both an apology for?"

"Well they found Mary Beth's body. As it turned out, Boy didn't kill her like everyone thought. The police can't figure it out exactly, but they found her body in Old Man Winters's property. They think he killed her because she could point him out to the IRS and where he was hiding. She must have not known he was dangerous."

"You're kidding me?"

"I ain't fooling with ya at all, Curtis. They even found Old Man Winters's son dead nearby. Who knows what went down between all of them, but whatever it was, they took poor Mary Beth with them, and she got herself killed at their place. There is strong evidence that there was someone else in the house who may have seen everything, but they never found a trace of anybody."

I was frozen with disbelief.

"And Curtis, there's something I owe you an apology for as well."

"What's that?"

"Ain't nothing wrong with Dawson either. I was just sore at you guys because I thought y'all had something to do with Mary Beth. I was just trying to scare you home. That's all."

"You mean that bastard is still alive?"

"Livelier than a rooster on a pile of ants. But he ain't gonna mess with ya anymore."

"What makes you say that?"

"He lost his job on account of being too rough with people. Not even his daddy could save him. He moved somewhere near Odessa to work at some railroad out there. I'm really sorry, Curtis. Can we just forget all about it?

"I reckon so, Angela. Hey, listen I'll call you back. I gotta go."

I was quite excited about what Angela had related to me. The thought of both Boy and I being able to go home was a remarkable feeling. We could always say we left because we were just tired of Tomball and stick to it. I got back to the abandoned house, realizing that it wasn't so abandoned after all. A man had Boy at gunpoint yelling things at him in Spanish.

"Oh shit!"

"Curtis, this guy is about to blow my head off. You best be going."

While this was happening, Jimena was probably getting impatient at the bar. She had earlier returned to the club where she had removed the $300,000. To her surprise, the boss was already at the bar and had already noticed the money missing. His name was Marcos Tobias, and he was sitting calmly at the bar. They already had the bar manager on his knees. He had endured a minor beating and had guns pointed to his head. Jimena walked in prepared for what came next. "Khalia, please come have a drink with me." He spoke in Spanish.

"Tobias, it is good to see you again."

"Is it?"

"Why, of course, it is."

"Now, explain to me why a young woman who takes money from me would be so happy to see me," he demanded from the bar manager.

"I will explain," Jimena said.

This got Tobias interested and caught off guard. "Do you mean to tell me that you actually did take my money?"

"Hold on a minute, Tobias, I didn't say that, but I do know where your money is. Just listen."

"Is that so?" He looked around to the many armed men who were in his company. "Gather around, gentlemen, this whore is expecting me to be so generous today in understanding why she took money that belongs to me."

"I saw the man who took your money. He took my daughter from the old Peña house and said he would not give her back if I told on him. He has her hidden away somewhere. Now, wants me to be his whore and is waiting for me in my apartment."

"So then what are you doing here? And why would this fool let you leave?"

"He sent me here to take alcohol for him, Mr. Tobias."

Tobias snapped at one of his men who instantly knew what the boss was asking. He called the lead man at the old Peña house. He spoke for a while and then hung up. "She is telling the truth, boss. Her daughter is missing."

Tobias signaled to let the manager go. He stood up and put both hands on each side of Jimena's face. He kissed her forehead and handed her some money. "You will need this for a new apartment, Khalia. The one you live in now is about to be destroyed. Talk to me later about finding your daughter."

The men all left in a group. Jimena had limited time to get out of town. The group of men would certainly find Alfonso in her apartment with the money under his bed, not realizing it was from Peña's house and not the club. As for the money in the Peña's house, it would not be missed until Max returned since that money belonged mostly to him.

"I am sorry, Felipe," she said to the manager of the bar before running out.

Max always made sure Jimena did not have a car that could go very far. She could not take a car from the mansion she was house sitting, which obviously belonged to Marcos Tobias. Her only choice was to get as far as she could in her old Toyota with her daughter and money in the trunk. She must have been more impatient than a hoot owl waiting for a field mouse to come out of its hole. But Boy and I were quite engaged at the time with 12-gauge shotgun pointing right at us.

"No, Boy, I ain't leaving ya like this."

"Ain't no sense in both of us getting shot, partner."

"We can talk this out."

"How? He doesn't even speak English."

Over the years in the United States, I had gotten rather spoiled with myself. I never imagined the house being occupied because I couldn't register people living like that. I needed to come to my senses and realize we were in Mexico, and people got by quite differently than most folks in Tomball. I tried to explain this to the old man, but he wasn't paying much mind to anything that was leaving my mouth.

"Okay, Boy, just walk slowly–and I mean very slowly–toward me. Once you get to the sidewalk, we're just gonna run!"

"Are you sure about that?"

"You bet. He'll see we're on our way and don't mean no harm and let us be."

"Alright then, but if he shoots me, I'm kicking your ass when you get to hell."

"That's fair enough."

He began to take baby steps back, but Boy began to run a little faster than I had expected him to. He ran into me, but we managed to stay on our feet as we darted down the street. My plan failed. The old man was not forgiving at all and took a shot in our direction. What happened next is unclear to me. The only thing I can say with great certainty is that it was me and not Boy who was hit. I was on a bench outside the local hospital of Nuevo Laredo, Mexico. I could hear Boy's voice telling me to hang on and Jimena telling me that I was going home. I don't know if she meant Tomball or heaven, but either place would have been fine with me at the time. They were doing something to my chest, but I didn't know what it was. It felt as if they were writing on me. I felt Jimena stuff something on the inside of my shirt pocket. Other people came to assist, and she told them to be sure I got the money. At that time, I had no way of knowing it was the money she received from Marcos Tobias for a new apartment. The doctors may have known Jimena by reputation and knew not to take Tobias's money from me.

I tried with every ounce of energy I had left in me to speak to Boy. I was trying to tell him what Angela had told me. He needed to know that he did not need to stay in Mexico. We could both return to Tomball and be safe. Every time I tried to get the words out, blood would shoot from my mouth, and Boy would tell me to keep quiet and do what I was told. I grabbed his shirt and tried to force myself to tell him to go home, but my efforts did not result in anything good. I could see Boy looking directly down at me. Suddenly, he became fuzzy, and my vision was going from white to black. I made one last effort to tell Boy what Angela had told me, but the words would not come out when I tried. I looked up and made eye contact with my long-time buddy. I tried to give him the message with my eyes instead, but I simply could not deliver it. I could see Boy crying for the first time in my life. I looked at him, smiled, and put my head back. It was the last time I would ever see Boy Jenkins.

Chapter 30

Gary Rodgers

He couldn't spit out more than ten words a day if a mule kicked him in the back of the head forcing his tongue to move.

My vision began to slowly return. I thought for sure I would open my eyes to meet my own maker looking down at me. Instead, I saw Angela in the form of an angel she had always been.

"Curtis Cash, are you coming to?"

"I reckon I am," I said with a dry mouth and a rusty throat. "Where am I?"

"You're in Tomball, cowboy. Welcome home."

"Tomball? What happened? I mean, why am I still alive?"

"Don't know, I guess it was Boy who wrote your Tomball address across your chest with someone's lipstick, so they'd know where to send your body. Poor fella must think you're dead."

"I reckon he does."

"Enough talk about Boy, stranger. You need to get some rest. You had several surgeries you need to recover from."

"What happened?"

"Looks like you were shot. Now, enough talking. Get some sleep."

"How did I get to the hospital?"

"Well, cowboy, I reckon they left you there. Why are you asking me? I wasn't a tick's hair near you. How would I know all this? Now, get some rest."

I didn't remember anyone cutting me up, but I would have preferred to sleep through that anyway. I was in a complete state of confusion. It felt like everything that had happened was nothing more than a dream. I was in the hospital for almost a month before I was allowed to leave. Tomball had grown quite a bit, and many of the people who lived there had no idea who I was. Many of the town gossips had passed away or moved on. I got lightheaded when I began to walk for the first time. Angela was the only help I had.

"Why are you being so nice to me?"

"I miss you, Curtis. I really did miss you. I don't know why you ran off like that."

"I feel foolish about that now."

"You think we can start over civil-like and all?"

"I don't see why not, Angela. But I ain't got nothing. You understand that, don't ya? I need to find a job. I need to shake off that stigma of whatever the paper printed about me and Boy."

"I understand completely. It's going to be a wild horse we have to tame, but we'll be alright. In the meantime–here." She handed me two envelopes. "What's this?"

"One envelope has some money that apparently was in your possession, so I imagine its yours. The other is a letter that got to my house from Boy explaining to me what happened."

It was through this letter that I learned what had transpired with Jimena and how I got back to Tomball. Boy still thought he was in trouble with the law down here, so he did not include a return address. I was certain now he thought I was dead, but they sent the money with me anyway so I could have a proper service. I couldn't stop thinking about how Boy was getting along. I never got to tell him that the blame for Mary Beth's death had already been assigned to something other than himself. I am sure that he would have loved nothing more than to come home. Mexico was a whole lot of country, and I was sure Boy kept himself concealed tight for his own sake. I had Angela do the research to get me the number to *La Sombrilla*, but Khalia didn't work there anymore. It frightened me to think that writing my address across my chest was Boy's dying wish and that those men got the best of both him and Khalia as well.

Either way, I was sure it was pointless to go on looking for Boy. He would be keeping himself well-kept in a country where I would not even begin to know how to look out for him. I don't speak the language, I don't know anyone, and I did not even know if he was alive. I would, in turn, be looking for a ghost. After months of debating with myself, I thought it was the smartest thing to leave my experience behind me and start my life over. I wanted to stay in Tomball, but it was tainted now. The entire town was covered in a blanket of memories of Mary Beth, Angela, Boy, and everything that happened in between.

I made a promise to Boy along the way that I intended to keep. My life had quickly turned into a tall Texas tale about mischief, and I did not want to add another dishonest thing about myself. I promised Boy I would go to the Dakotas, and once I felt strong enough, that is exactly what I did. I did go back on one thing. That is, I never gave me and Angela a chance. She woke up one morning to my departure letter. I cannot say for sure how she reacted to her discovery, but I imagine she wasn't too pleased about it. I wanted to explain in much better detail and in person why I decided to take to the road the way I did again, but I learned that I couldn't explain what I did not have an answer to.

I don't know if this is just a cowboy thing or if it happens to common folk too, but there are times in our lives when we are driven by something that is inside us. It comes in the form of a feeling that is rarely felt, so when it comes around, we just know what it is—not because the feeling is familiar but because it isn't. The old feeling told me to work for a ranchman in Tomball who wasn't there before I left. I did so for a couple of months doing various things. Mostly, I learned how to fit horseshoes on his horses. That was his thing. His name was Joseph Buchanan. He was a man advanced in age and widowed by cancer. God blessed him with ten beautiful children, but eight of them were women and two of them had no business being born men of the saddle. Poor Buchanan had no choice but to tend to the manly duties of the ranch all by himself. For him, it was a curse. For me, it was a blessing. Six months of savings and sleeping in his barn was all I needed to have enough to get out of Texas. I added that to the funeral expenses Boy and Khalia left me, and I was set. I was born in Tomball, but I had no interest in dying there.

Old Joseph Buchanan never had much to say. He couldn't spit out more than ten words a day if a mule kicked him in the back of the head forcing his tongue to move. But the day I told him I would be leaving, he made it known I'd be missed. It was tempting to stay. He was paying me much more than I deserved. I wondered how much of that was compensation for my company. Over the years, however, Tomball had become a den of unwanted memories. After everything I had been through with Boy, I never even returned to the old house I lived in. The landlord had probably gotten rid of all my belongings, and the house was sure to be falling apart. I don't think I could go back to that house anyway, at least not without seeing images of me and Boy carrying out Mary Beth's body. He may not have killed her after all, but we'd done wrong by that. What the world knows in a physical sense is so different than what the conscience knows. Everyone in Tomball had formulated their own theories about what happened with Mary Beth, but I knew the truth. This truth continued to haunt me, and the spirits of those affected by that truth were pushing me out of Tomball faster than a raccoon sticking his head in a beehive.

I was now on the bus headed toward Dakota. I would have to change bus lines in Topeka, Kansas and should be in North Dakota in three days. The ride to Topeka was quiet, but a stranger on the bus from Topeka to Bismarck gave me some idea as to where I should settle once I was there.

"I imagine if we're going to have to sit next to each other for all these hours, we may as well talk a little. My name is Gary Rodgers. Who I am talking to?"

"Curtis."

"Well, Curtis, where do ya hang your hat?"

"Texas but looking for a new hat stand."

"Going far, are ya?"

"As far as I can."

"Where ya getting to?"

"North Dakota."

"No kidding? I lived there some years before retiring."

"How was it?"

"Best place in the world. I think it's heaven. Doesn't have all that wild hustle and bustle that the big city has. I mean Texas has its share of quiet ranchland, I'm sure. But that damn state is so big, it has to co-exist with the city. North Dakota don't share shit with the city. It's all peaceful-like."

"Where would you go there?"

"Depends what you want to do. Personally, you might want to look into Keystone. Now that's a nice little place for ya. It's green, quiet, and peaceful. At times, you can't hear nothing but the Western Mead-owlark for miles."

"Sounds great."

"Oh, it's wonderful. Medora, Devil's Lake, all them small towns make for some comfortable living. You might want to stay clear of the Bitterroot Valley, though, especially if you want to grow something."

"Why is that?"

"Our old ancestors left a mess of old mines buried under the soil. Didn't do the dirt any good."

"Thanks."

"Oh, that's for free. For a spell from your flask I'll tell ya something else."

I took my flask out of my shirt pocket. It must have been sticking out a bit for him to have noticed. He pulled out a small shot glass from the tote bag he had with him and held it out to me. "Whiskey?"

"Yeah, straight from Nashville."

"I'll drink to that."

"So, what did I just pay for?"

"Now you just make your way down to Fort Ransom. Old little town doesn't hold more than 100 people in it. You ask at any farm-house for Garland Bedford's place. Tell them you're his grandson. They'll point ya in the right direction. Once you get there, the place is yours."

"Mine? You mean Garland will give me a job?"

"No, I mean the place is yours. He left it to his grandson and moved on to Canada."

"What about the grandson?"

"Died in an accident about three years ago. Poor guy was never any good with tractors."

"I'm sorry to hear that."

"You won't be once you get this land. I knew Garland pretty well. He wouldn't have wanted it to go to waste. Obviously, you won't be the rightful owner of the land, but it would be some time before anyone bothers to look into the place."

"Did he die too?"

"Nope, bastard killed his wife and went on to Canada."

"Killed his wife?"

"Yep, that's the rumor. He went to your neck of the woods to hide out in Texas for a while. Once everything was clear, he went off to Canada to live out the rest of his days. I promise you, he ain't ever going back to that house. It's yours unless some very distant family makes claim to it. That's doubtful too. He didn't have much in the form of family."

"I don't imagine people will take a liking to the grandson of a killer."

"They don't know, cowboy. They think she's out and about with him. You just tell them they sent you to watch over the place, and you're set." The old man was very sure of this plan, so I thought it was worth exploring. We both lowered the rims to our hats and slept the rest of the way.

Chapter 31

Fort Ransom

I remember thinking to myself that a man can get lost both physically and spiritually in a place like North Dakota.

We arrived in Bismarck at dark, so I wouldn't set off to Fort Ransom until morning. I had to wake Gary. Poor old man was fast asleep. "Gary?"

"Yeah? We here?"

"Yeah, we're in Bismarck."

"Damn it, Curtis. I would have missed my next bus if it weren't for you."

"The next bus?"

"Oh yeah, I ain't got no business in Dakota. I'm going further north. It sure was a blessing knowing ya, Curtis." He smiled and shook my hand. I shook it back thinking he would have been kind company for me in Fort Ransom. "You stop by some time at Bedford's place. I'll set a place at the table for ya." He smiled and turned to leave. I thought it was a strange reaction to the invitation. It got stranger when he turned one last time as he was leaving. "Oh Curtis, do me a favor, will ya? Get the mail when you get to Bedford's place. There's probably a clutter of it by now."

"You bet, Gary." He was gone.

The next day proved to be a difficult task. Fort Ransom didn't have a bus going through there, and it was three hours from where I stood. I found a small café to get some breakfast and had to take off on boot to pavement to thumb to the wind. This too proved to be much more difficult than it would have been in Texas. Not much traffic passed me on my voyage, so my thumb got plenty of rest. I walked for over an hour before a truck pulled over. "How far you going?"

"Fort Ransom."

"Hop on."

"Much obliged to ya. Curtis Cash."

"Milo Garrison, and no problem. The sheriff around here don't take to hitchhikers much. I'd hate for ya to get jailed over such a small matter."

"I appreciate that."

"Not much in Fort Ransom. Got family there?"

"No, just trying to start something new with my life."

"Not too many people come to the Dakotas for a start."

"I'm gonna try."

"How did you come to decide on Fort Ransom?"

"Business opportunity."

"Not much business there–the best of luck to ya."

"Thanks."

The rest of the way was mostly quiet. I could understand the appeal the Dakotas had on Boy. It was pleasant scenery with a green that was much different than the colors I would see in the Texas mesquite lands. The trees were tall and green. The mountains went high to the sky. I remember thinking to myself that a man can get lost both physically and spiritually in a place like North Dakota. I couldn't help but wonder if it would have been this easy for Boy and me to get this far north the first time we made our way out of Tomball. Sometimes when a person is under a great deal of stress, it's hard to have a good mind to think of things. As it turned out, it was safe for us to have gone back home after all that.

I arrived at Fort Ransom to the sounds of the Western Meadowlarks and a slight breeze coming in from the Dakota mountains. It was quiet, and I didn't see too many people to ask about the Bedford place. I walked over to an old church parish and saw an elderly woman watering the grounds. "Excuse me, ma'am. I'm looking for Garland Bedford's place."

"Ain't nobody home."

"Um, yes I'm aware. I've been asked to get their mail for them and look after the place for a spell."

She turned to face me and looked over me from boot to hat over the rim of her glasses. She gestured with her head that I was walking the right way. "It's the first road on your left. It's gonna be quite a walk, but there ain't no other road going left. So, when you see it, go down it for about the same distance it's gonna take you to get there." She returned to her watering.

The walk was considerably farther than I had envisioned, but my head was so full of thoughts of Boy that it felt like minutes before I was there. I wondered how he was and what he was doing. More than anything, I couldn't help but worry about whether he was safe or not. I imagine he felt as alone as I was feeling, but he was feeling it in a foreign country. I wish there was a way I could send him a message letting him know it was more than safe to go back to Tomball. For now, I had to worry about stabilizing myself, and it all began with this unlikely opportunity of free-living at Bedford's house. When I walked up the narrow, dirt pathway, I found the cabin concealed behind a lot of brush. The grass certainly needed some attention, but it probably snowed quite a bit and once the sun melted the water down, it kept the grass greener than I had ever seen grass be.

Everything about the beauty of the place was consistent with how Gary described it. The first thing I did was walk over to the mailbox, but there was no mail to collect. It was curious to not see any mail there if the house had been abandoned as long as Gary said it was. I soon learned there was a good reason for no correspondence in the mailbox. The house wasn't as vacant as Gary thought. One of the most beautiful things about North Dakota was standing on the front wooden porch holding a twelve-gage shotgun. "Is there a good reason you're standing on my property?"

"Not a good reason, I'm afraid–probably miscommunication or a wrong turn somewhere. I was looking for Bedford's place."

"You're standing in it."

"Oh, well I do beg your pardon, ma'am, but Gary Rodgers told me I could watch over the place while it was empty. I guess he didn't figure on someone being here. I'll be on my way."

She lowered the twelve-gage slowly and leaned it against one of the posts that held the roof over her porch. "Gary Rodgers, huh?"

"Yeah. Ya know him?"

"I have an idea."

"You're talking to Curtis Cash, ma'am."

"I hadn't asked you, but since you're getting all formal-like, I'm Blaze Saddlehorn."

"Nice to meet you, Blaze. Pardon the intrusion."

I turned to walk back toward the main road. I thought I was going to have to find a nice tree to sleep under before Blaze stopped me.

"Hold on a minute. You seem harmless enough, and well, Gary did send you. There's a lot that needs tending to around here that ain't much in my interest to do. Come on in and get something to eat. You can sleep in the bunk house out back. It has a bed and a place to read the Bible, but your washing and relieving yourself is done the old-fashioned way out in the woods. There's a clear stream out back just below the backyard that makes for some good washing water."

"That'll be fine, ma'am."

"If you keep saying ma'am, I'm going to strain my neck from turning back to look for my mother."

"Well, thank you, Blaze. I appreciate your help."

A few months went by. I had Blaze's place looking presentable. The yard was trimmed, the hay was stacked, and I made deals with local farmers to get a chicken farm going. I looked hard to find someone to make a deal on a horse, but that deal was still pending. I had earned Blaze's trust enough for her to allow me to take my meals in the kitchen with her. We spoke a lot and learned from one another. I didn't want to fool myself into thinking this was how it was going to be for the rest of my life. Blaze was a beautiful woman, and I knew that it wouldn't be much longer before my heart gave in to her kind. She played the role of a tough girl, but I could see an innocence in her eyes that penetrated my soul and made me see the gentler side of her. So many times, I came close to leaning over and kissing her. I could not take this kind of risk though. She was providing me shelter and a good living. I was certain it was temporary, but I didn't want to lose the sudden joy of enjoying life as a free man with a woman.

Our living arrangement remained this way for a year before she let me use the bathroom inside the house. I never thought she had one.

"You mean all this time you had a bathroom inside the house?"

"I never said I didn't, did I, cowboy?"

I couldn't justly argue with her. She never said she didn't have a bathroom inside the house. Personally, it was a relief knowing she had been taking care of her business lady-like and not in the woods as I had been. December rolled around, and the weather got very cold. The snow fell harder than I had ever seen in my life. We had already prepared with plenty of food, firewood, and with securing the chickens so they wouldn't freeze. I wouldn't have known to prepare in advance for this.

"Ain't you a cowboy?" Blaze would ask me.

"Cowboy yes, but I ain't no Eskimo. The most we ever got back in Tomball was frozen rain."

"You mean to tell me it wouldn't snow at all out there?"

"Sure, it would snow, but it would all be melted by the evening. The snow down here seems to stick around for a while."

"You bet it does. Don't care for it much, do ya?"

"Quite the contrary, Blaze. It's the prettiest thing I ever did see. I love the lands out here. The green, the mountains, and the beautiful snow. If I had coyote paws instead of boots, I'd love to go off exploring."

"You may not have to wait to do that."

"How do ya reckon that?" She smiled and put on her coat. She took an old abandoned coat off the hook and threw it to me. She said Gary Rodgers had left it there.

"Where are we going?"

"You'll see, cowboy."

I followed her out back. There was a lock on the barn door. "Why did ya put a lock on the barn door for?"

She put her index finger over her lips asking me not to speak anymore. She unlocked the door and opened it. There it stood. The most beautiful horse I had ever seen in my life was sticking its head in a barrel of apples mixed in hay.

"Blaze, where did you find him?"

"Well, the deal we had going was pending for so long, I looked somewhere else."

"Wow! He's amazing."

"He's yours."

"Mine? You're crazy!"

"Yeah, I am, but not for the horse."

"Then for what?"

She walked over to me with her eyes fixed on mine. She kept walking toward me until our lips were locked. She kissed me longer than any other first kiss I had ever had in my life. I picked her up without losing the lock on our lips and continued the passion through the night. It was one of the most magical moments I had ever experienced.

The time went by, and the winter's snow began to fade. Blaze and I spent a quiet Christmas together as romantic as anything anyone could ever read about. She was an amazing woman both inside and out. I felt like everything that had ever transpired with Boy and being on the run was necessary for me to be at that particular moment and that particular place in time with that specific person. I asked myself if I would go through all that again if it meant being at that exact place with Blaze, and the answer was always, "yes."

As the snow became water running down between the rocks that drained into the river just below the cabin's backyard and the flowers began to show their colors, there was a sudden change. Blaze was just as loving as ever, but she was much quieter than she had been in recent months. I was afraid to bring it up because I didn't want to ruin what we already had built together. We made romantic love and often. We laughed an awful lot and shared more than any two people I had ever personally known. Now it was time for both of us to share the more extreme aspects of our life. I needed to do this in the gentlest manner I knew how.

"I took the saddle off Rushmore. How about we bareback up the mountain?"

She was shy about it, but she was willing. "Okay, but not too far, okay? I have to get the duck in the oven for supper."

"We'll just be a while. I'm getting hungry anyway."

Once again, she was quiet. I rode up the large grassy hill Blaze called Lucky Hill because lucky charms grew by the millions in the area. I found a nice soft, flat area where Rushmore could eat some fresh grass while we sat on a rock that looked as if nature intended for someone to use as a bench.

"This rock sure screams out to people to sit on it, doesn't it?"

Blaze smiled. "Yeah, my daddy used to bring us here all the time.

In the spring, the lower part of the canyon gets lit up by fireflies."

"Your daddy, huh?"

"Yeah."

"Gary Rodgers?"

"Yeah."

"There's no Bedford, and there is no dead grandson, is there?"

"No, Curtis, there ain't. How did you figure on that?"

"You said something about giving me Gary Rodger's coat. If he was just a friend, what would it be doing here?"

"You got some good thinking in ya, Curtis."

"Something happen with your ma?"

"He told you?"

"Well, he surely didn't take no credit for it."

"He shouldn't take credit for it, Curtis. It ain't his to take."

I looked at her with curious eyes. I wasn't sure I was ready for what came next. "Did you kill your mama?"

"Had to, Curtis. She was a mean bitch and was gonna kill my daddy."

"Was she?"

"Mean as hell, Curtis. More than I can ever tell you."

Chapter 32

Blaze's Story

"Nobody knows. I suppose it will just stay a mystery."

Blaze told me her entire story. It was one worth relating to anyone willing to hear it. She was just a little girl when her parents started fighting. They didn't live in Fort Ransom at the time. Her father was trying to raise some cattle just outside the Bitterroot Valley of Montana. It didn't take him long to realize that he had chosen a patch of land with the poorest dirt God ever made. He couldn't grow anything worth living for. Young Blaze must have been no more than six years old when the family decided to move to North Dakota. Things got much better there. Gary Rodgers went to work for a local timber mill that paid him handsomely. He was the foreman before long and eventually worked his way to the front office.

It seemed that the more money Gary made, the more his wife would hound him about things she wanted, things she needed, things that wealthy people should have. Gary was more in favor of saving for older age and tending to their farm. His wife wouldn't have that. She began to drink and leave for days. When she was home, she was an abusive woman and often took out her anger on Blaze. By the time Blaze was twenty, the family had grown apart, and the couple slept in separate rooms in the house. Gary began to feel sick quite often, and his wife would blame it on the stress between the two. Blaze had much different ideas, and she shared them with her father. "Daddy, I think mama is trying to poison you."

"Oh, she throws a fuss, honey, but it isn't in her to kill nobody." He would defend her in this way for reasons Blaze did not understand. He defended her, that is, until a co-worker, Cecil Feldman, at the lumber mill had a strange conversation with him.

"So, how's that rat problem coming along? Did ya take care of it?"

"Rat problem?"

"Yeah, my son is working at the Rusty Wagon Market and said your wife said something about a rat problem. She's been buying up the rat poison by the case out there."

"Oh yeah, well it's getting better." He pretended.

"You best see to them rats. They'll not only eat all the feed–they'll get them chickens sick too."

"Will do, Cecil, thanks for the tip."

It was after this conversation that poor Gary Rodgers confirmed with Blaze that his wife was out to get him. She must have been poisoning his food in small doses, which is why he'd been getting sick so often. Soon, she started doing something beyond reproach that took both Gary and Blaze by surprise. She began being much kinder to both of them. She spent some serious quality time with Blaze. She bought her things and took her out. Gary didn't mind his money being used on his daughter like that. After about a month of this treatment, her motives became more apparent.

Blaze's mother was doing nothing more than grooming her daughter. She had offered her the world of riches in insurance money to kill her own father. "Hasn't this past month just been marvelous, honey?"

"Yes, momma."

"Well, don't ya wanna live like that with me all the time?"

"It would be nice momma, but what about daddy?"

"Don't ya think he'd want that for us too? I mean he's sickly and all, darling. You've seen how often he gets sick."

"Yeah, mama, but he ain't been getting sick lately, and I love him."

"You're gonna do this– and you're gonna do this tonight."

She changed her demeanor instantly. She threatened to set the entire place on fire while they slept if Blaze didn't. Her mom then returned to her calm voice.

"Please, honey. Do this for us. I'll help you. I'll romance him, and we'll be in the same room tonight. I put the shotgun in your closet already. It's loaded, honey."

She left the room confident that Blaze would carry out the crime. It was here that Blaze stopped telling me the story. It must have been difficult for her to continue as she wanted me to draw my own conclusions.

"You shot her instead, didn't ya?"

"Had to, Curtis. I really had to. She would have eventually killed my daddy. Look at him now. He ain't even close to dying. He is full of life, and my momma would have killed him."

"It sounds very much like she had a mind to."

"Is it true she's on this property somewhere?"

"Yeah, but I don't know where exactly. My daddy wanted to protect me so much and thought it would be best for me to go on for a while. The less I knew, the better."

"But you came back."

"This is my favorite place in the whole world, Curtis, and I wanted to experience it one last time before I left for good."

"Wait a minute, girl. Are you trying to tell me you're leaving?"

"Listen, baby, we're lucky we've been here as long as we have. Momma had family that cared for her. I've been writing to them for her, but they'll want to see her soon. I got a letter about a week ago about them being in the area by April. They'll want answers, Curtis. I won't know how to act. I just can't be here."

"What about me?"

"Well, you don't have to go. You have nothing to do with this. All you have to say is that you bought the place from Gary Rodgers Saddlehorn. You wouldn't know anything else."

"I could still do that and keep you somewhere on the farm, can't I?"

"I'm too scared, Curtis. I can't do it. I just need to get away, that's all."

"Well I'm going with ya, then!"

"I can't take you from here, Curtis. You've done too much work, and there's no other place in the world you can stay for free."

"Look here, Ms. Blaze. I've done just fine for myself to this day. Now I'm a grown man and can rightfully judge what I want to live with or without. I can do without this house, Blaze Saddlehorn, but I can't part with you. I just can't."

"Do you mean that truly?"

"I'm more serious than a snake bite, honey!"

"You know, maybe sometime after the spring we can come back and see how things look."

"You bet."

"We only have two months left before we have to go."

"Yeah, I reckon so, but how did I come about seeing your daddy on the bus?"

"It was just coincidence, honey. He went to Texas and then Kansas to see some family before going off for a longer time to Canada. He may have seen your honest face and that you were alone and thought you'd be good to tend to his land. He didn't think I'd come back."

"Aren't you gonna see him again?"

"I'll find him. Do you think I'm awful for what I've done?"

"Not even close."

"So, what about you?"

"Me?"

"Yeah, ain't it about time you told me about those gunshot scars you got all over your body?"

"I reckon it was time a long time ago, pretty lady."

"So, what of it?"

"I'll tell you what. Let's go get that duck in the oven. I'll tell you the entire story over dinner. You need to get ready for this one."

It felt good getting things out in the open for both of us. I was feeling lonely thinking she was losing interest in me. It was selfish to feel a relief knowing that her sudden quiet nature was provoked by something else. I still had some good money that Boy and Jimena left me with. There wasn't a need to spend it at Gary's place, and I actually made a profit. In the following two months, we sold the chickens, the barn by itself, but the most painful of all was selling Rushmore. I guess Blaze hoped we'd be there much longer. She must have thought no one would ever come calling on her mother. Now, this was a real possibility, and it was time to go. We also sold the furniture and some farming equipment. We had a good amount of money and even got Gary's old 1966 pickup running. The motor still sounded strong, and we knew it would get us far. The only thing left to decide was where we were going.

Before we got to the point of deciding where to go, I decided to call on Angela while in town one evening. I'm not sure exactly why I called her. I felt I owed her an apology and wanted to make my new start a completely new one. "Hello."

"Hey Angela, it's Curtis."

"Hey back at ya."

"You angry?"

"No, I knew it would be difficult for us, Curtis. I just want you to be happy. Are you happy?"

"I am. Are you?"

"Yeah. I met a cowboy from Amarillo. I think it's the real deal this time."

"I'm happy for ya."

"Thanks."

"You don't seem surprised I called."

"I expected you to call at some point."

"I see. Nothing from Boy, I reckon?"

"No. He's lost, Curtis."

"Yep, I guess he is."

"Funny thing though . . ."

"What's that?"

"Turns out they confirmed Old Man Winters didn't kill Mary Beth."

Now this was something shocking to me. I had no immediate response. "How is that?"

"It was all over the papers in Tomball and even Houston. The medical examiner said poor Mary Beth had a pre-existing condition in her head."

"You mean like a tumor or something?"

"I can't tell ya for sure because I don't know about medical things, but whatever it was seems to have busted in her head. Poor Mary Beth was sick, and nobody knew better."

"What about her being on Old Man Winters's property?" I asked only to know what they were saying about that.

"Nobody knows. I suppose it will just stay a mystery."

Chapter 33

Peter "Boy" Jenkins

"I could slap a beehive as hard as I slapped her,
and nothing would come out of it."

Taxco, Mexico, 1983

Three long years had gone by since we left Curtis outside that emergency room of the hospital. The dry Mexican land was cracked over the honorary burial site I had made for him. I never knew exactly what happened after Curtis was taken to the hospital, and while death by my own hand remained an option for me, I held firm to the idea of life. I found a job as a ranch hand in a small town just outside Taxco. I was given two acres of my own to work on and live by, and this was just fine with me. Jimena made all the arrangements to have a memorial set up for Curtis in Taxco. The memorial was erected at the edge of our new property which overlooked the beautiful mountain sides. At night, the city lights below glittered like stars that were released by the ancient Aztecs.

I leaned over and reflected on my role in Curtis's death. I thought it was a matter of days before Maxwell's men caught up to me to send me to join him, but the day never arrived. I thought it was an intentional act of God to keep me alive. Having to live with the guilt of responsibility for my best friend's death was worse punishment than death itself. On the third-year anniversary of Curtis being shot, the wound was still very fresh in my chest, and I could not help but round up tears every time I leaned over my friend's memorial. My beautiful little girl ran up behind me as I tried to forgive myself.

"Are you crying, daddy?"

"Just a little, princess."

"Are you crying for your friend again?"

"Yeah, princess, I reckon I am."

A beautifully manicured hand came from behind me and rubbed my shoulder gently. "You alright, cowboy?"

"I'll be alright, Jimena, it's just–"

"I know, baby, today is the day."

"Yeah, it should have been me."

"Don't say that, Boy. God knows what he's doing."

My little girl rejoined the conversation. "Daddy, Esperanza and I wanna ride horse."

Esperanza was nine years old now and acted more like a teenager. She had grown into a beautiful little girl who didn't speak much, but when she did, she always had something clever to say. Jimena named our daughter Cassidy. It was a nice cowgirl name and tribute to Curtis. She was just over two years old now, and I always described her as one smart firecracker.

I was doing well in my job, which I got to not draw attention to myself or Jimena by using the money she tricked the cartel out of. The only thing we took out was to have my leg repaired. Every now and then, the mountains bring in a cold chill that makes the weak nerves in that leg start to dance inside me, but for the most part, it feels good. The rest of the money we buried in a barn I built. I created a trap door just large enough to push the bag through underneath the bales of hay.

Above that trap door, there is a second one to make matters more difficult for anyone who looks there. They will open the first door to find nothing inside.

Jimena and I happened by accident. Once we left Curtis at the hospital, our next order of business was to find a new vehicle. We found someone to trade for their vehicle, which was in worse shape, but it was something no one would be looking for us in. I had it in mind all along to separate at some point, but the beautiful young lady seemed scared. She didn't want to be alone, and this was not something she had to tell me. I could see it as clear as the Texas sky that she didn't want to move on. I thought there would be no harm in letting her settle in with me until some time passed. The more time we spent together, the closer we got. Eventually, little Cassidy caught us by surprise, and it seemed right and proper to be a family. I love Jimena with all my heart—I just wasn't expecting a little girl.

I decided to make my past the past. I never told Jimena what Curtis and I were running from. I didn't think she would trust me much if she thought I could go off on her the way I did on Mary Beth. I swore that to my dying day I'd never lay a hand on another woman again. Even with this promise to myself, I knew I had to come clean soon. There wasn't a point in living a lie in a relationship.

I didn't feel completely free. The first two years after arriving in Taxco, I kept looking out the window just waiting for Max and his men to drive up looking for both Jimena and their money. Jimena couldn't remember whether Max ever knew her real name or not. It helped that all her proper documents still had her real name. Khalia was nothing more than an illusion. Now, I wasn't educated in Mexico or how things work in this country, but I knew enough about drug cartels to learn they don't take a liking to people messing with their money. I lived in constant fear that we would be found out.

Jimena and I talked about when the right time to move on would be. It was a question neither of us could answer. We were quite comfortable where we were, but we just didn't know how long it would be before our past caught up to us.

"How long do you think we can stay?" She would ask me.

"I don't know, pretty lady. It sure is nice out here, ain't it?"

"Yes, it is."

"Well, you know Mexico much better than me. What are the chances we get found out here?"

"I don't know, Boy. The entire country is run by the cartel now. I don't know what the right thing to do is."

"Well I'm a bit trapped, Jimena. I've thought of going back to the United States and working on getting your papers fixed. As it turns out, I'm just as illegal up there as you are."

"Illegal? How?"

"Remember when you thought Curtis and I were robbing banks?"

"Yes, I remember."

"We weren't running from no bank robberies."

"What were you running from, Boy?"

"Murder!" I just blurted it out. I didn't want to take too much time with it.

She backed up a little from me, and this concerned me. "Murder? Who, Boy? Who did you murder?"

"My wife." Jimena darted to the inside of the house. I ran after her pleading with her to stop. She ran into the bedroom and closed the door. Our girls were still riding the horse, and I hoped to finish the conversation before they got an ear of what I had done. I could hear Jimena crying on the other side of the door. I didn't want to show my angry side by forcing it open, so I spoke through the damp wood.

"Sweetheart, you've got to believe me that it was an accident. I didn't mean to hurt her that badly, and Curtis could have vouched for me on that. I'm no more danger to you or the girls than a rabbit to a rattlesnake, honey! Please come out."

It took a few minutes, but the door slowly began to open. Her eyes were red, and her makeup was smeared. "Accident?"

"I promise you, baby, I didn't mean to hurt her. I had a thing where I couldn't control my anger, but I've changed. I didn't mean to ever slap her hard. I don't know, Jimena, it puzzles me how she hit her head awkward-like or something because I could slap a beehive as hard as I slapped her, and nothing would come out of it. I can't explain it pretty lady, but I can tell you this for sure, I didn't mean to hurt her. I ain't no killer."

She hugged me hard, but things were a little quiet between us the rest of the day. I figured she just had to process everything I told her. I can see she appreciated me telling her the truth. She might have felt I was placed in a criminal position the same way she was. By later that night, she seemed to be herself again. She laughed with me and the kids during supper and sent the girls to bed early so we could make love. A man can always tell if his girl is sore at him by how they make love. She didn't seem to be sore at me anymore. We opened the large two pane windows of the bedroom to look outside and see the stars. She loved doing that after a romantic evening. We got quiet for some time and my mind drifted off thinking about Curtis.

"What are you thinking?" She asked me curiously. "I was just wondering if Curtis felt any pain that day."

"I think he was alright, Boy. You shouldn't think about that."

"I can't rightly help it. He was like a brother to me."

"He was trying hard to talk to you. I guess he wanted to say good-bye or something. He was really trying hard. What do you suppose he wanted to tell you?"

"Oh darling, I know exactly what he was going to say."

"You do?"

"Oh yeah, I had him call his old girlfriend that day before he was shot. She probably told him that Tomball was a hotbed for the both of us, and he was pleading with me to let him stay with us."

"You think so?"

"Oh yeah, that had to be it. He must have known that going back to Tomball could never be an option for either of us without going to prison."

THE END

CPSIA information can be obtained
at www.ICGtesting.com
Printed in the USA
LVHW040841121020
668551LV00001B/55